Saving Olympus

The Dark Army

Book One

Second Edition

Written By:

R.D. Wolfe

To my son, Hunter. You can do whatever you want to in life, if only you work hard enough and keep the goal in sight.

Acknowledgements: J.R. Rain, J.T. Cross, and C.J. Urban This work exists because of your endless advice, help, and support. Thank you, from the bottom of my heart.

Cover Art: John Henry Esteban (Art) Sketch Study (Text)

Table of Contents

Chapter I: The Career

The Academy had been Darien's home for as long as he could remember. Left at its gates as an infant by an unknown guardian, he had been raised within its walls, surrounded by teachers, students, and the very foundation of the institution itself. The Academy was a place of learning in the traditional sense—its curriculum covered chemistry, history, biology, trigonometry—but for Darien, its true value lay elsewhere.

What set it apart was its sports, though they were nothing like the ones played in the outside world. There were no football teams or baseball leagues. Instead, students trained in ancient, time-honored disciplines, skills that tested not just the body but the mind, forging discipline through mastery of weapons from a long-forgotten era. These skills, outdated as they might have seemed to the wider world, carried lessons that would last a lifetime—or so the Academy claimed.

For Darien, the claim rang true.

Darien rounded a corner, making his way toward his mentor's office. Master Whyn had been one of his favorite teachers from the moment he had been old enough to train. As head of the swordsmanship department, Whyn had guided Darien through years of training, instructing him on the positions to perfect, the moves to commit to memory, and the tactics to master.

Darien led his team of three, competing against other student teams in the Academy's Arena. His team was the best—and he intended to keep it that way. He had spent countless hours practicing, studying, and refining his understanding of swordplay and small-scale battle tactics.

His chemistry teacher had once sighed and told him, "If you spent half as much time on the periodic table as you do memorizing battle formations, you'd be my best student."

Darien had laughed it off, returning to the mental strategies playing out in his head. He didn't care about the atomic weight of molybdenum or the number of electrons in an atom's outer shell. He cared about winning.

After several minutes of walking, he reached a corridor lined with evenly spaced doors. On the left, classrooms. On the right, the faculty offices. The swordsmanship department.

Stopping at a door near the center, he read the brass nameplate.

Headmaster Kenneth Whyn.

Taking a deep breath, he knocked.

A firm voice from inside called, "Enter."

The room was cool and dimly lit, casting an illusion of dusk despite the bright daylight beyond the windows. Darien stepped inside, meeting Master Whyn's piercing gaze.

The swordsman was not an old man, but he had more days behind him than ahead. His brown hair was flecked with gray, and his sharp, grey eyes were both stern and thoughtful. He stood just about Darien's height, carrying himself with an air of quiet authority.

"Please, sit," Whyn said, motioning toward one of the two chairs opposite his desk.

Darien complied, casting a glance around the sparsely furnished room. A desk, a reading chair, a few floor lamps, and towering bookshelves lined with row upon row of ancient tomes.

Silence stretched between them.

Whyn sat, his eyes never leaving Darien's face, studying him with an intensity that made him shift uncomfortably. Finally, the headmaster rose, crossing the room to pull a tattered book from one of the shelves.

"Do you know why I called you here?" he asked, flipping through the pages.

Darien hesitated, unsure if he was supposed to have an answer. "No, sir, I don't."

Whyn replaced the book, turned, and fixed Darien with a serious expression.

"The Academy has trained tens of thousands—perhaps hundreds of thousands—of students in its lifetime. Even the Academy Council does not know when it was founded. We have records dating back centuries, yet no one alive today remembers a time before this place existed."

He walked to the window, gazing out at the freshly cut lawn beyond.

"Master Whyn, I don't—"

"Why did you pick the sword?" Whyn interrupted, his voice sharp.

Darien frowned. "I don't understand what you mean."

Whyn turned, half of his face shadowed by the light streaming in. "Why, in your third year, did you choose the sword? You could have taken up the bow, the axe, the staff. Any weapon was open to you, and I have no doubt you would have excelled at any of them. So why the sword?"

The question caught Darien off guard. He had never really stopped to think about it. It had never felt like a choice.

From the time he was three years old, watching the older students battle in the Arena, he had known he wanted to be a swordsman. It felt like the sword had chosen him.

"I suppose I like the challenge," he said slowly. "You have to be graceful and fierce at the same time. Cautious and daring. It just... made sense."

Whyn watched him for a long moment before nodding. "Why do you study as hard as you do?"

Darien didn't hesitate. "Because I want to be the best."

"No," Whyn said impatiently, shaking his head. "Why do you stay here? You have friends who would gladly welcome you into their homes. Why choose to remain at the Academy when you could seek a life beyond these walls?"

Darien stiffened, the question making him uncomfortable.

Philip, his closest friend and roommate, had invited him every year to visit his home during the holidays. Darien had always refused, opting instead to remain at the Academy to train, study, and explore its endless halls. He had never really questioned why.

"Because the Academy is my home."

Whyn studied him, nodding slowly. The only sounds were the muffled voices of students hurrying to class beyond the closed door.

"What do you intend to do after you graduate?" Whyn finally asked. "Once you receive your diploma, the world will be open to you. Will you travel? Pursue further studies?"

Darien shifted. "I don't know. Probably travel. See the world. Try to build a life for myself somewhere."

The truth was, he didn't want to leave the Academy.

But he couldn't say that.

Whyn leaned forward, hands folded on his desk. "What if I told you that you didn't have to?"

Darien sat up straighter. "What do you mean?"

"I mean stay. Not as a student. As a teacher."

Darien's breath caught.

Whyn gave him a rare smile. "You would continue your studies, of course, particularly in the subjects you've 'simply slipped by.'" His smile faded. "The Academy is a secret. Its existence is protected because it contains knowledge the world has long thought lost. History hidden beneath its foundations. There are things kept here that are better left unknown."

Darien's curiosity sparked. "Like what?"

Whyn shook his head. "That's for another time."

He continued, "Because of the nature of the Academy, finding qualified instructors willing to live and teach in secrecy is difficult. You have been noticed—not just by me, but by others. After much discussion with the Council, we have decided to offer you a position."

Darien stared. He jumped to his feet, pacing across the room. Students were never offered staff positions while their classmates were still attending. It had never happened before.

Whyn's voice cut through his thoughts. "You don't have to answer now. We wanted to wait until after the year-end tournament, but you must have time to make an informed decision. Think well, Darien. This will change everything."

Darien's mind immediately leapt to Kara. He had to talk to her.

They had planned to leave the Academy together after graduation, to move into the wider world and start a life beyond these walls. He had always imagined the two of them, just the two of them, free to be alone without the constant pressures of competition, exams, and training schedules dictating their every move.

But this offer changed everything. If he accepted, he would stay.

The life he had imagined with Kara would be gone, left behind in favor of the one thing he loved more than anything else. The one thing he had always felt drawn to.

Master Whyn's voice cut through his thoughts. "You must tell no one of this, Darien. Regardless of your decision, we cannot afford to make this public so close to the end of the year. It would only serve as an unproductive distraction for the students. No one must know until the Academy Council decides otherwise."

Darien nodded, then hesitated. "Sir, may I tell my team?"

Whyn studied him for a long moment before speaking. "Teams must be able to trust each other implicitly, without reservation. If you believe they can be trusted to keep this secret, then you may tell them—only so that no secrets impede your progress together. But be certain, Darien. They must keep it in the strictest confidence. Not a word to anyone else."

Darien stood in the center of the office, still lost in thought, trying to grasp the magnitude of what had just happened.

Whyn's voice softened. "I believe," he said, "that you have an exam to get to, if I am not mistaken?"

Darien jolted, glancing at his watch. Five minutes.

He had to go up four stories, through two hallways, and somehow make it to his classroom before the test started.

"Yes, sir! May I be dismissed?"

Whyn nodded, and Darien bolted from the room, racing through the halls toward his exam. He wasn't sure how he was going to focus on European history or chemistry after a conversation like that.

Despite his distraction, Darien thought he had done well enough on the exams, but by the end of the day, his patience was running thin.

Philip, who was in the same chemistry class, had been relentless in trying to pry information out of him.

"You've been staring off into space all day," Philip said as they walked out of the exam room. "It's like you're a thousand miles away."

Darien shrugged. "I'm fine. You're imagining things."

Philip wasn't buying it.

Philip O'Conner was seventeen, but looked older due to his early beard growth and the shaggy brown hair that always fell into his eyes. His dark, unreadable gaze rarely gave anything away, but Darien had long since learned to read between the lines.

Short and stocky, Philip reminded Darien of a bull—a fast one. More importantly, he was a formidable ally and an even better friend.

But Darien had spent all day dodging his questions, trying to decide if and how he would tell the rest of the team about Whyn's offer.

They walked together toward their shared dormitory, Philip still pestering him as Darien practiced his forms.

Then, just outside the dining hall, they spotted Lia.

Lia was the captain of another team—and Darien's closest rival.

She also fought with a sword, and while she was good, she had never quite been able to beat him. Even when she cheated.

Their final match was tomorrow, the outcome of which would determine who placed first for the school-wide tournament at the end of the year. This was Darien's last tournament at the Academy. He intended to win.

Her voice cut through the hallway.

"Look, loser, I don't care where you got it, just give it to me!"

Darien followed her glare to a young kid, no older than twelve, backed into a corner. Darien recognized him—he had seen the boy hanging around the Arena, watching the older students after their matches.

Philip leaned in. "Darien, just leave it alone."

Darien ignored him and stepped forward.

The boy clutched a model fighter jet in his hands, holding it tightly against his chest.

"Please, my mom sent it to me. It's the same plane my dad flies. It makes sounds, see?"

He pressed a button, and the jet let out a mechanical roar, mimicking the sound of a real engine.

Lia smirked. "Oh, your mommy sent it to you? I don't care. Give it here."

The boy shook his head, gripping the toy tighter.

"Leave him alone."

Darien's voice was flat, emotionless—but it was enough to make Lia turn in surprise.

"Stay out of this, Glade. Why do you care if he gets to keep his stupid plane?"

Darien shrugged. "Because it's his. That should be enough."

Lia rolled her eyes and ripped the toy from the boy's hands, ignoring his frantic attempts to get it back.

"Hey!" Darien snapped. "Give it back. Now."

Lia turned, a wicked grin spreading across her face. "Or what? You gonna fight me? You wouldn't risk your perfect record."

She tossed the plane into the air, catching it, tossing it again.

Darien watched the rhythm carefully.

In one swift motion, he drew his practice sword, struck the underside of the plane with precision, sending it flipping through the air—straight into Philip's waiting hands.

"Hey!" Lia shouted, clearly not expecting that.

Her expression twisted into a snarl. She drew her sparring sword, holding it at her side. The blade wasn't sharpened, but it could still do some serious damage if it struck someone.

Darien's voice dropped into a low, dangerous whisper. "Lia, it's over. Don't do anything stupid."

A voice cut through the tension.

"What is going on here?"

All four of them turned.

Master Akira, head of the archery department, stood in the doorway, arms crossed.

Philip jumped in immediately. "Lia was taking the plane from him!"

Too late.

Akira's eyes narrowed. "Both of you, put those swords away and come with me! You're going to Master Whyn. I'm surprised at you, Darien, particularly after your conversation with him this morning. I knew we had overstepped."

Darien's stomach dropped.

Did she mean the offer? Was this going to ruin his chance to stay at the Academy?

"Master Akira, I—"

"Silence, Mr. Glade. Nothing excuses fighting in the halls—especially not with a sharpened sword!"

Darien's heart pounded.

Lia smirked past him, clearly enjoying the turn of events.

As they followed Master Akira back to Whyn's office—the very place he had been that morning—Darien felt the opportunity he had always dreamed of slipping further away with every step.

Chapter 2: The Transition

Darien kept his gaze steady as the three walked into Master Whyn's office. He wasn't going to show any sign of weakness, not after what had happened. It was this or beg for mercy. He told himself there was a better chance that Whyn would understand why he had taken the course of action he did.

He was wrong.

After Master Whyn gave Lia a stern dressing down, sentencing her to extra days of physical training as punishment, he dismissed her and turned to Darien. He leaned against the edge of his desk, a stern look on his face.

"Why?"

The question was simple, calmly spoken, but it hit Darien like a slap. He wasn't even sure he'd heard it correctly.

"I'm sorry, sir?" Darien replied, unsure of what was being asked of him.

"Of all the stupid things to do, especially after this morning," Master Whyn continued, his voice tight but controlled. "Why, oh why, would you draw your sword—your sharpened sword, no less—on another student in front of a second year?"

"Lia was—" Darien began to defend himself, but Master Whyn cut him off, his voice growing more intense.

"I don't care what Lia was doing, has done, or will ever do." He wasn't yelling, but his calmness made the words sharper. "Nothing justifies pulling a sword in the hallways. Nothing. You know that, Darien." Whyn sighed, rubbing his brow. "I don't know what will happen now. Master Akira had significant reservations about allowing you to join the staff. You don't know how many favors I had to offer on your behalf to convince her to relent. Now, it may have been in vain."

Darien's stomach twisted with guilt. Master Whyn had offered him the chance at the career he'd always dreamed of. He wasn't even sure he wanted it before, but now that it was in jeopardy, Darien realized there was nothing he wanted more.

"Sir, isn't there anything I can do?"

"There may be," Master Whyn said seriously. "But I need to know if you're committed. I left the offer open before, but I am not going to try to undo the damage you've done without knowing for sure that this is what you want."

Darien hesitated. He needed to talk with Kara. This was everything he had ever wanted, sure, but if he made this decision without talking to her first, she would never forgive him.

"Sir, can I let you know after the match tomorrow? I have to talk to someone first," Darien asked, hoping he wasn't being too presumptuous.

Master Whyn paused, his expression unreadable. Then he gave Darien a knowing smile. "Tell Miss Knight that I wish you both the best of luck tomorrow."

Darien's cheeks flushed with embarrassment. He hadn't realized that word of his relationship with Kara had reached the staff.

"Yes, sir."

Darien left the office, heading toward his room, his mind racing. After reaching the dorm, he went to the showers he shared with Philip and the other tenth-year students. He cleaned himself up and put on some comfortable clothes. Battle gear always made him feel like a fight was just around the corner.

When he and Philip arrived at the dining hall, Darien finally filled his friend in on the conversation with Master Whyn. Philip was shocked at the offer to stay on at The Academy. But being the friend he was, Philip didn't ask what Darien's plans were. He understood that Darien had someone else to talk to first, and he kept his peace.

After filling their plates, they found a table near the back of the hall. The space was enormous, enough to seat the entire student body at ten large tables. Darien and Philip sat down and dug into their meal, talking about their plans for the match tomorrow. They caught sight of Trey, another member of their team, sitting alone at the end of a table across the room.

"Think he'll ever stop being so grumpy?" Philip asked with a mouthful of potatoes.

Darien shrugged, letting the subject drop. Trey was the newest member of their team, and he hadn't quite found a way to fit in yet.

After finishing their meal, the two started back toward their dorms. Darien stopped at an intersection, allowing Philip to walk ahead without him.

"Hey, you coming or what?" Philip called back.

"You go ahead. I'll be there later."

Philip nodded with a smirk and turned away. Darien stood still for a moment before heading in the opposite direction, toward the arena. He needed some time alone, and he knew the arena would provide the solitude he needed.

When Darien arrived at the arena, he pushed open the unlocked doors, relieved to find the space empty. He walked forward, his mind replaying his many matches, each footstep echoing in the stillness. The dust from today's match still lingered on the floor, a reminder of the challenges and victories that had marked his time at The Academy.

He took a moment to study the footprints, analyzing the marks they left. After a moment of quiet reflection, he moved forward and looked out over the familiar terrain of the arena—trees, boulders, dirt, and gravel—all bathed in the soft glow of the moonlight. The arena had been designed for combat training, with various terrains to simulate real-world conditions.

He turned toward the boulders, climbing up to the highest point in the arena, where he could see everything laid out before him.

As he reached the top, he froze in surprise. Kara was already there, waiting for him. Her long blonde hair was pulled back, and her slender frame was seated comfortably, her legs crossed as she stared at him with soft green eyes.

"Took you long enough," she said with a teasing smile.

Darien smiled back as he finished climbing the rest of the way up. "I got... slowed down." He paused. "I didn't see you in the dining hall. How long have you been waiting here for me?"

"There are some things you just don't get to know." She winked, her voice full of playful mystery.

Darien sat down beside her, lying back on the smooth stone. Together, they gazed up at the stars, their quiet company filling the space between them. The arena was far from the noise of the school, providing the best view of the sky anyone could hope for without sneaking into the surrounding forests.

They stayed like that for several minutes, the world quiet around them.

"Are you ready for tomorrow?" Kara asked, her voice barely above a whisper.

"Yeah," Darien replied, glancing at her. "We'll win, just like I said we would last time."

"Yeah, you were right again." Kara lay back, resting her head on his chest, forming a T shape as she made herself comfortable. Darien sighed, feeling the weight of the moment. It was easy to be at peace here with her.

"I heard you had an interesting day." Kara turned her face toward him, her voice soft and knowing.

"I did," Darien said, and began to recount the events of the day—the offer from Master Whyn, his encounter with Lia, and his second conversation with Master Akira.

"I don't know how you can learn from her. She's so... rigid." Darien shook his head, recalling the stern demeanor of his mentor.

"You get used to it." Kara smiled softly. "So, what are you gonna do?"

Darien sighed, standing up. Kara moved to lean against the raised rock as he paced, deep in thought.

"I don't know. There's so much to think about. This is all I've ever wanted to do—teach at The Academy, like Whyn. But then I met you, and everything that's happened this year with... us."

"It's been nice, hasn't it?" Kara smiled. "The last six months?"

Darien nodded, stopping his pacing. Something in her voice made him look at her more closely. He noticed tears running slowly down her face.

"What's wrong?" Darien asked, confused.

"Darien, you know what you have to do. I won't let you throw your whole life away just for a chance to have a life together after this."

"But what about all the places we wanted to go and see? What about all the—"

"Darien, stop." Kara interrupted, her voice firm. "Can you honestly tell me that when Whyn offered you the job, the first thing you thought about was where we wouldn't be able to go?"

Darien kicked the dirt in front of him, shrugging as he avoided her gaze.

"That's what I thought, and it's okay." Kara stood quickly and came over to him, slipping her arms through his and squeezing him tightly. Darien wrapped his arms around her.

"I didn't want to just say yes before I talked to you," he said quietly.

Kara looked up at him, standing on tiptoes, and pressed her soft lips against his. Darien kissed her back, enjoying the moment before pulling away.

"Can we still have our time here?"

"I wouldn't have it any other way." She smiled, pulling him in again. "Just promise, if you ever decide to abandon your dreams and explore the world on a grand adventure, you'll come find me."

"I promise." Darien smiled.

The two stayed in the arena, watching the stars pass overhead. They shared stories of their day, distracting themselves from thinking about a time when they might be apart. When the moon had moved directly overhead, they left the arena. Darien peeked out the door to ensure the way was clear before they parted.

"Get to bed, 'captain.' We can't have our illustrious leader falling asleep in his last regular season match. Especially not against Lia."

Darien smiled. She always knew what to say. He went to bed that night strangely at peace. He was looking forward to the position at The Academy, and especially grateful that Kara had insisted he take the job. There would, of course, be the sad day when their last year together was over, but Darien refused to think about that. Instead, he chose to remind himself of the time he had left with her. For now, everything seemed to be falling into place.

The next morning, Darien woke to the sound of Philip putting on his battle gear, testing his sparring axe to ensure it functioned properly. All of their weapons were specially crafted, so no permanent injury would result from an unprotected blow. Darien wasn't entirely sure how they worked, but there had been times when he was glad they had such a safety measure. When Philip saw that Darien was awake, he smiled, standing and securing the handle of his axe into a loop on his belt.

"Morning." Darien yawned, stretching his arms out to loosen his muscles.

"Morning. How'd you sleep?" Philip asked.

"Great. Ready to take on Lia again. In the arena this time."

Darien began putting on his battle gear: leather boots, forearm bracers, a loose brown shirt, and cargo pants, to which he strapped his sword belt. He considered wearing his hauberk over the shirt for the match, but decided against it, opting to stay light and agile for this particular contest. When they were ready, the two locked the door behind them and made their way to the dining hall. They ate a quick but filling meal before heading to the arena. Their match was the first of the day, and it was bound to attract a crowd.

Halfway to the arena, Darien cursed under his breath. He hadn't swapped out his real sword for the sparring one after his practice session the night before.

"What is it?" Philip asked, concern in his voice.

"I gotta go back to the room," Darien said, showing Philip the problem. "If I hurry, I'll make it back in time."

"Go then! I'll let everyone know where you are."

Darien ran back through the hallways, finding his key and rushing into his room. He dug frantically through the clutter, fished out his sparring blade, and turned back to the door. Removing his sword belt, he tossed it onto his bed and quickly strapped the sparring belt around his waist.

Darien stopped. Something was off. He paused in the doorway, scanning the room. He could hear a strange sucking sound coming from his bed.

He moved cautiously back into the room and looked at the source of the noise. Flicking the light switch, he surveyed the sheets, but the sword belt he had just tossed there was gone. He looked under the bed, around the floor, and even checked Philip's bed, but it was nowhere to be found. Maybe it had slipped between the blankets? Darien ripped the sheets off his bed, but the sword wasn't there. Then his breath caught.

Floating above his bed was a sphere, pulsing in varying shades of blue. It cast strange shadows across the room, and a quiet rhythm filled the air. Darien felt it thumping faintly in his chest.

Curiosity rising, he stepped closer, staring at the orb as it spun slowly above him. He waved his hand in front of it. Nothing. He waved behind it. Again, nothing.

Tentatively, Darien reached out to touch the orb with an outstretched finger. Just half an inch away, he felt a jolt of electricity shoot through him, and his body locked rigid. The sensation morphed, as if he were being ripped from the ground, his whole body compressed simultaneously. The sucking sound grew louder, the rhythm of the orb returning as the blue sphere expanded around him.

Darien tried to scream, but no sound came out. He felt himself being pulled, almost like being sucked through a straw. Everything around him turned pitch black. His arms were pinned to his sides, and for what felt like ten minutes, he could only feel the sensation of movement without seeing anything.

Then, suddenly, a light appeared ahead, quickly rushing toward him. As it drew nearer, the sensation began to slow down. The light grew so bright that Darien shut his eyes in fear, expecting it to hurt. He felt weightless and then falling—THUD.

Darien found himself lying face-first in a grassy field, heat beating down on his back. Dazed, he lifted his head, only to be hit by a wave of dizziness. Crawling to his knees, he felt sick and lost his breakfast. He wiped his mouth with the back of his hand and crawled away from where he had landed, before collapsing back into the grass.

The rhythmic pounding in his head seemed to emanate from the ground. It sounded different from the orb's thumping, but there was an eerie similarity. A set of horse legs came into view, and then his world went black.

Chapter 3: The Story

Darien's eyes fluttered open to the steady rhythm of pain pounding behind his left temple. The sensation spread outward, blooming like a bruised flower beneath his skull. He pushed himself upright, feeling the strange, coarse texture of the bedding under his fingertips. Straw and animal hide—definitely not his room at the Academy.

Taking a cautious breath, he swung his legs off the raised platform he realized served as a bed and placed his feet onto a floor of packed clay, sprinkled with fresh straw. Sunlight filtered dimly through cracks in wooden planks that formed the walls, sending dusty golden beams slicing through the semi-darkness. The air was heavy with earthiness, scented like damp soil after rain, carrying hints of herbs he couldn't identify.

Darien's throat felt parched, each swallow painful. Beside the bed sat a metal cup, its surface reflecting faint ripples of light. He took it carefully, sniffed the clear liquid within, then sipped. Cool water washed down his throat, immediately easing the roughness and dulling the ache in his head. Greedily, he drained the rest.

Where am I?

He looked around, eyes scanning his unfamiliar surroundings once more. Nothing here held any sense of the Academy's structure or the polished corridors he'd known his entire life. Instead, this place felt rustic, almost primitive.

He stood slowly, wavering briefly as dizziness surged and receded. Gathering his balance, he moved cautiously toward a window set oddly high on the wall—almost six feet up. Frustration flickered through him as he cast around for something to stand on, but just as his eyes settled on a small wooden table, a sound froze him in place: the rhythmic clop of hooves echoing clearly just beyond a curtain hanging across a doorway on the far side of the room.

Darien instinctively retreated to sit back on the bed, gripping the now-empty cup, trying to appear casual despite the thundering beat of his heart. The curtain shifted, and a massive shadow moved into the room.

He had expected a rider, perhaps a visitor on horseback, but his breath caught sharply as his eyes widened. It wasn't a rider—it was the horse itself, or rather, something astonishingly impossible. Where the horse's neck should have risen, there was instead a muscular torso, broad shoulders, and a face—weathered yet gentle, framed by strands of graying hair. The creature halted just inside the doorway, hooves shifting as it took a few steps forward.

Darien stared, words evaporating from his mind. This was a creature he'd only ever read about, a centaur straight out of mythology. His throat tightened again, but this time, no amount of water could ease it.

"Ah, good, you're awake," the centaur spoke, his voice deep yet strangely soothing, accented in a way Darien couldn't place. "I thought I heard you moving around."

Darien opened his mouth, but confusion choked out any attempt at speech. He merely stared dumbly, lowering the cup to his lap. Questions battled in his mind, each vying for dominance, but none emerged.

The centaur tilted his head slightly, concern creasing his brow. "Are you well? You look pale."

Darien slowly nodded, then shook his head. "I… I don't understand. Where am I? Who are you?"

The centaur's lips curved into a patient smile, and he took another step closer, bringing with him the faint scent of leather and meadow grasses. "Of course. You wouldn't know, would you?" he mused softly, more to himself than Darien. "You are in the village of Taitron, in the lands known as Altruis one of many lands in Olympus—this is the home of my people, the centaurs. As for me, my name is Chorrun. I'm the healer and teacher here."

"Taitron? Altruis?" Darien echoed faintly, his brow furrowing deeply. He gripped the cup tighter as though it might anchor him to reality. "Is that anywhere near the Academy?"

Chorrun frowned slightly, clearly puzzled by the question. "Academy? There are no academies nearby. None except perhaps in the histories or distant lands far from here."

Memory suddenly flooded Darien—Master Whyn, the match with Lia, the strange orb that pulled him through darkness. His pulse quickened, panic clawing at his chest. "The Academy—I was just there! How long have I been here? I have to get back! Master Whyn, Kara—they're probably worried—"

Ignoring the concerned calls from Chorrun behind him, Darien rushed toward the open doorway, bursting into bright sunlight. He stumbled onto a cobblestone street lined by buildings that looked carved and shaped from nature itself, surrounded by lush, thick forest pressing in from every direction.

Around him, other centaurs halted their activities, staring curiously at the strange, panicked figure in their midst. Their confused murmurs faded into a hum of background noise as Darien stood, mouth agape, overwhelmed by the stark realization of just how far he was from home. Fear, disbelief, and dread rose in waves, threatening to drown him completely.

His knees buckled beneath him, hitting the cobblestones with a dull thud. Time stretched, each passing moment heavy with realization as emotions cascaded through him—confusion tangled with grief, hopelessness battling disbelief, and a deep, resonant despair anchoring it all.

Then a desperate thought surged clearly through the chaos.

I must be dreaming. This has to be a dream.

Darien pushed himself up, legs trembling, eyes darting wildly as the centaurs finally turned their gazes toward him, their eyes filled with curiosity and mild concern. Ignoring their murmured questions, Darien bolted down the street to his right, shoving past surprised centaurs who called out after him. Their voices faded quickly as he veered off the main road, plunging into the cool embrace of the dense forest.

Branches clawed at his clothes and face as he raced blindly through the foliage, his heart pounding in rhythm with his frantic footsteps. Guided by the sound of running water, he broke into a clearing, where a gentle brook wove through the moss-covered stones, oblivious to his desperation. Darien stumbled forward, dropping to his knees at the water's edge and scooping handfuls of icy water onto his face, each splash a pleading cry for reality to return.

"Wake up!" His voice echoed sharply through the trees. "Wake up! Please, wake up!"

Water dripped from his face, soaking his shirt and chilling him to the bone. He fell back onto the bank, breathless, his chest heaving as exhaustion mingled with terror. Slowly, fearfully, he opened his eyes.

Nothing had changed.

Darien squeezed his eyes shut once more, feeling tears sting behind his eyelids. Thoughts swarmed relentlessly, battering his resolve.

Where am I? What's happening to me? Why is this happening to me?

Minutes passed in agonizing silence, only the brook's soft murmur breaking through his spiraling thoughts. Gradually, the discipline ingrained by years at the Academy began to assert itself, calming his breathing, steadying his pulse. He slowly opened his eyes and sat upright, glancing back toward the trees.

Chorrun stood quietly several feet away, his powerful frame poised with quiet dignity. He'd clearly been there for some time, respectful of Darien's turmoil but protective, ensuring privacy from prying eyes.

"Are you well?" Chorrun asked softly, his voice gentle but laced with genuine concern.

"I—I don't know," Darien stammered, trying to control the shaking in his voice. "I don't know how I got here, who you are, or if any of this is even real. I just want to go home."

Chorrun watched him carefully, his golden eyes studying Darien with an intensity that made him feel small and exposed. The silence stretched between them for a long moment, broken only by the occasional rustle of leaves overhead and the faint sound of hooves outside the room.

"You truly don't remember how you arrived?" Chorrun asked, his voice low and cautious, as if trying to gauge whether Darien was simply in shock or hiding something. "Not even the smallest detail? The cycle, the weapons, the Eldric?"

Darien's pulse quickened. He shook his head slowly, the panic from before simmering just beneath the surface. The memories felt fragmented, like pieces of a puzzle that didn't fit together. He tried to recall how he got here, but the effort only made his head throb with a deep, aching confusion.

"I—I don't remember anything," Darien managed, his voice barely a whisper. "I just woke up here... Where am I?"

Chorrun exhaled softly, and for the first time, Darien noticed a shift in his demeanor. The centaur's brow furrowed slightly, his expression betraying a flicker of concern.

"That could be a serious problem," Chorrun murmured, almost to himself.

Darien remained silent, his mind still racing. This wasn't how things were supposed to be. This wasn't normal. He had been a student—he wasn't supposed to be here, in Olympus, surrounded by creatures he had only read about in myths. The world felt unreal.

The silence stretched again, the tension in the air thickening. Finally, Chorrun moved, stepping closer to Darien, his large form imposing yet oddly steadying. He extended his strong hand toward Darien, not as a command, but with an almost gentle urgency. Darien hesitated but reached out, his hand trembling slightly as he gripped the centaur's forearm. There was a strange comfort in the strength that radiated from Chorrun. It grounded him, but it didn't quell the rising anxiety.

Chorrun helped Darien stand, his steady hands guiding him up, and for a moment, Darien just leaned into the support, his legs unsteady beneath him. "Come," Chorrun said, his voice soft but commanding. "You need rest, Darien. With your expected arrival we tried to make sure to have comfortable accommodations. Once you're feeling stronger, we can talk more clearly about how you arrived."

"Expected?" Darien repeated weakly, still trying to grasp the words Chorrun had spoken. "You knew I'd be here?"

Chorrun's expression remained carefully neutral, but Darien caught the slight hesitation in his eyes. The centaur stopped and turned to face him, his posture straight, but his tone suddenly more measured.

"Yes," Chorrun said slowly, his words careful, "Every fifty years, four warriors appear to challenge Cyprin and protect Olympus. It's a part of our history—our way of life. Your arrival isn't unusual, though we didn't know it would be you specifically." He paused, and his gaze lingered on Darien. "The issue is that you seem completely unaware of your role, the cycles, even Olympus itself. This is not how things have ever happened before."

Darien's heart skipped a beat. Cyprin? He didn't know what that meant, either. He felt his breath catch in his throat as the words registered, but he couldn't process them. He couldn't process any of this. The more Chorrun spoke, the more Darien's mind refused to catch up with the reality of his situation.

"Cycles? Warriors?" Darien's voice wavered as he struggled to understand, but the more he tried to make sense of it, the more foreign everything felt. "This makes no sense. I don't understand any of this."

Chorrun nodded slowly, his face solemn. "I know. And that's exactly why I'm worried."

The centaur's words carried a weight that settled heavily on Darien's chest. The idea that Darien didn't know what was going on was unsettling, and it was starting to become more disturbing by the moment. Chorrun's worry was clear, but the way he spoke also made Darien feel like something wasn't right—like the entire situation was somehow off-kilter.

Chorrun took a step back, as if trying to give Darien space to absorb the overwhelming information. "Your fellow team of warriors will be waiting for you," he said, his tone quieter, almost offhand. "They, too, have been summoned by the transitions. Traditionally, all four members of The Eldric meet at Farkland Reach, the city to our north."

The mention of the others felt like another thread pulling at him, unraveling his understanding of everything he thought he knew.

"The others will be there too?" Darien asked, the idea of meeting the three other members of his team filling him with a sliver of hope to unravel the strangeness of the situation he found himself in.

Chorrun nodded, looking at Darien with concern. "But that is after a long ride north. I can see it in your face, you're tired. I encourage you to rest. I have never had the honor of going through the transitions, but they seem to have taken a toll on you."

Darien nodded, the weight of the conversation as well as the lingering effect of the strange journey here pressed onto him. The sun was still shining through the window as he tried to calm his mind using meditation techniques from The Academy. It took some time, but eventually he drifted off to sleep.

Darien's eyes shot open. The chirping of birds and the warm early glow of late afternoon sunlight flooding the room brought a sense of reality crashing down on him. He blinked rapidly, trying to make sense of his sur-roundings. For a moment, he forgot where he was, be-fore the crushing realization hit.

I'm still here.

A sick feeling curled in his stomach, but he couldn't quite place it. Homesick? He had heard the term used by other students at The Academy, but he'd never thought much about it. Now, with everything unfamiliar around him, it hit him harder than he expected. He groaned and let himself fall back onto the bed, staring at the ceiling.

I don't want this. I don't want to be a hero for some world that isn't even real.

Darien threw his legs over the side of the bed and stood, rubbing his face. His head still ached from whatever had happened during the journey here, but he could manage. He had to.

As he got up, he noticed the sword—his real sword—hanging on a hook inside the door. That explained where it had gone. It had come through the transition just before him.

His mind was still reeling, but there was no time to waste. He stepped out of the room and into the main area. Chorrun was there, speaking with a young centaur, who quickly left the house after a few words.

"Good afternoon, Darien," Chorrun said, turning with a smile. "I trust you slept well?"

Darien shrugged, trying to sound neutral. "Yeah, I guess. How long was I asleep for?"

"Only an hour or so. I expected you to sleep longer, actually." Chorun set a piece of parchment down on the small table in front of him. "Darien, I don't wish to leave you alone so soon, but there's a situation I must attend to. A girl has fallen ill, and I need to go. I had planned to show you around Taitron, but if you're up for it, you can explore on your own for now."

Darien nodded, his thoughts still jumbled. "I can do that."

"Good," Chorrun said. "Food's on the table for you. Take your time." With that, Chorrun left, leaving Darien to his own thoughts.

Darien ate quickly, his stomach growling after the strange morning but feeling at least lightly refreshed from his nap. He was surprised at just how tired he felt. Once finished, he decided to explore, hoping the walk would clear his mind. As he left the small house and stepped onto the cobbled streets, he tried to keep his thoughts focused on his surroundings instead of the crushing weight of uncertainty.

The village was quiet and calm, with centaurs passing by, some acknowledging him with nods. He walked for a while, losing himself in the natural beauty around him. It wasn't much different from his home, except the people here were... different. His boots crunched on the gravel as he wandered further from the village.

It wasn't long before he realized he had wandered too far. The familiar buildings were gone, and the dense trees surrounded him, closing in. He hoped he could still find his way back, but with no signs of life, he was starting to feel the weight of the situation again.

Then he heard voices. With a sense of relief, he hurried towards the sound, hoping it would lead him back to where he needed to be. As he emerged from the trees, he stumbled into a meadow. In front of him, a group of centaurs were playing some sort of game. Darien blinked, momentarily confused by the sight of them. A ball, about the size of a cantaloupe, was being passed around, kicked between the players' legs and heads. Darien hesitated, unsure how to approach, but finally called out.

"Hey, is this a game?" he asked.

One of the centaurs, looked at him, his face breaking into a smile. "It's called hooper," Torin said. "Ever seen it?"

Darien shook his head, intrigued. "No. How do you play?"

"You can't use your hands," the boy explained, "only your legs or your head. It's tougher than it sounds."

Darien laughed, amazed. "I don't know if I could manage that."

"You should give it a try sometime," he grinned. "It's a lot harder than it looks."

Darien took a seat on a nearby hill, watching them play. The game was fast, rough—nothing like any game he'd ever seen back home. It reminded him of basketball, soccer, and football all mixed together, but more chaotic.

As he watched, he caught himself wishing that Philip, Kara, or Trey were there, that they could be a part of this experience with him. He hoped wherever they were, they were making their way to the same place Chorrun had planned for them to travel to.

The feeling of longing grew heavier, and Darien tried to push it down, but it wouldn't go away. After a while, Torin came over to him, his group dispersing.

"Need help getting back?" the young centaur asked.

Darien nodded, relieved. "Yeah, I think I got lost. Hey, what's your name by the way?"

"Torin," he said simply.

Torin began walking alongside Darien as they made their way through the forest. As they walked, Darien tried to distract himself by looking at the natural surroundings. The paths seemed almost to have grown through the trees, the centaurs working with nature to create their roads, blending them seamlessly into the world around them. It was impressive, but Darien couldn't stop his mind from drifting back to his own world.

The weight of his situation was becoming harder to ignore. He was a stranger in this place, and all he wanted was to go home. He couldn't stop thinking about his friends, his life back at The Academy. He wasn't supposed to be here, in this strange world, with no idea how he'd get home.

"Are you okay?" Torin's voice snapped him out of his thoughts.

Darien quickly wiped the troubled look from his face. "Yeah, I'm fine," he said, his voice a little too quick. "Just... adjusting. This whole place is just... a lot to take in."

Torin seemed to accept the answer without further comment, and the two continued walking in silence for a few moments. Darien, still trying to compose himself, looked around, trying to appreciate the calm, the quiet, and the strange beauty of the world around him.

"How old are you, Torin?" Darien asked, wanting to change the subject and keep his mind occupied.

"I'm seventeen," Torin replied. "I'll be eighteen soon, and then I can undergo the rights to become a man. I'll be able to build my home after that."

Darien nodded, taking in the information as another question rose to the surface. "How many days are there in a year here, in Olympus?"

Torin thought for a moment. "About 372 days, though sometimes a day is added or subtracted. Not sure how it works exactly. We mostly tell by the seasons. How many days in a year for you?"

"365," Darien said. "But sometimes we add a day, too. So, I guess we have that in common."

Torin's ears perked up. "Can I ask what your world is like? Chorrun talks about the other worlds as the histories tell of them, and they sound amazing. But that's from thousands of years ago."

Darien couldn't help but laugh at the thought of Earth being called "amazing." He stopped walking for a moment to catch his breath.

"What did I say?" Torin asked, a bit confused.

"Nothing," Darien said, shaking his head with a smile. "It's just... hard to imagine. There's nothing too magical where I'm from. Though, we have some things you might not."

"Like what?" Torin's curiosity was evident.

"Well, we have things like big buildings, lights everywhere, and screens."

Torin's face lit up with interest. "We have lights here!"

Darien shook his head, amused. "Not lights like these. At least, not from what I've seen in Taitron."

He began explaining, describing the concept of lights that could light up entire streets, how computers could capture images and play them back. For Torin, it all sounded like magic. Darien laughed at how alien even the simplest things from his world seemed here.

By the time they'd spoken about Earth and its wonders, the village was in view once more. The sun was dipping lower in the sky, casting a golden glow over the forest.

As they walked, Darien couldn't help but feel a growing fondness for Torin, who was so eager to learn about Earth. The village itself had started to feel less strange, blending so naturally with the forest. The trees had shaped the homes, the paths, even the shops, creating a peaceful, harmonious atmosphere that Darien couldn't quite explain. The more he looked around, the more he realized how much this world and its people had embraced nature rather than fight against it.

When they reached the dwelling where he had woken up, Darien waved goodbye to Torin, thankful for his company. He entered the building, the cooler air of the evening immediately soothing him. An incredible hunger hit him then as he remembered he hadn't eaten since the morning. He walked over to the small table where another plate of fruit, cheese, and bread awaited him. Beside it sat a pitcher of water.

Darien sat back against the wall, his fingers still gripping the strange fruit, but his thoughts were far away. He thought of Kara, her laughter, the way her eyes lit up when she spoke about their future. But here, in this new world, there was nothing familiar. He was alone. He pushed past the feeling, praying that in just a few days he'd hopefully see his friends again, and tried to enjoy the strange flavors. They weren't bad, but they were incredibly different.

He was surprised at how tired he felt. Between the mental toll of where he found himself, the feeling of the food in his stomach, and the excitement of watching Torin and his friends play, he was tired again already. His eyes closed, and before he knew it, sleep overtook him, his body too tired to fight it. His mind filled with a whirl of images, a familiar face, holding a sword—bloody and ready for battle. A monstrous creature held Kara, his vision blurring as her scream reached his ears.

"Darien!" she called, her voice fading as he stood helpless, watching her fall over the edge of an endless abyss.

Chapter 4: The Departure

"Darien!"

A firm shake rattled him from the depths of his nightmare. He lurched awake, breath ragged, fingers curling into the coarse bedding beneath him. Chorrun's face hovered above him, lined with concern, his earthy scent mixing with the remnants of Darien's terror.

"You were screaming," Chorrun said, his voice low and measured. "I had to wake you."

Darien stared at him, heart hammering against his ribs. The images clung to him, stubborn as shadows—flashes of blood, fire, a familiar voice crying his name before vanishing into darkness. He pressed his hands against his temples, grounding himself in the sensation of rough fabric and solid earth beneath him. "It was just... a bad dream," he muttered, voice hoarse.

Chorrun studied him for a long moment, stepping back as Darien swung his legs over the edge of the bed. The cool air of morning met his skin, a stark contrast to the feverish heat still clinging to his body. "Do you need anything?"

Darien exhaled slowly, forcing steadiness into his limbs. "No thanks," he said, shaking his head. "I'll be fine."

Chorrun remained unmoving, eyes narrowed slightly. "You were screaming quite loudly. Are you sure I can't make you a tonic? Some water, at least?"

Darien hesitated, running a hand through his damp hair. He could still feel the ghost of the dream slithering beneath his skin, but admitting that wouldn't help. "It was just a nightmare," he said, more to himself than Chorrun. "Nothing more."

The healer sighed but let it drop. "What time is it?" Darien asked, glancing toward the slivers of light stretching through the wooden slats.

"Just after sunrise," Chorrun said.

Darien blinked. "Sunrise?" He turned to the centaur, startled. "I slept all day?"

"You were exhausted," Chorrun replied. "I returned late last night after tending to a sick child. The fever finally broke, but it took most of the day. I saw you sleeping and thought it best not to disturb you—until, well..." He gestured toward the space between them, where the weight of Darien's screams still lingered.

Darien's cheeks burned. "Sorry I woke you," he muttered.

Chorrun waved the apology away with a flick of his hand. "I have preparations to make before we leave, so I needed to be up early, anyway."

Darien latched onto the shift in topic like a lifeline. "When are we leaving?" he asked, urgency creeping into his voice.

"As soon as everything is ready," Chorrun replied. "An hour, maybe two. If you're prepared?"

Darien nodded. "I'm ready."

Chorrun studied him for a beat longer, then turned and exited, leaving Darien alone with the lingering remnants of his dream. He took a deep breath, steadying himself. The shadows were fading, slipping into memory, but restlessness gnawed at his muscles. He needed to move.

He rose, stretching his stiff limbs before moving toward the corner where a set of folded garments hung from a wooden hook. Fresh clothes. He hadn't even noticed them before. Tugging off his sleep-wrinkled tunic, he changed quickly, relishing the feel of clean fabric against his skin. The fit was slightly looser than he was used to, but comfortable. He secured his sword belt around his waist, testing the weight of it as he rolled his shoulders. Good enough.

Stepping outside, he inhaled deeply. The air carried the crisp scent of morning dew, tinged with the faint aroma of damp earth and distant firewood. The village was beginning to stir—centaurs moving between huts, voices murmuring in the early quiet. Overhead, the sky stretched in soft hues of pink and orange, the sun still hidden beyond the treetops.

Darien closed his eyes for a moment, feeling the tension ease slightly. But only slightly. The restlessness remained, coiled in his chest like an unspent breath. He needed motion.

Turning down a side path, he found a small clearing, half-shielded by the tall trees. The earth here was compact, firm beneath his boots. It would do. Drawing his sword, he took his stance, exhaling through his nose. The morning sounds faded as he focused, his mind slipping into the familiar rhythm of movement.

Thrust. Parry. Sidestep. Lunge. His blade cut the air in precise arcs, his body following each motion with practiced ease. The weight of the weapon was an extension of himself, a seamless flow between thought and action. He imagined an unseen opponent before him—a faceless enemy pressing forward. He countered, his footwork light, his strikes measured. Block. Pivot. Dodge. Attack. The world narrowed to the dance of steel and breath, muscles burning with the effort. He pushed harder, losing himself in the motion, in the discipline, in the control.

He halted mid-swing, chest heaving. Turning, he saw them. A small group of centaurs had gathered at the edge of the clearing, watching in complete silence.

Darien swallowed hard, suddenly acutely aware of his flushed skin and sweat-dampened shirt. He hadn't even noticed them approach. For a long moment, no one spoke. Then—applause. A ripple of appreciation spread through the gathered onlookers, some nodding, others murmuring in approval. Darien's face burned. Clearing his throat, he gave them a sheepish nod, hastily sheathing his sword. Without another word, he turned and strode back toward Chorrun's hut, heart still pounding—not only from exertion, but from the weight of unexpected eyes.

When Darien stepped outside, he found Chorrun waiting near the edge of the dwelling, holding the reins of a sturdy brown horse. The animal stood patiently, its ears flicking at the occasional morning insect, while packs bulged from the simple saddle strapped to its back. Supplies, no doubt, though Darien couldn't begin to guess what all was inside.

"Hello again," Chorrun greeted, his voice light and chipper. "Are you ready to leave?"

Darien nodded, his gaze shifting to the horse. "What's that for?"

"You, of course," Chorrun chuckled, giving the reins a light shake. "You didn't think you'd be walking all the way to Farkland Reach, did you?"

"I guess I hadn't thought about it." Darien stared at the horse for a moment, realizing just how unprepared he was for this kind of journey. "How far is this place we're going again?"

"The ride to Farkland Reach is about nine or ten days north from here—if we take it slow," Chorrun said. "We could push the pace, but there's no need to exhaust ourselves or the horse. You'll be traveling with me and two others, so we decided it'd be best to lend you a horse."

Darien nodded but couldn't ignore how odd it felt to hear a centaur speak about owning and riding horses. He tucked that thought away, thanking Chorrun before slipping back inside the hut to collect himself before departure. A wave of unfamiliar emotions stirred within him. He had spent his entire life within the walls of the Academy, structured, secure, and predictable. The idea of traveling, of moving from place to place with no certainty of what lay ahead, was... unsettling. Sitting on the edge of the bed, he ran a hand over his face, forcing himself to push past the uncertainty. One day at a time. That was all he could do.

Taking a deep breath, he looked around the room. What did he even have to pack?

His belongings were minimal. He grabbed the animal-hide bedroll he had been using, rolling it as tightly as he could before securing it with the leather straps attached to the ends. Slinging it under his arm, he stepped back into the crisp morning air, squinting against the golden sunlight now filtering through the canopy.

Chorrun handed him a pack. "Some extra clothes for the journey," he explained.

Darien took it, rummaging through the contents. Two sets of pants, a second shirt, a pair of gloves—simple, practical. He tied the pack shut and slung it over his shoulder before glancing back at the centaur. "Back home, I had other things I wore when I fought sometimes. Where could I find those? Or maybe get some money to pay for them?"

Chorrun let out a deep, hearty laugh. "Pay?" He shook his head. "You won't be paying for a thing while you're in Olympus—at least not in this village, and likely not in Farkland Reach, either. Tell me, what do you need?"

Darien hesitated, considering his answer carefully. If centaurs existed here, what else might he come across? Trolls? Dragons? Mermaids? The thought almost made him smile, though the mental image of Kara rolling her eyes at him quickly wiped it away. He straightened, focusing back on what mattered. "A shield, about the width of my arm. Bracers, a hauberk, and heavy leather greaves if you have them."

Chorrun nodded after a moment's consideration. "We can provide most of that, save for the greaves. My people don't use that sort of armor, so we don't have any in the village. But I believe we have a hauberk that will suit you. As for the greaves, the king of Farkland Reach will likely be able to supply them. They have some of the best smiths in all of Olympus, and if they don't have what you need, they'll make it for you."

Chorrun turned and called out to another centaur— Jodin, Darien learned his name was. After a brief exchange, Jodin gave a nod and trotted off toward the village center.

Darien approached his waiting horse, taking a closer look at the setup. It looked clunky, the various packs strapped haphazardly to its frame, but the horse stood firm, patient beneath its burden. He reached out, running a hand along its neck. The animal didn't shy away. That was a good sign.

And then another realization struck him.

He had never ridden a horse before.

For all the Academy's combat training, its medieval-styled tournaments, its practice with blades, bows, and shields—horsemanship had never been part of the curriculum. He made a mental note to bring that up to Master Whyn if he ever made it back home.

Jodin soon returned, carrying the requested armor. He handed the pieces to Darien, who accepted them with a quiet nod of thanks, feeling a strange guilt at receiving all of this for free. He slipped the hauberk over his head. The weight settled comfortably over his torso, the mail light but durable. The craftsmanship was unlike any he had seen before—the gaps in the chain links were smaller, woven tighter. The fit wasn't perfect, but it would do.

Testing his range of motion, he stepped back, examining his horse once more. The arrangement of supplies still seemed chaotic, but he figured he'd have time to make adjustments during the journey. He drew his sword and shifted it against his hip, checking the weight. The motion was fluid, familiar. That, at least, felt right.

Chorrun watched him for a moment before motioning toward the saddle. "Mount up."

Darien stepped forward, placing his foot into the stirrup as he had seen others do. He pulled himself up, but the motion felt awkward, foreign. His balance faltered, and before he knew it, he was tumbling backward. The impact sent a jolt through his tailbone, and he let out a sharp grunt, staring up at the sky as he heard Chorrun stifle a laugh.

Heat crawled up Darien's neck, but he swallowed his embarrassment and climbed back to his feet, dusting himself off. On the second attempt, he managed to get into the saddle, though the effort left him gripping the reins tightly as he steadied himself.

Chorrun gave him a knowing smirk. "It gets easier."

Darien wasn't convinced.

The two other centaurs approached, their own supplies already secured. Chorrun turned to them with a nod. "Are we ready?"

Darien and the others gave their confirmation.

"Then off we go."

The three centaurs took the lead, trotting forward in a steady, rhythmic motion. Darien followed in single file, his horse moving at a measured pace beneath him, each step sending a new jolt through his body as he adjusted to the movement. He held tight to the reins, trying to appear more confident than he felt.

As they left the village of Taitron behind, the weight of the journey ahead settled over him. There was no turning back now.

Darien could only describe their first day of travel as quiet and beautiful. The landscape shifted from dense forests to sprawling meadows, where golden fields stretched beneath an endless sky. Creeks wove through the terrain, their gentle gurgling the only sound besides the steady rhythm of hooves against the lightly worn road. Though they passed no other travelers, the well-trodden path suggested this route saw frequent use.

It didn't take long for Darien to find a rhythm in the saddle, though his body disagreed with the experience. The horse moved differently than anything he was used to, its rolling gait forcing his muscles into patterns they weren't accustomed to. His hips protested at every shift, and his legs felt stiff from holding a position for so long.

Chorrun led the small group, with Jodin following behind him, Darien in the middle, and Lotry taking up the rear. Darien had hoped to ride closer to Chorrun, to ask more about the world and its history, but with the other two centaurs so near, he wasn't sure how much the elder would be willing to share. For now, he resigned himself to the quiet, letting his thoughts drift as they moved through the ever-changing landscape.

By late afternoon, the horizon burned in deep oranges and purples as the sun descended. Chorrun slowed his pace before calling out, "We'll make camp here."

He led them off the path, through thick grass that swayed in the evening breeze, until they reached a shallow dip in the landscape, shielded from view. The location was well-chosen—hidden enough to deter unwanted attention, yet open enough to see any approaching movement.

Darien dismounted, immediately regretting the decision as his legs nearly buckled beneath him. His whole body screamed in protest, stiff from hours spent in an unfamiliar position. He gritted his teeth, suppressing a groan as he forced his feet to hold firm on solid ground.

Turning to his horse, he began fumbling with the saddle's straps and buckles, feeling the weight of the animal's patience as it let out a deep, expectant snort. The saddle refused to budge. Darien tugged harder, only for the horse to shift its weight with an irritated huff. Finally, after several long minutes of uncoordinated struggle, the saddle came loose, nearly toppling him backward as it slid to the ground. Darien exhaled sharply, muttering under his breath as he shook out the blanket that had sat beneath it, laying it over a low branch to dry.

Once the horse was secured and left to graze, he returned to the others, who had already gathered around a freshly built fire. The orange glow flickered against their figures, casting long shadows into the night as the scent of woodsmoke mingled with the cool evening air.

Taking a seat near the flames, Darien turned his gaze skyward. The constellations above were unfamiliar, scattered across an alien canvas. A crescent moon hung low, smaller than he was used to, its soft glow illuminating the world in an eerie silver sheen.

"Is this place so different from your home?" Jodin asked, his tone carrying genuine curiosity.

Darien considered the question before answering. "It's different from where I grew up," he admitted. "I'm sure there are places on my world that look like this, but I've never seen them. Nothing here feels familiar. Not even the stars."

"What is your world like?" Lotry asked.

Darien hesitated. He had described Earth to Torin just the day before, but now the words felt harder to find. He had never truly stopped to consider the scope of the world he had lived in, never thought to appreciate what it meant beyond the walls of the Academy. He had learned about it through books, maps, and lessons, but the reality of it felt distant—something he had always planned to see but never truly experienced.

"Earth is..." He paused, searching for the right words. "It has massive cities, sprawling across land and water, filled with millions of people. But there are also places where no one lives for miles. There are deserts, forests, oceans stretching farther than the eye can see. Mountains that touch the sky. It has everything."

Jodin tilted his head. "Have you traveled all of it?"

Darien let out a small chuckle, though there was no humor in it. "No," he admitted. "I haven't seen much of it at all. I spent most of my life at the Academy. I never really left."

The weight of the words settled heavily in his chest. He had always planned to leave, always imagined seeing the world alongside Kara, but now that future felt like a fading dream. He caught Chorrun's sharp gaze flick toward him from across the fire, the centaur saying nothing as he stirred their meal over the flames.

This is going to be harder than I thought.

Jodin shifted slightly. "What is the Academy?"

Darien hesitated. "It's a school," he said finally, choosing his words carefully. "A place where we train for battle, where we study... everything, really."

"You went to this Academy to prepare for your time here in Olympus?" Lotry asked.

"Yeah," Darien replied. "You could say that, I guess."

The conversation faded, and Chorrun's posture relaxed slightly as silence settled over the group once more.

A few moments later, the elder centaur began passing out bowls filled with steaming soup. The scent of herbs and roasted vegetables filled the air, and Darien realized just how hungry he was. He accepted his portion gratefully, the warmth of the meal seeping into his chilled fingers as he took his first bite. The taste was simple but hearty, and as he ate, a drowsiness crept over him, the exhaustion of the day finally catching up.

The others stretched out by the fire, the centaurs laying flat against the ground in a way that seemed second nature to them. Darien followed their lead, spreading out his bedroll and sinking into its rough fabric. The fire crackled, and in the distance he saw flashes of lighting and the distant roar of thunder.

Beyond the glow of the flames, a single shooting star cut through the darkness, vanishing as quickly as it had appeared. Darien watched it fade, wondering if Kara was seeing the same sky from wherever she was.

His eyes drifted shut, the weight of sleep pulling him under before he could finish the thought.

Chapter 5: The Tower

Darien was the first to wake. The world around him was still, save for the quiet hum of morning insects and the distant trickle of water. He stretched, rolling his shoulders to ease the stiffness from the previous day's ride. His muscles ached, his hips sore from the unnatural motion of the saddle, but it was nothing he couldn't push through.

His horse stood exactly where he had left it, lazily swishing its tail. With a yawn, Darien made his way to the nearby stream. He crouched at the water's edge, cupping his hands and splashing the icy water over his face. The chill jolted him fully awake, washing away the last remnants of sleep. The water was crisp and clean, tasting fresher than anything he'd had back at the Academy. He ran wet fingers through his hair, pushing it back before rinsing out his mouth. It wasn't much of a morning routine, but it would have to do until he could figure out something better.

By the time he returned to camp, the others were stirring. Chorrun and Lotry were dousing the last embers of the fire while Jodin was busy looking through a bag of belongings for something buried at the bottom.

"Good morning," Darien greeted them, surprised by the energy in his own voice. The cold water had done more to wake him than he'd expected.

"Good day, Darien," Chorrun yawned, scattering the ashes with practiced efficiency. "Sleep well?"

"As well as I could," Darien said, rubbing his neck. "Soreness is setting in."

"That'll happen," Jodin smirked as he continued gathering his gear. "You'll get used to it."

"You ready to go?" Chorrun's voice was steady, but there was something more beneath it—a kind of quiet reassurance.

Darien nodded, though he still wasn't sure he felt ready. The whole thing felt wrong, like he was waiting for someone to tell him it was all a mistake, that he was going home and he had been brought here by accident. But that moment didn't come.

The group set off in silence, the soft crunch of their steps and the rhythmic clip-clop of hooves filling the air. The early morning air was cool, though it carried a hint of moisture that made Darien's skin prickle. As they moved forward, the land around them seemed endless—rolling hills, dense forests, and the occasional break in the trees that revealed the horizon.

The pace was slow at first. Chorrun led them on a winding path, careful to avoid any dense woods that might slow them down. For the first time since arriving in Olympus, Darien felt like he could breathe.

A distant flash. Lightning.

It was almost too faint to make out at first, just as the one the night before had been, but it was unmistakable. The storm was on its way. He felt the air shift, the temperature dropping sharply as the sky darkened.

"Storm's coming," Darien said, the words catching in his throat. His mind was racing again, and the unease in his chest seemed to grow with each flash of lightning.

Chorrun glanced up, his eyes narrowing. "I see it. We've got time, but we need to keep moving. We don't want to get caught out in it."

Lotry, walking up beside Darien, spoke up. "Let's push on as far as we can. The faster we move, the less likely we are to get caught in the worst of it."

Darien didn't argue. He didn't know much about traveling in a storm, but Chorrun seemed confident. They quickened their pace, trying to make up for the lost time they would inevitably endure as they waited out the storm.

The sky darkened further as they moved; the wind picking up and stirring the trees. Beginning with small, scattered droplets, the rain quickly intensified into a steady downpour.

Darien felt it hit, the chill of the rain biting through his cloak. The storm was closing in fast.

Chorrun pulled his hood tighter and pushed himself forward. "We'll need to find shelter soon. There's an old watchtower nearby that we can use."

"Good," Darien muttered, pulling his cloak tighter around his shoulders. He didn't mind the rain, but there was something about the urgency in the air that made his nerves flare. The unknown, he thought. This place, Olympus—it was so different from the Academy.

The rain was picking up now, and the wind had started to whip through the trees. The path before them, once open, seemed to narrow as the landscape began to shift, the trees growing thicker and the earth more uneven. Darien's horse shifted beneath him, its hooves sinking into the mud as they moved forward.

"We're getting close," Chorrun said, looking ahead toward the dense woods. "The tower should be just up ahead."

But Lotry and Jodin, walking behind them, exchanged uneasy glances, and Darien caught the flicker of hesitation in their eyes.

"The tower?" Jodin muttered under his breath. "You're not seriously thinking of staying there, are you?"

Lotry shook his head. "No one goes there," he added quietly, his voice edged with something that bordered on superstition. "It's... it's cursed, isn't it?"

"Cursed?" Darien asked, unsure how much to set aside his disbelief at this point. "Why would it be cursed?"

Jodin nodded. "It's one of the ruins of the last battle with Cyprin, built during the great war. They say it's haunted by wraiths."

"Wraiths?" Darien frowned, hearing the unease in their voices.

Lotry nodded solemnly. "They're said to linger there. People say it's forbidden to go there, a place of respect... but also a place to be avoided. No one's supposed to disturb the resting place of those who fought there."

Darien turned his head slightly to look at Chorrun, who had remained silent during the exchange, his gaze forward as the storm continued to rage around them. Chorrun's lips barely moved, but he didn't seem worried in the same way.

"That's superstition," Chorrun said, his voice steady. "The wraiths of the battle are stories passed down by the people who don't understand the history of Olympus. It's just a ruined tower now, a relic. There's nothing to fear. The wraiths that do exist all live in caves far from here."

"But Chorrun," Jodin said, his voice rising slightly, "they say the people who go there disappear. Some never come back at all."

"Who do you know who has ever seen or known someone who entered?" Chorrun replied firmly. "It's an old building, yes, and a sacred place to some. But there are no wraiths haunting it."

Despite Chorrun's reassurances, the tension still hung in the air like a storm cloud. Lotry and Jodin were clearly unconvinced. They exchanged a glance before Lotry spoke again.

"I don't like it," he said, his voice quieter. "It's taboo, you know. Just... being near it."

The rain was only getting worse, turning the path into a slick, muddy mess. Darien didn't want to stay out here, trapped in this growing storm and the uneasy tension that seemed to hang in the air. The watchtower was a place of shelter—nothing more. He needed somewhere dry. The rumors about the place didn't matter. He just wanted out of the rain.

Lotry eyed the structure, his brow furrowed in reluctance. "I still don't like it," he muttered under his breath, his voice tight. "But we'll have to do something. We can't stay out here in this."

Darien looked at the storm swirling around them, the lightning flashing in the distance, and then at the crumbling tower ahead. Without another word, he nudged his horse forward, the path leading them toward shelter.

"I don't know about you, but I'm tired of the rain. I'm going inside," Darien said. His tone wasn't harsh, but the resolve was there. "You can stay out here if you want."

Lotry and Jodin exchanged another uneasy glance, but it was clear that neither of them was particularly eager to remain exposed to the storm. With a collective sigh, they finally relented and followed Darien into the tower's shadow.

The wind howled, and the first few drops of rain began to fall heavily, quickly soaking them through. As the others reluctantly followed, Darien spurred his horse faster, the shelter of the watchtower now an urgent refuge.

Darien followed Chorrun into the ruins of the old watchtower, the remnants of an ancient battle still hanging heavy in the air. He had never felt anything like it before—this place was more than just stone and dust. It felt like history itself had settled here, waiting to be understood.

The tower stood like a ghost, its stone walls weathered and cracked with age. Some of the walls were barely standing, and the roof had long since collapsed, but the structure still had a kind of majesty, as though it had once been more than just a defensive position. There was a quiet sacredness to the place that Darien couldn't shake.

He ran his fingers over the stone walls, careful of the rough texture, trying to make sense of the symbols etched into the surface. His mind wandered back to Chorrun's earlier words. The last battle. The weapons. The cycles. So many questions.

"The Eldric. You said every fifty years they come back to Olympus, right?" Darien's voice was quiet, almost hesitant, as he turned to Chorrun, still grappling with the enormity of what he was hearing. "But... why? What's the point? Why does this happen over and over?"

Chorrun's golden eyes glinted in the dim light, his expression soft but serious. He didn't seem surprised by the question. It was the same one, after all, that everyone asked when they first learned of Olympus's history.

"The Eldric come every cycle to keep Cyprin locked away," Chorrun explained, his voice steady. "Without them, the gates to Olympus would remain closed, and the balance would tip. We've done this for three thousand years. Every fifty years, a new group of warriors must come to retrieve the weapons, complete the ritual, and reimprison Cyprin."

Darien looked at the walls, tracing his finger in the chiseled runes that he could not read, taking in the significance of the words. Three thousand years. A cycle of rebirth and death, with the Eldric constantly coming, gathering the weapons, and locking away Cyprin once again.

"The weapons," Darien said slowly, his brow furrowed in confusion. "What are they? Why can't Cyprin be stopped without them?"

Chorrun smiled faintly, the curve of his lips almost melancholic. "The weapons are the key to opening the gates to Olympus. They are what make it possible for us to imprison Cyprin—to ensure he remains locked away. Without them, the gates would remain closed, and we would never be able to face him."

"Where are these weapons?" Darien asked, his curiosity piqued.

"The weapons are scattered across the land," Chorrun said. "The cities that hold them guard them jealously. There's a sword and bow, but those are the only I know of for certain."

"The weapons are the key to everything," Chorrun continued. "Without them, Cyprin cannot be imprisoned again. They were created during the first rise of the Eldric. With the spell cast by Whytaren the last free spellcaster to oppose Cyprin. They are not simply tools—they are symbols of the balance we must maintain."

Darien felt the tension in his chest tighten, the weight of the information pressing down on him. There was so much more he didn't understand. "But why does it have to be this way? Why does Cyprin come back every fifty years? Why do the Eldric always have to face him?"

Chorrun paused, his eyes clouding with a mix of thoughts Darien couldn't quite read. "I don't have all the answers, Darien. But this is how the cycles have always worked. The Eldric must come, gather the weapons, and perform the ritual. The world is built on these patterns."

"But who decides this?" Darien pressed. "Who decided that we need to keep doing this?"

Chorrun looked at him, his gaze thoughtful but steady. "When Whytaren cast the spell, it set everything in motion. Cyprin was winning. The histories say all was lost, and he, along with the first Four, were able to lock Cyprin away. Not victory, but not defeat."

Darien felt his mind start to race with more questions, but Chorrun's voice interrupted. "There are some things we will never fully understand, Darien. This world was shaped long ago, and the cycles are now simply part of Olympus's nature."

Darien stood there, silent for a moment, trying to wrap his mind around it. Three thousand years of this cycle, each generation choosing warriors to gather the weapons, perform the ritual, and imprison Cyprin. But there was more to it than just the ritual. There had to be. Hi mind turned though to something more practical.

"How are we able to understand each other?" Darien asked. "This is a whole different world. I couldn't read anything on your map, so we must have a different language. How is it that we speak the same?"

"That is part of the magic of the transitions," Chorrun explained. "It has always been this way. Those who travel between worlds can understand the language of the place they enter. In Olympus, we all speak Olveery, but you will have no trouble communicating with anyone you meet. It is one of the few remaining traces of magic outside the mountain."

Darien stared at the weathered stones around him. The weight of the tower, the mystery of Olympus, pressed on him, and a deep sense of alienation settled in his chest. This place was so foreign, even the small bit of it he knew was so different from everything he had ever known. He didn't belong here. "I don't... I don't know how to do this," he muttered, his voice low, frustration lacing his words. "Everything here feels wrong. I don't belong here, Chorrun."

Chorrun turned to him, his gaze steady but understanding. "You are exactly where you need to be, Darien. Sometimes, finding your place means walking through the unknown. Olympus may seem strange now, and I know your entry into it was not what the histories describe, but life has a way of showing you where you're meant to go. Trust that you're not here by mistake."

Chorrun shuffled his feet to find a better grip for his hooves on the weathered stone. "The ruins—like this tower—are remnants of a past we cannot change. They are a reminder of the price we pay for peace. We cannot let that peace go so easily."

Darien nodded, though he wasn't quite sure what in the centaurs words he was nodding to. He turned back to the tower, his eyes searching for answers, but they were hidden beneath layers of time. The cycle would continue, whether he accepted it or not. Whether he was part of it or not.

The group spent the night waiting out the storm. When Darien emerged the next morning, he felt as though something had been washed away. The air was clearer now, and the sky above them had softened into a pale blue, the last remnants of the storm retreating into the distance. His horse, still uneasy from the rain, adjusted its footing on the wet earth, and the group began moving again.

As they made their way down the winding path, the land began to change, the dense forest giving way to more open meadows bathed in soft sunlight. The scenery was peaceful, almost surreal after the chaos of the storm. The quietness between them stretched, broken only by the occasional sound of hooves and the soft rustling of grass as the they moved.

Darien's mind, however, was far from quiet. The Eldric, the weapons, the ritual—it was all starting to make sense in a way, but with each answer, new questions surfaced, more than he could grasp at once. The more he learned, the more there seemed to be. He turned his head to look at Chorrun, his questions rising to the surface of his mind again, but before he could speak—

A distant sound split the air.

A horn.

Chorrun immediately tensed, his body going rigid as he turned toward the noise, his golden eyes scanning the horizon. "Blast it!" he muttered under his breath. "The reports said they had moved east!"

Jodin's voice was sharp, his expression suddenly alert. "It's a marauder group!"

Darien's pulse spiked, his instincts screaming at him to be ready. His hand tightened around the reins, his body going still, trying to make sense of the urgency in Chorrun's voice. What was a marauder?

The horn sounded again, closer this time, and Darien's heart skipped. The riders were moving fast, closing in.

"We have to run," Chorrun said quickly, his voice steady but urgent. "These marauders rob, steal, and take prisoners for ransom—when they aren't killing their captives first."

Darien froze for a moment, his mind racing. He was still trying to process Chorrun's words when the urgency of the moment hit him. Run? How fast could they go? What was he supposed to do? His hand gripped tight around the hilt of his sword, but it felt heavier than it had before. He was just a student, not some hero like Chorrun seemed to think. Not part of this world, not part of this fight. His mind was locked, not sure if he should move or stay still.

Chorrun's eyes scanned the terrain, calculating their options. "There!" he pointed toward a dense patch of trees in the distance. "We can lose them in the western forests if we move quickly. Darien, stay with me. Jodin, Lotry, follow close behind."

Without hesitation, Chorrun surged forward, galloping toward the trees, his hooves pounding against the wet earth. Darien's horse startled, but he spurred it into motion, struggling to keep pace with Chorrun's speed, his heart racing as the wind picked up.

The ground blurred beneath him, the pounding of hooves filling the air. He risked a glance over his shoulder. A cloud of dust rose in the distance, and within it, Darien could make out the unmistakable shapes of masked riders, closing in fast.

The horn sounded again, louder this time, nearly deafening.

Darien barely had time to brace himself before his horse veered quickly to avoid a rock in front of him. He felt himself go up in the air, slam down hard onto the saddle, and his balance quickly went over the side. His breath was knocked out of him in a sharp gasp as he slammed into the hard ground. Pain shot up his wrist as he hit the earth, the world spinning as dust swirled around him.

He scrambled to regain his bearings, blinking rapidly to clear his vision. The thunder of hooves grew louder, and before he could react, he looked up to see a green-skinned rider towering over him.

"We got one," the rider growled, his voice rough, laced with amusement. "Let's see what we've caught."

Chapter 6: The Marauders

The green-skinned rider dismounted smoothly, his boots landing heavily in the dirt as he approached Darien's crumpled form, still sprawled on the ground. The sound of hooves faded as Chorrun and the others disappeared into the distance, leaving Darien alone with the hard-eyed bandit. His mind raced, still trying to process the chaos of what had just happened.

Darien's heart pounded in his chest. His thoughts scrambled, trying to form a plan, but everything felt so out of reach, so foreign. His world had collapsed around him—he had no idea how he had arrived here, no idea who these people were or what they wanted with him. His one link to the outside world had vanished into the forest, and now he was left facing this stranger with no clue how to protect himself.

The rider crouched down to meet Darien's gaze, his expression unreadable. His black eyes were intense, as though sizing Darien up. The air felt thick, heavy with tension.

"I don't recognize your kind," the rider said, his voice cold, detached—an emotionless tone that sent a chill through Darien. "I've traveled nearly every scrap of land, but I've never seen someone like you. What are you?"

Darien's heart raced, the tension in the rider's voice making his chest tighten. What was he supposed to say? Chorrun had warned him about the risks of being taken hostage, but Darien had never imagined anything like this. He opened his mouth to speak, but the words seemed to stick to the back of his throat. His hesitation cost him. The slap came fast, snapping his head to the side.

"I asked you a question, whelp," the rider snarled.

The sting of the slap burned on his cheek, and Darien fought to keep his breath steady. His mind raced, scrambling for any coherent response that wouldn't get him killed. "I—I'm not really sure," he stammered, the words coming out strained. "No one's been able to tell me. I woke up a few days ago with no memory. We were heading north to see if the trolls could help."

The rider studied him closely, the black eyes narrowing. He seemed to scrutinize every word Darien said, searching for signs of deception.

After a long moment, the rider straightened and motioned to one of his men.

Darien barely had time to react before a pair of rough hands yanked him to his feet. His sword was stripped from him, the motion swift and practiced. His armor was removed piece by piece, with no care for his discomfort, each movement harsh and unfeeling. The cold rope tightened around his wrists, and Darien winced as it dug into his skin, the rough fibers cutting through his senses. His injured wrist throbbed, the sharp pain distracting him for a moment as he glanced back toward the forest. But no one came.

"Did you recover the horse?" the leader called over his shoulder.

A second rider approached, wielding a crossbow. "No," he said flatly. "I had to put it down. Snapped leg."

The leader gave a small nod before turning his full attention back to Darien. "You said you were heading north to the troll city?" His lips curled into a smirk. "Well, I think we need to take a bit of a detour. You'll be heading east now." He motioned to one of the others. "Krat, get him on your horse. We'll decide what to do with him tonight."

A pudgy, broad-shouldered man with a scar running down his cheek gave a grunt of acknowledgment. Without much ceremony, he hoisted Darien onto his saddle, securing him behind him with an iron grip.

Darien looked back toward the trees once more, but there was no sign of his companions.

"Don't even think about it," Krat muttered. "No one's ever escaped Totra-Dal's camp. The ones who tried didn't live long enough to regret it." He let out a low chuckle as they spurred their horses eastward.

The ride passed in silence, the steady rhythm of hooves the only sound filling the air. Darien focused on piecing together what little he knew. Chorrun had called them marauders—robbers, slavers, and killers. That meant they wanted one of two things: coin or blood. If he could convince their leader, Totra-Dal, that he was worth something, maybe he had a chance.

Chorrun could find a way to pay for him. The king of Farkland Reach could be convinced. There was a way out of this.

Besides, I am one of the Eldric.

The thought steeled him as they passed through a thick grove of trees. When they emerged into a small clearing, Darien spotted the camp. Fires flickered in the dimming light, casting long shadows against the ring of trees surrounding the settlement. The air smelled of damp earth, woodsmoke, and old sweat.

As they neared the center of camp, a deep voice called out. "Ho there! Was the ride worth the risk?"

"That's yet to be decided," the leader responded.

Darien turned his gaze toward the man who had spoken. He was larger than the others, built like Philip but broader, his skin a dull gray. A thick red beard framed his angular face, and his dark eyes gleamed with intelligence behind a casual air of menace. A strange weapon was slung across his back, and his light leather armor was patched with scraps of fur, some still holding strands of hair.

The riders dismounted. Krat helped Darien down without much ceremony, though he at least made an effort not to jar his injured wrist further.

"Well, well, well," the bearded man said, stepping closer. "What do we have here? What are you, boy?"

Darien bristled at being called "boy" but forced himself to keep his composure. He needed to be careful.

"I don't know," he said, keeping his expression neutral. "I woke up with no memory of who I was. Some centaurs found me wandering and offered to take me north to see if anyone recognized me. That's when they attacked." He gestured toward the masked rider still mounted nearby. "I lost my horse in the chaos and got caught."

The large man studied him for several long seconds before shaking his head. "I think you're lying," he said bluntly. "You know exactly what you are. You just don't want me to know." His lips curled. "That means you're valuable. A prince, maybe? A half-breed? A mix of mer and fairy?"

Darien let genuine confusion slip into his features. Whatever the man had expected, that wasn't it. He seemed both satisfied and frustrated at the same time.

"Nicely done, Kort," the leader said to the green-skinned rider. "Come see me when you've cleaned yourself up." He motioned to Krat. "Take him to where we have the girl. We'll see if I can get anything useful out of him later."

Darien barely had time to process that before he was being led across camp. They passed the fire pit, its embers still softly glowing from the previous night, before arriving at a three-walled tent.

Inside, four metal rings were hammered into the ground. Darien's eyes flicked to one of them, where a small figure was bound, their wrist secured by thick rope. A hooded cloak obscured the child's face.

"Sit," Krat ordered, securing Darien's hands to another of the rings. "Don't try anything stupid. We have eyes all over the forest. You wouldn't make it fifty steps before an arrow found your back. But, hey—" He grinned wickedly. "Feel free to try if you want to give us some entertainment."

With that, Krat left him alone with the other prisoner.

Darien flexed his fingers against the rope, testing its hold, but there was no easy way out. His wrist throbbed in protest, sharp and insistent. He clenched his jaw against the pain, forcing himself to breathe evenly.

He turned toward the small figure beside him. "Uh, hello?"

No response.

"Can you hear me?" He kept his voice low, wary of drawing attention.

Still nothing.

Darien exhaled sharply, glancing toward the entrance of the tent. "Listen," he said, barely above a whisper. "I have people looking for me. We'll get out of here, alright?"

The child didn't stir.

Darien shifted his focus to the camp outside. It was chaotic, but not in a way that suggested disorganization—people moved with purpose, working, laughing, talking. Yet every time Totra-Dal stepped into view, the energy shifted. No one cowered, but they avoided his gaze. A man who commanded fear without needing to show it.

As the sun dipped below the tree line, Darien's stomach growled. He hadn't realized how hungry he was until now.

A shadow appeared at the entrance of the tent. A woman stepped inside, her gray skin smooth, her solid black hair falling to her waist. She was striking in an austere way, her expression cold and unreadable.

"Totra-Dal wishes to dine with you tonight," she said flatly. "To discuss your... options."

She pulled a dagger from her belt; the tip gleaming in the firelight. "I'm going to release you. Don't make me regret it."

Darien nodded as she stepped forward, slicing through his bindings with a single flick of her dagger. The tension in his wrists eased as the ropes fell away, leaving behind deep red marks where they had dug into his skin. He flexed his left wrist cautiously, wincing as a dull throb flared up. It wasn't broken, but it would take time to heal.

The woman stepped behind him, pressing the cold steel of her dagger against his back. "Walk," she said flatly.

Darien obeyed, moving through the dimly lit camp, his mind working through the possibilities ahead. Shadows stretched long in the fading light, figures drifting in and out of view, their faces obscured by the glow of scattered torches. The camp bustled with activity—marauders tending to weapons, sharing quiet conversations, or watching the newcomer being escorted through their midst with mild curiosity.

As they neared the largest tent in the center of the camp, Darien felt the dagger leave his back. His escort stepped ahead, pulling open the thick canvas flap. A flood of warm golden light spilled out, momentarily blinding him. He raised a hand to shield his eyes, taking a cautious step inside.

The air was thick with the scent of roasted meat and spiced ale. A long wooden table sat at the center, laden with food—not just dried rations or simple fare, but a lavish spread of fruits, cheeses, freshly baked bread, and cuts of meat still steaming from the fire. It was a stark contrast to the rough, weather-worn camp outside.

A deep voice boomed across the tent. "Ah! Our newest guest!"

Darien turned to see Totra-Dal lounging at the far end of the table, his broad frame draped in a red-striped tunic and loose-fitting trousers. He looked far more at ease than when Darien had first seen him. The wild, mangy appearance was softened, but not gone entirely. His presence filled the space, commanding attention with nothing more than his sheer size and confidence.

"Come in, come in!" Totra-Dal gestured to the chair closest to the entrance. "Sit, sit!"

Darien hesitated, his gaze flickering toward the now-closed tent flap.

"No need to fear Hodra," Totra-Dal said, following his glance. "She speaks in sharp tones, but she won't harm you—unless, of course, you give her reason to." He chuckled, clearly amused by himself. "We're a rough bunch, but not uncivilized."

Darien didn't move.

The moment stretched, and Totra-Dal's expression darkened. His jovial air shifted as he leaned forward slightly. "I don't like to repeat myself, boy," he said, his voice dipping into something lower, more dangerous. "You are in my camp. You are under my command. I extended an invitation for you to dine with me so that we might talk, but make no mistake—you are my prisoner. You will do as you are told. Now... sit."

Darien's pulse quickened, but he forced himself to keep his expression neutral. His gut told him pushing back would be a mistake, but backing down too quickly would mark him as weak. He needed to walk a careful line.

Totra-Dal studied him for a moment, then exhaled in amusement, shaking his head. "Come now, you must be famished!" He grinned, waving toward the food. "You haven't eaten since you arrived. And surely you have questions—particularly if what Kort says about you is true, and you weren't lying to me before. Perhaps I can help you. And if luck favors you, perhaps you can be of use to me as well."

Darien remained standing for several beats longer before finally stepping forward and sinking into the offered chair.

"See? That wasn't so difficult, was it?" Totra-Dal smirked, pouring himself a goblet of ale.

Darien didn't answer, his mind working through his next move.

Totra-Dal leaned forward slightly, his gaze sharp and calculating. "I'm sure you're just as curious about me as I am about you. What's your story? You seem... peculiar." He chuckled darkly, leaning back in his chair. "Don't worry, I'll get it out of you, eventually."

Darien felt the pressure mount. Totra-Dal wasn't just asking for information—he was sizing him up, testing him, like a snake playing with its prey before it struck. The sudden weight of his gaze made Darien's pulse quicken, and the unease swelled in his stomach.

"Now, let's start with introductions." Totra-Dal gestured toward himself. "I am Totra-Dal, leader of this family of outcasts and free men." His gaze sharpened. "And you are?"

"Darien," he said simply.

"Darien." Totra-Dal repeated the name as if testing how it felt in his mouth. "A pleasure, though I imagine the circumstances are not to your liking." He leaned back in his chair, taking a slow sip from his goblet.

"Now that we know each other's names, let's get to the more pressing question. What exactly are you?"

Darien felt the weight of Totra-Dal's stare. He had to be careful here. Should he lay his cards on the table and risk revealing too much? Or keep his story vague enough to stay interesting—but not suspicious?

He chose the latter.

"I'm not sure," he admitted, letting just enough uncertainty into his voice. "I woke up south of here. A few centaurs found me wandering alone and offered to take me to Farkland Reach to see if anyone recognized me. That's where I was headed before we were attacked." He gestured toward the leader of the raiding party. "I lost my horse in the chaos and got caught."

Totra-Dal studied him for a long moment before picking up a hunk of roasted meat from the platter in front of him. He tore off a piece with his teeth, chewing thoughtfully.

"That's quite a story," he said after swallowing. He reached for a plate, tossing a generous portion of food onto it before sliding it across the table toward Darien. "Eat. It would be rude of me to let a guest go hungry."

Darien's hands tightened around the goblet in front of him. He wanted to push back, but he could already hear the snaps of rope and feel the cold weight of the chains again. He couldn't escape yet. He couldn't run. Not now. Anger flared up in him again, but he fought it down, burying the defiance inside.

For now, he needed to eat.

"Alright," he said, his voice low and clipped, his jaw tight. "I'll eat. But don't think for a second that I'm going to just give up."

Totra-Dal grinned widely, a spark of delight dancing in his eyes. "Ah, now that's the spirit." He gestured to the food. "Eat, then, Darien. Let's see how much you're worth."

Darien hesitated only briefly before picking up the plate. The food smelled rich, the spices unfamiliar but inviting. He thanked his host but didn't immediately eat, his appetite dulled by the tension in the room.

Totra-Dal's smirk widened, as if he could see the doubt in Darien's eyes. He poured himself a goblet of ale, the amber liquid glimmering in the light. "See? That wasn't so difficult, was it?" He let out a low chuckle, relishing Darien's discomfort.

Darien didn't answer, instead taking a slow breath, trying to steady his racing heart. He couldn't afford to show weakness. Every part of him screamed to resist, to stand up and shout at Totra-Dal, to demand answers. But that would only get him killed. Right now, survival was all that mattered.

Totra-Dal leaned back in his chair, swirling the ale in his goblet. "I have to admit, I didn't expect you to play along so easily. Most people in your position... well, they don't make it to the table."

Darien glanced at him, feeling the weight of every word Totra-Dal said. Manipulation was thick in the air, and Darien knew he had to be careful. "I'm not here for you to play games with," Darien said, his voice steady, but his mind screamed at him to think more clearly. "My stay here won't be long. I'm going to find my way out."

Totra-Dal's grin faltered slightly, but he recovered quickly, as if he found Darien's resolve amusing. "That's the spirit, boy. But let me make something clear to you, Darien." He leaned forward slightly, his voice softening, but the intensity in his gaze was palpable. "You can think you're going to escape, but you're in my camp now. There's no way out unless I say so. And believe me, I'm not in the habit of letting people walk away."

Darien's stomach tightened. He had heard the subtle threat in those words, and they sent a chill down his spine. He tensed, his fists clenching beneath the table, but he didn't dare show the fear that was starting to boil beneath his skin. This wasn't some game to Totra-Dal; it was a game of life and death. Darien knew he had to tread carefully.

"Surviving is all I'm trying to do," Darien said quietly, his voice rougher than intended. "I don't care about your games. I just need a way out."

Totra-Dal's laughter filled the air, rich and full of mockery. "Oh, you think I'm playing with you, Darien?" His voice dropped to a more serious tone, the change immediate and unsettling. "You don't get it, do you? You're already playing my game. You just don't know it yet."

Totra-Dal's words rang in Darien's ears like a bell. The game. Darien had never been good at games—especially the ones with high stakes. And now, it seemed, he was deep in one. A game where the rules were set by Totra-Dal and the penalties were life and death.

Darien forced himself to lean back in his chair, trying to hide how much Totra-Dal's words had affected him. He needed to stay calm, but his mind was a mess. This wasn't how he imagined Olympus, or the role he was supposed to play. He had thought he'd be a hero, fighting to save the world. Now he was a prisoner at the mercy of a group of marauders, and the way forward seemed more uncertain by the moment.

Totra-Dal didn't miss a beat, pouring more ale into his goblet. "I'm going to give you a choice, Darien." His voice dropped again, low and dangerous. "You'll work for me, and I'll let you live. Do something useful, and maybe I'll even help you get the answers you're looking for. Fail me, and I'll have you killed."

Darien didn't speak for a long moment. He let Totra-Dal's words sink in, the finality of them settling in his gut like a rock. There was no escaping this. There was only survival. He had no choice but to play Totra-Dal's game for now, and that thought made him sick.

But it wasn't about escaping—not right now. It was about staying alive.

"I'll work for you," Darien said finally, his voice hoarse. "For now."

Totra-Dal smiled, the wickedness of it sending a ripple of unease through Darien. "Good. I knew you'd come around. You're going to be very useful, Darien." He leaned back in his chair, his expression pleased. "And remember, boy, this is your choice. You'll have a chance to prove your worth. If you can do that, you might just find your answers. But I'll warn you again..." He leaned forward, his voice low and menacing, "No one gets out of here unless I say so."

Darien nodded slowly, the weight of the situation sinking in. He didn't know how long he could keep playing along before Totra-Dal would ask for something more, but he didn't have a choice. Not yet.

"You have quite the mind for survival, Darien," he said, shaking his head in clear amusement. "I like it." A wicked grin spread across his face. "I also like that this will drive Kort mad. He hates new people. Especially ones that he brings in himself."

After the meal, Darien was escorted back to the small tent by the woman, Hodra. She didn't speak as she led him through the camp. The quiet murmurs of the marauders filled the air, but no one approached them, keeping their distance as if Darien were already an outcast among them.

As they entered the tent, Darien's mind raced, still disconnected from the events unfolding. He had eaten, played along, and agreed to work for Totra-Dal, but his stomach churned with guilt and fear. Every bite he'd taken had felt like a small betrayal of his own resolve. How had he come to this? He had no memory of how he had arrived in Olympus, no understanding of why he had been pulled into this cycle. And yet, here he was, doing everything in his power to stay alive.

The tent was small, just large enough to house a bedroll and a few simple supplies. The air inside was stale with the scent of dust and the remnants of yesterday's meals. There was a small firepit in the center, still warm from the night before, casting soft shadows against the canvas walls.

Hodra gestured to the bedroll at the far side of the tent. "You'll stay here." She didn't wait for a response. "Get some rest. Tomorrow, you begin working. Totra-Dal will expect you to pull your weight."

The words settled heavily on Darien's shoulders, more so than he cared to admit. As he sat down on the bedroll, a wave of exhaustion washed over him. His body ached from the rough ride, his wrist still throbbed painfully, and his mind was a chaotic mess of fragments. Farkland Reach felt like a distant dream, and The Academy even less than that.

Chapter 7: The Observer

Darien jolted awake, heart racing. His breath came in sharp, rapid bursts, and it took him a moment to remember where he was—the rough tent, the marauders' camp, Totra-Dal's unsettling hospitality. He touched his wrists instinctively, grimacing at the lingering ache from yesterday's bindings. The dull pain was an unwelcome reminder of just how precarious his position truly was.

Slowly, Darien rose and stepped into the morning chill. The camp stirred quietly around him, muted murmurs blending with the thin wisps of smoke drifting upward from dying fires. Marauders moved about, sharp-eyed and cautious, their wary glances occasionally flicking toward him. Darien avoided meeting their gaze directly, feeling vulnerable beneath their suspicion.

"Awake already?" Kort's sharp, sneering voice shattered his fragile sense of calm. "What a pity."

Darien turned reluctantly to face him. Kort's green skin and jagged features were as unsettling as ever, and his narrowed eyes conveyed open hostility.

"Morning, Kort," Darien said evenly, careful to hide his unease.

Kort stepped dangerously close, his expression twisted in contempt. "Don't pretend we're friends. Totra-Dal might find you interesting, but I see right through you. You're nothing but dead weight—a stray dog he'll tire of soon enough. And when that happens, I'll gladly end you myself."

Kort's voice lowered, becoming a threatening whisper. "One wrong move, one misstep, and I'll bury you without a second thought."

Darien forced himself to hold Kort's stare, feeling a cold pit forming in his stomach. "Understood."

Kort smirked cruelly, clearly dissatisfied that Darien hadn't crumbled outright. "Good," he sneered, turning sharply away. "Watch your back, outsider. No one else here will."

Darien remained perfectly still until Kort disappeared from view, then sank onto a crude wooden stool near the fire, letting his breath steady. His hands trembled slightly, adrenaline still rushing hotly through his veins.

"Don't let him bother you too much," came a smooth, measured voice from nearby. "Kort treats everyone with equal disdain. It's practically admirable, in a twisted sort of way."

Darien glanced up sharply, startled. A thin, grey-skinned figure stood at the edge of the firelight, observing him calmly. His features were finely chiseled, his eyes sharp and quietly amused. Darien recognized him vaguely from the previous evening—another of the camp's inhabitants, though unlike Kort in almost every respect.

"Easy for you to say," Darien replied cautiously. "He seems especially eager to kill me."

The stranger's lips curved into a faint smile. "Oh, that's Kort's particular talent—he makes everyone feel especially chosen for his violence."

Darien studied him thoughtfully. He hesitated before asking cautiously, "Forgive me for not knowing...but what exactly are you? I've never met anyone quite like Kort—or you, for that matter."

The figure raised his eyebrows in mild surprise. "Really? Fascinating." He stepped forward slightly, eyes bright with curiosity. "Kort is a goblin. Unpleasant, aggressive creatures known for their stubbornness and cruelty. I, however, am a troll—generally more diplomatic, though perhaps that's only my personal pride speaking."

Darien absorbed this new information quietly. "Are there other... types here? Like you, or Kort?"

The troll smiled faintly, eyes glinting with amusement. "Of course. Olympus is home to many races, each with their own unique... charms, shall we say. You've already met trolls and goblins—neither known for their gentle natures, though trolls usually display better manners."

He paused thoughtfully, voice smooth and instructive. "Then there are the Peronia—lizard-like, cunning, ruthless traders mostly, fond of hissing every word. Their speech can be a bit unsettling at first, but you grow accustomed to it. Cyclops, too, of course—solitary, strong creatures. One-eyed, prone to keeping to themselves unless there's coin or battle involved."

Darien listened closely, trying to commit each detail to memory. "And what about... fairies?"

The troll smiled softly, amused. "Fairies? Small, purple-skinned, winged creatures. Short-lived, frail—delicate beings unsuited for marauder life. You won't find them here, I'm afraid. Too easily broken."

Darien frowned slightly, considering the implication. "Yet, all these other races—you're all willing to band together here? Even though you're so different?"

The troll's smile widened knowingly. "Oh, we aren't exactly bound by camaraderie or loyalty, Darien. More like mutual necessity and convenience. After all, Olympus itself is far harsher than the company we keep."

Darien tensed slightly, realizing abruptly that the troll had casually spoken his name. "You... you know my name?"

"Of course," the troll said calmly, eyes glittering in quiet amusement. "I make it my business to know interesting things. And you, Darien, are quite interesting."

Darien's unease deepened, a faint chill running down his spine. He couldn't help noticing how this troll's curiosity reminded him of Totra-Dal's interest, though this felt less utilitarian, more intellectual. But still dangerous.

"Who exactly are you?" Darien asked cautiously.

"Garik," the troll replied smoothly. "Just an observer, gathering bits of information here and there."

"Observer?" Darien echoed, wary.

"Precisely. Observation is far safer than direct involvement—especially in a place like this. Kort's violent methods work for him. But I prefer subtler tools: knowledge, information, secrets." Garik tilted his head slightly, curious. "I suspect you understand how valuable those things can be."

Darien exhaled slowly, measuring his next words carefully. "Totra-Dal seemed curious, too. But his interest felt... different."

Garik's lips curved slightly in acknowledgment. "Ah, yes. Totra-Dal's interest is rooted in practicality—usefulness. Mine is simpler: the pure, intellectual pleasure of an unanswered question, a puzzle." He paused thoughtfully. "And you, Darien, seem quite puzzling."

Darien fell silent, absorbing Garik's words carefully. He briefly considered how strange it was that he kept expecting human kindness, human reason here, among beings so utterly inhuman. He silently chastised himself for that naïveté—expecting familiar behaviors in an unfamiliar world was foolish.

Garik's voice softened, breaking through his thoughts. "Still with me, Darien?"

Darien nodded quickly, taking a slow breath. "Sorry, just... it's a lot to take in. This place, all these races—it's overwhelming."

Garik inclined his head gently. "Interesting perspective. My advice? Accept that you're an outsider. Don't try too hard to blend in—it'll only draw attention. Remain observant, cautious. People here underestimate outsiders; use that to your advantage."

Darien nodded carefully, appreciative of Garik's quiet sincerity despite his unease. "And if Kort decides I'm too much trouble?"

Garik's eyes narrowed slightly, seriousness replacing amusement. "Then you'll find yourself in trouble—fast. Kort doesn't hesitate, and he doesn't bluff."

Darien swallowed, understanding the gravity of Garik's warning. "Thanks. I'll keep that in mind."

Garik stepped slowly backward, already fading into the camp's morning shadows. "Stay vigilant, Darien. Olympus itself is a brutal teacher. Trust your instincts. I'd hate to see our future conversations cut short prematurely. I suspect that I will enjoy them."

Then Garik was gone, leaving Darien standing alone, heart racing. He was grateful for Garik's counsel, cryptic though it was—each new detail about Olympus and its diverse inhabitants was a fragile thread connecting him to survival, to understanding this strange world.

And despite Kort's open threats, Garik's mysterious knowledge left Darien feeling less isolated. Perhaps even among marauders and monsters, there could be unexpected allies if he stayed observant and careful enough to find them.

Darien moved quietly through the waking camp, avoiding direct eye contact. The morning had fully broken, casting sharp sunlight over the mismatched tents and crude shelters. Marauders moved briskly around him, their wary expressions dismissive, marking him clearly as an outsider.

He felt deeply uneasy but forced himself into action, seeking out the pile of supplies that he had been instructed to work through. Finding a scattered pile of supplies near the camp's edge, he knelt and began sorting through straps, rusted blades, and spare bits of armor. His injured wrist still ached slightly, but he worked slowly and deliberately, careful not to draw attention to his weakness.

As he worked, Darien's attention was drawn to two tall, lizard-like creatures near a cooking fire. Their green and bronze scales shimmered slightly in the morning sun. Peronia, he remembered Garik saying earlier. They spoke quietly, their words carrying in soft, deliberate hisses. Their eyes flicked sharply, alert and calculating. The sound of their conversation unsettled him, reminding him just how alien and unfamiliar Olympus truly was.

Nearby, a lone cyclops sat hunched on a rough stool, massive arms methodically sharpening weapons with practiced ease. The single eye in his wide, weathered face focused intently on his work, paying no mind to those who passed carefully around him. His quiet, deliberate movements radiated a confidence born of strength; other marauders noticeably kept their distance.

Absorbed in watching the cyclops, Darien didn't realize he'd drifted from his task until he felt himself collide softly against something hard and scaled. He spun sharply, meeting the narrow, suspicious gaze of a Peronia who had approached silently from behind.

The Peronia hissed softly, head tilting slightly, sharp teeth briefly visible. "Ssstupid to linger ssso clossse, outsider. Watch your ssstep."

Darien drew back quickly, holding his palms up slightly in a gesture of peace. "My mistake," he said quietly, "I meant no offense."

Before the Peronia could respond further, Garik appeared smoothly beside them, his tone mild and diplomatic. "Forgive him—he's still adjusting to our ways." Garik inclined his head respectfully, addressing the Peronia. "I assure you, he'll be more cautious from now on."

The Peronia eyed Garik warily, considering. "Sssee to it," it said coldly, turning back toward its companion. Darien released a quiet breath, relaxing slightly as they moved away.

"You're fortunate I was nearby," Garik murmured lightly. "Peronia don't take kindly to anyone they don't know."

Darien gave a short nod, grateful but still wary. "I noticed. And the cyclops?" He glanced toward the hulking figure still sharpening weapons. "He seems... different."

Garik nodded slightly. "Kanos. Strong, capable, and smart enough to avoid petty disputes. He likes his quiet. Even Kort leaves him be."

Darien considered that carefully, returning quietly to sorting through supplies. "And the Peronia—they seem...tense."

"They always are," Garik replied calmly. "Peronia deal in information and favors. It's profitable work, but it leaves them inherently suspicious. Don't underestimate their reach—they listen, observe, and trade secrets."

Darien paused, thoughtful. "Why would they stay here if everyone distrusts them?"

Garik smiled faintly. "Mutual advantage. They can gather and sell information Totra-Dal needs. He offers them protection, connections, resources. It's an arrangement—fragile but effective."

Darien looked around carefully. "This whole place feels fragile."

"Very," Garik agreed quietly. "Peace here is moment-to-moment. One mistake, one slight, and things spiral. Totra-Dal holds it together through intimidation and strength—but it won't last forever."

Darien glanced toward the goblins clustered by their fire, noting how closely they watched the trolls nearby, tension crackling quietly in the space between them. "It seems everyone is just waiting for a reason to fight."

Garik inclined his head slightly. "Exactly. Which is why caution is essential. If violence erupts, the weak and the outsiders suffer first."

Darien felt the implication clearly. "And I'm both."

Garik's eyes glinted subtly. "Precisely."

They fell briefly silent, sorting quietly through the supplies. After a pause, Darien hesitated, his curiosity getting the better of him. "Garik, why are you here? You seem... different."

Garik glanced sideways at him, expression mildly amused. "Do I? Perhaps because I never intended to stay long. My curiosity brought me here, and curiosity keeps me. Olympus is endlessly fascinating—but never safe. Don't mistake my calm for security."

Darien nodded slowly. "You seem confident, though."

Garik smiled faintly. "Confidence and caution go hand-in-hand. I observe carefully, I speak carefully. Both have kept me alive."

Darien hesitated again, then spoke cautiously. "If things fall apart here—will you leave?"

Garik raised an eyebrow slightly, gaze subtly curious. "Of course. I owe Totra-Dal no more loyalty than he owes me. My interests align with his, for now. If that changes, I'll disappear quietly—assuming I'm fortunate enough to leave unnoticed."

Darien absorbed this carefully, recognizing clearly that even Garik considered himself expendable. "Then I suppose I have even less chance than you."

"Perhaps," Garik admitted quietly. "But remember, Darien, even outsiders have their advantages. Most underestimate you—use that. Watch, listen, learn. The camp is full of cracks and quiet rivalries. Exploit them."

Garik rose abruptly, brushing dirt from his trousers. "I must go. Be careful—keep to yourself, but notice everything. Small details make large differences."

Darien nodded, watching Garik move swiftly back toward the heart of the camp. Alone once again, he continued sorting quietly, reflecting carefully on Garik's subtle warnings. Olympus felt impossibly dangerous—tensions hidden beneath fragile alliances. Yet Garik's words offered guidance, a cautious path forward.

Darien glanced around again, his gaze lingering on the Peronia, the cyclops, and finally the rough groups of goblins and trolls. He was vulnerable here, yes—but perhaps not entirely powerless. Information, Garik had hinted, was valuable currency. If he observed carefully, if he understood the tensions clearly, maybe he could navigate safely through the uncertainty ahead.

With that quiet resolve, Darien returned carefully to his task, determined not to repeat mistakes. If Garik had taught him anything, it was that survival here depended on noticing things others overlooked—and being ready to use that knowledge when the time came.

Later that night Darien sat quietly at the edge of the camp, sharpening a rusted blade by the faint glow of dying embers. Around him, the marauder camp had settled into a softer rhythm, the tense energy of the day fading gradually into weary calm. Looking around, Darien felt a strange sense of detachment—it was hard to believe only a single day had passed since he'd woken here, confused and terrified.

He glanced across the camp, discreetly studying the groups that clustered separately around their fires, isolated islands of uneasy companionship. Trolls kept to themselves, exchanging quiet, wary conversation, while goblins whispered tersely, casting suspicious glances toward others. Two Peronia sat slightly apart, their hissing conversation barely audible, yet strangely unsettling.

Darien's eyes caught briefly on a tall, grey-skinned troll near one of the central fires, clearly in command of a group preparing horses and weapons. He didn't know who she was, but her calm presence drew his attention. She moved confidently, directing others with a casual authority that clearly marked her as respected, even feared.

He felt a subtle curiosity about her—one of the few individuals in this camp who didn't seem openly hostile or indifferent toward those around her. He wondered briefly what her role was, what respect or fear kept others deferential to her commands.

Quiet footsteps drew Darien's attention suddenly. He looked up to see Garik slipping quietly out of the shadows and taking a seat on a rough stool beside him without invitation.

Garik inclined his head slightly, eyes flicking briefly toward the grey-skinned troll preparing supplies. "That's Evatra," he said softly, answering Darien's unspoken curiosity. "She leads raiding parties. Effective. Capable. If she notices you, it might prove advantageous. Joining her would be dangerous—but perhaps no more dangerous than staying here, passively."

Darien nodded slowly, considering Garik's careful words. "I haven't spoken to her," he said quietly, uncertainty clear in his voice.

"You won't need to," Garik replied calmly. "She'll find you, if she has reason to. Evatra watches carefully—she doesn't miss much." He rose silently, brushing dirt from his trousers. "Remember what I told you: hesitation rarely ends well."

Without another word, Garik vanished back into the shadowy camp, leaving Darien alone again, the blade heavy and cold in his hands.

For a long moment, Darien remained still, gazing thoughtfully toward Evatra's quiet preparations. Garik's words had been carefully cryptic, yet clear enough in their meaning. He understood now that an opportunity might present itself—one that could offer safety, or at least protection. He also understood clearly the risk: any choice he made here would come at a cost.

His thoughts drifted briefly to Kort's silent threat, the inevitable danger waiting if he remained passive.

Evatra was unknown—dangerous perhaps—but Kort was familiar, and the certainty of his threat was far worse.

Darien rose quietly, slipping the blade carefully into its sheath. The marauder who was in charge of examining his work took the blade with a thankless glance. Darien took the approval, and, glad to be done with the immediately assigned work. His movements felt steadier now, determination settling within him, quiet but certain.

He turned silently back toward his tent, suddenly feeling the exhaustion of the day settle heavily into his bones. There was nothing more he could do tonight, nothing more to be gained by worrying. He ducked inside, lay back slowly onto the bedroll, and closed his eyes, hoping to find at least a few hours of sleep before morning brought new uncertainty.

Chapter 8: The Offer

Darien woke abruptly to a harsh kick against his ribs. A squat, rough-featured goblin stood over him, dropping a filthy shovel at his feet. "Up," it barked impatiently, already turning away.

He dragged himself upright, muscles protesting as yesterday's exhaustion surged painfully back. Stepping outside the tent, he was greeted by an overpowering stench drifting from the ramshackle horse stalls across the camp. Darien sighed, picking up the shovel reluctantly. It seemed the marauders had no shortage of unpleasant tasks to test him with.

By midday, sweat and grime streaked his face and clothing, the ache in his injured wrist deepening with every load he shoveled. Pain shot up his arm in dull, persistent waves, slowing his pace despite his efforts to push through it. Darien's hands shook from both the labor and the anxiety of constantly being observed, judged, and controlled.

"You'd best speed up before we decide you're not worth our trouble," Kort's voice sneered suddenly from behind, dripping with mocking amusement.

Darien's jaw tightened, resisting the urge to fling a shovel full of manure in Kort's direction. Instead, he kept his head down and shoveled harder, focusing his anger into the work. Kort chuckled softly, clearly enjoying his discomfort before moving off again.

Throughout the afternoon, Darien discreetly studied the camp as he worked, looking for patterns among the marauders. But the camp operated in disorganized chaos. Guards came and went unpredictably, and watchmen abandoned their posts at seemingly random intervals, making careful observation futile.

Yet one group caught his attention—two or three pale-skinned beings moving silently among the tents. They were unsettling, their appearances strangely androgynous and impossibly symmetrical, with skin so pale it seemed nearly translucent. Their eyes disturbed him most: instead of white, each eye was a pool of blackness with stark white pupils suspended within. Darien found it hard not to stare, yet something in their quiet movements filled him with instinctive dread.

Garik hadn't mentioned creatures like these—though Darien suspected that omission was intentional. Knowing Garik's wry sense of humor, it was probably his idea of a joke to have Darien find them all on his own. It seemed to fit him.

As Darien worked closer to the tent where he had been held the day he arrived, he noticed again the small child bound to a metal pole. Her wrists were raw, and she appeared to have been given no food or water since yesterday. Darien's chest tightened painfully with sympathy.

He glanced around quickly, seeing no immediate threats. Grabbing the waterskin from his cart, he ducked into the tent and knelt beside her, whispering urgently, "Hey—I brought some water."

She didn't stir, remaining eerily still.

Concerned, Darien reached toward her shoulder—

"Stop!" A sharp voice called from the entrance of the tent, freezing him instantly.

He spun around, heart racing, to find himself face-to-face with one of the pale, unsettling figures he'd seen earlier. Those unnatural black-and-white eyes stared at him intently, expression disturbingly calm.

"Do not touch the child," the figure warned, its voice quiet yet firm. "The wraith inside her would take you immediately. If it fails, it would kill you instead."

Darien recoiled instinctively, pulse thudding in his ears. He stumbled back a step, away from both the child and the strange figure before him. "I—didn't know," he stammered, quickly lowering the waterskin.

The figure tilted its head slightly, studying Darien with an unsettling intensity. "Clearly," it replied simply. "You must learn caution quickly. Ignorance can kill."

Darien swallowed hard, regaining a bit of composure. "What is a wraith?" he asked carefully.

For a moment, the figure seemed surprised, but quickly its expression smoothed again. "You truly know nothing, do you? Wraiths are spirits twisted by dark magic when Cyprin stole Olympus's power millennia ago. Souls trapped in eternal torment. Sometimes they possess the living, using weak bodies to regain form." It glanced at the motionless child. "She was weak, vulnerable and in the wrong place at the wrong time. Now the wraith controls her completely."

Darien stared quietly at the child, his stomach twisting with quiet dread. "There's nothing anyone can do?"

The pale figure shook its head slowly. "If we kill her, the wraith would likely move on and claim another. For now, she is beyond our help. But Totra-Dal, for reasons his own, refuses to allow us to simply leave her behind."

Darien felt a shiver, nodded solemnly, exhaling softly. He hesitated a moment, then spoke again. "What are you, exactly? I've never seen anyone like you before."

A faint smile tugged at the corner of the figure's pale mouth. "We are called Scillan. My kind rarely leave the islands beyond the mainland. We observe, learn, and gather knowledge. Occasionally we travel, seeking truths to share with our people." Its gaze briefly sharpened, almost inquisitive. "You interest me, Darien. But remember—truths in Olympus are often dangerous to learn."

As the Scillan's pale figure faded into the chaos of the camp, Darien stood rooted in place, his heart thundering in his chest. He glanced again at the bound child, still and lifeless, save for the occasional rise and fall of shallow breaths. She seemed smaller now, impossibly fragile, and the weight of what the Scillan had revealed pressed heavily upon him.

A wraith. The very thought chilled him to the bone. This wasn't just another unfamiliar creature of Olympus; it was something far more sinister. Something capable of possessing, of destroying—something that embodied the corruption and decay beneath the surface of this strange new world.

Darien stepped away slowly, leaving the tent and the girl behind, his thoughts tangled in confusion and dread. He moved toward the edge of camp, needing space, needing air. As he passed by the various marauders working, talking, laughing, he caught fragments of whispered conversation. Each voice was laced with the same underlying tension, each glance toward the tent containing a quiet but unmistakable fear.

A voice nearby made him slow his steps, catching his attention.

"Forty-two days," a marauder murmured to his companion, echoing the Scillan's earlier words with dark fascination. "They usually don't last more than thirty."

"Can't believe Totra-Dal's keeping it around," the other grumbled. "It's dangerous."

"They say wraiths get stronger the longer they hold onto a body," the first one continued, dropping his voice even lower, glancing nervously toward the tent.

"What if it breaks loose? What if the Scillan are wrong?"

Darien felt a chill ripple through him at their words. The fear was contagious, hanging in the air like a thick fog. He felt it settling deep within his chest. Could the wraith truly escape? Could it take another body—could it take his?

He quickened his steps, moving toward the outskirts of camp, his mind racing. This wasn't his fight. He had stumbled into a world filled with monsters, magic, and myths, but he was still struggling to understand his place here.

Once safely away from the others, he found a secluded spot near a half-collapsed tent, the fabric flapping softly in the evening breeze. His wrist ached sharply again, and he flexed his fingers, grimacing. His injuries from Kort's capture were a constant reminder of his vulnerability. He wasn't ready for this. He wasn't prepared for any of it.

His thoughts drifted back to the girl—the wraith's host. The idea that a young child could be reduced to little more than a hollow shell, her body nothing more than a prison for some dark, corrupted spirit, made his stomach twist painfully. She was just a child, innocent and undeserving of such a fate.

And yet, he felt a strange kinship with her. Both of them trapped, both of them victims of forces beyond their control. Darien's hands curled into fists, frustration simmering beneath his fear.

Was this what Olympus was truly about? Fighting endless battles against enemies that never truly disappeared, facing horrors that couldn't be defeated, only held at bay? Was this what the Scillan had meant when they warned him of dangerous truths?

He knew he couldn't stay hidden away forever. Soon, Totra-Dal would summon him again, and he would have to make his choice—ride with the raiders, or risk the cruelty of Kort and his men. Neither option felt safe, neither felt right, but what other choice did he have?

Darien exhaled slowly, forcing himself to calm. The sun was beginning to set, casting the camp in a golden, almost peaceful glow that felt painfully at odds with the turmoil inside him.

But he knew he couldn't linger here any longer. Drawing a final, steadying breath, he rose to his feet. He had survived this long. He could keep going. For now, that was enough.

He turned back toward the heart of the camp, ready to face whatever came next.

By the time twilight painted the camp in shadowed hues, Darien had finally finished clearing the last stalls, his entire body sore and weary. When the evening meal arrived, he hardly tasted the thick, bland stew, his hunger overtaking any concern for flavor. Even after finishing, his stomach still growled impatiently, demanding more.

He hesitated for only a moment before stepping toward the food tent again.

"I wouldn't do that if I were you."

Darien paused mid-step, turning to find Evatra, the troll woman Garik had spoke of, leaning casually against the side of a nearby tent. Her expression was carefully neutral, though her eyes glinted faintly with wry amusement.

"Do what?" he asked cautiously.

She straightened slightly, eyeing him thoughtfully. "Going back for seconds. You only eat your fill here after a successful raid, or if Totra-Dal grants you special privileges." She smiled slightly, dryly amused. "In your case, that means you eat only when invited."

Darien returned her faint smirk, his exhaustion making him bolder than he felt. "I'm not sure I'd let Totra-Dal hear you say that."

She chuckled quietly, clearly unconcerned. "I won't."

She stepped away without further explanation, motioning subtly for him to follow. He hesitated only briefly, curiosity outweighing caution. After all, it wasn't as if returning to his own tent offered anything but more solitude and questions.

Inside her tent, Darien sank onto a low stool, his aching muscles grateful for even this small reprieve. Evatra sat across from him and resumed eating in silence, finishing her meal without further comment. Darien waited patiently, quietly observing her calm movements, sensing there was more to this conversation.

At last, she set aside her bowl and leaned back slightly, eyes sharp and assessing as they met his own. "So— how did you enjoy your first full day in camp?"

An involuntary chuckle escaped Darien, dry and humorless.

"You enjoyed cleaning horse stalls that much?" she asked lightly, one eyebrow raised.

"Hardly," Darien admitted, shaking his head. "If you'd told me a few days ago I'd end up here, doing this… well, I wouldn't have believed you. Part of me still wonders if I'm dreaming."

He shifted slightly on the stool, wincing sharply as his injured wrist protested the careless movement. Evatra's eyes narrowed immediately, noticing his discomfort.

"Not a dream, apparently," she remarked quietly, genuine concern flickering briefly in her gaze. "What happened?"

Darien rubbed gingerly at the sore joint. "My wrist. Kort's group was rough when they caught me—hurt it pretty badly. It's mostly fine now, just sore."

Without hesitation, Evatra leaned forward and took his wrist gently in her calloused hands. Darien froze briefly, caught off guard by her unexpected touch. She methodically rotated his wrist, gently testing its range of motion with practiced efficiency. Her touch was careful yet firm, professional and surprisingly gentle.

Finally, she released him, nodding thoughtfully. "Worse than a sprain, but it's healing well. Give it another week or so."

Darien nodded gratefully. "Thanks."

She turned her attention toward the tent flap, and for a few moments, they both sat silently, the muffled sounds of camp life drifting between them.

Eventually, she broke the silence again, her voice suddenly direct. "What skills do you actually have?"

Darien blinked, momentarily startled by the bluntness of the question. "Sorry, what?"

Evatra exhaled softly, her patience clearly limited. "Skills. You had a sword when they found you. Can you use it? Track, shoot, hide? I'm trying to figure out if Garik has actually found something useful—or if he's just playing one of his subtle jokes again."

Darien hesitated, considering carefully how much truth he could afford. "I'm good with a sword—very good. But the rest... tracking, hunting, archery—I'm not sure. I don't remember clearly. I just know I can fight."

She watched him quietly, her expression unreadable, assessing. "Hmm."

The single sound carried heavy meaning, and Darien couldn't help asking, "Why?"

"Because I need someone," she said bluntly. "We lost a rider on our last raid. Guard shot him through the chest. Totra-Dal wants me to fill the gap, but all he offered were Kort's lackeys." She grimaced slightly at the thought. "Then Garik approached me. Said you might be worth trying."

Darien tilted his head slightly, intrigued by her reaction. "Garik said that?"

Evatra nodded slowly, her eyes narrowing thoughtfully. "He rarely recommends anyone. Rarely even speaks unless it's important. Yet somehow you caught his attention enough that he specifically asked me to consider you. Which makes me curious—why?"

Darien shrugged slightly, uncertain himself. "Honestly, I don't really know."

"You don't know," Evatra said calmly. It was a statement and not a question. "I lead raiding parties. It's dangerous work. Garik's recommendation carries weight—but it doesn't guarantee you'll survive. It certainly doesn't guarantee you'll be good at it." She paused briefly, letting the warning sink in. "We have one final raid before we break camp. You're the best option I have right now."

Darien hesitated, her blunt honesty sobering him quickly. Raiding didn't exactly appeal to him, but neither did the thought of remaining vulnerable to Kort's malice. The choice seemed clear, even if it wasn't easy.

Evatra watched him closely, noting his uncertainty. "You're exhausted," she said finally, her voice softening slightly. "Think on it tonight. I'll speak with you again in the morning."

Darien nodded slowly, grateful for the brief reprieve. As he stood to leave, he hesitated briefly at the tent flap, glancing back toward her. "I appreciate you even considering Garik's advice, Evatra."

She regarded him for a long moment, a subtle smirk returning to her lips. "I'm not sure I had much choice. He made it sound intriguing—and Garik rarely takes interest in anyone without a very good reason." She paused, her expression unreadable again. "We'll see if his instincts are right this time."

Before Darien could reply, she turned away, clearly ending their conversation. He stepped out into the cool night, lingering for just a moment as his tired mind replayed their exchange. Garik's quiet influence weighed on him, raising as many questions as it answered. But for the first time in days, Darien felt a cautious flicker of hope.

Returning slowly to his tent, he sank onto his bedroll, body heavy and weary. The choice ahead felt daunting—but at least he now had one. Sleep claimed him swiftly, pulling him down into exhausted darkness.

Chapter 9: The Raid

Darien woke earlier than most of the camp. The thin fabric of his tent did little to shield him from the chill of morning, and a dull ache lingered in his wrist. He pushed himself upright slowly, the stiffness of yesterday's labor biting deep into his muscles.

Rising unsteadily, he grabbed his pack and made his way quietly toward the edge of the camp, mindful to remain visible enough not to arouse suspicion. He paused near a narrow stream, breathing in the crisp, cool air that filled his lungs with a sharp clarity. He stripped to his underclothes, grateful for the fresh bite of water against his skin, washing away the layers of grime and exhaustion he'd gathered since arriving here.

As he scrubbed his clothes against the smooth, moss-covered rocks, his thoughts drifted unbidden to Chorrun, Lotry, and Jodin. Had they reached Farkland Reach? Were they safe? More troubling, had they given him up as lost? The thought weighed heavily, adding to his already considerable anxiety. He placed his clothing carefully on a nearby stone, hoping the rising sun would dry them enough to wear.

As he finished cleaning himself, Darien waded out of the stream, shivering from the morning chill. He shook water from his hair, slicked it back, and quickly dressed in the spare clothes the centaurs had provided. He took one last steadying breath, bracing himself against the uncertain day ahead.

He returned to camp just as Evatra approached, leaning casually against a nearby tree as if she'd been waiting for him all along. Her black eyes studied him carefully, betraying neither hostility nor warmth, simply quiet appraisal.

"I spoke with Totra-Dal," she said finally. "He's agreed to let you ride with us today." She tilted her head slightly, curiosity evident beneath her composed expression. "Garik rarely speaks on behalf of anyone, you know. What makes you so special?"

Darien shook his head slowly, genuinely unsure. "Honestly, I don't know. But I'm not about to question his judgment—especially if it gives me a break from Kort and his work detail."

She nodded slightly, as if she'd expected that answer. "I suppose we'll find out soon enough whether his instincts about you are right."

She stepped closer, and Darien realized with mild surprise that she was slightly shorter than he was. Even so, the weight of her presence seemed larger, her posture confident and commanding. "Understand something," she continued, her voice calm but firm. "You might have Garik's favor, but that won't protect you out there. If you endanger me or my riders—if you make one false move—I won't hesitate to cut you down myself. Do we understand each other?"

Darien met her gaze squarely. There was no malice behind her words, only stark, uncompromising clarity. "Understood," he replied, his voice steady despite the sudden tightness in his chest. "I gave my word. I won't betray that."

She eyed him thoughtfully, as if measuring his resolve. After a brief pause, she inclined her head slightly, seemingly satisfied. "Very well," she said. "Grab some food and head to the stalls. You'll find your horse waiting there. I hope you're ready for a rough ride—one way or another."

Without waiting for his reply, she strode off purposefully toward the gathered riders. Darien watched her go, admiring the efficiency of her movements despite himself, her confidence something he found himself quietly envying.

Returning briefly to his tent, Darien draped his still-damp clothes carefully over the thin fabric roof, hoping they'd dry by evening. Then he hurried toward the food tables, grabbing dried meats, nuts, and fruits. He hesitated for a moment, his stomach still tight with anxiety, but forced himself to swallow a few bites, knowing he'd need the strength.

At the stalls, his mount waited—a palomino, smaller and leaner than the horse he'd ridden with the centaurs. It shifted restlessly, clearly sensing his tension as he awkwardly pulled himself into the saddle. The soreness of his muscles immediately flared to life again, but he pushed the discomfort away, knowing he had no choice now but to endure.

Across the camp, Evatra swung smoothly onto a powerful black horse. She raised her voice, calling out clearly and confidently to the gathered riders: "Mount up! We're heading out now."

The group rode out slowly, breaking through the early morning mists as they left the camp behind. Darien struggled at first to find his rhythm, his seat uneasy and uncertain as he watched the more experienced riders moving fluidly, effortlessly shifting their weight. He mimicked them as best he could, his awkwardness fading gradually as the miles stretched behind them.

Eventually, the landscape opened before them; the forest giving way to wide, rolling hills. Evatra signaled the group to stop near the crest of a hill, turning to a short, wiry goblin rider named Drack. She nodded silently, and Drack spurred forward, swiftly climbing to the top of the hill, where he raised a spyglass to his eye. Moments later, he returned with a tense expression, whispering quietly to Evatra.

Darien felt a cold thread of dread twist through him, aware something had changed. The raiders around him shifted slightly, their calm confidence subtly giving way to unease.

Evatra faced them, her expression carefully neutral but clearly strained. "There's a caravan ahead," she announced quietly, authority clear in her tone. "But it's already been attacked."

A murmur of unease rippled through the riders. Evatra raised her hand sharply, silencing them. "We'll approach cautiously, scout the area. Whoever attacked may still be nearby." She glanced at Darien, her gaze heavy with unspoken warning. "Eyes open. Move carefully. Let's go."

As the group began to move again, Evatra dropped back slightly, matching Darien's pace. Her voice lowered, quiet but clear. "Look, you're going to be pretty useless here. You don't know what to look for, and you definitely don't know what you're dealing with, so stay back and pay attention. You may be useless to me right now, but that doesn't mean I want to see you get yourself killed on your first raid."

Darien swallowed hard, his throat tight, but nodded. "Understood."

Evatra's gaze softened fractionally, just enough for him to see the human-like worry flickering behind her mask of calm. "Good," she replied quietly. "And remember—if anything goes wrong, don't be a hero. Just survive."

Darien nodded again, swallowing the tightness that had formed in his throat as Evatra rode ahead to rejoin the others. Her words echoed in his mind, mingling uneasily with his own anxieties. He shifted uncomfortably in the saddle, struggling to find rhythm with the palomino beneath him.

The terrain gradually flattened into broad fields of waving grass dotted with patches of shrubs, the vivid green dulled by an encroaching haze. In the distance, a thin, ghostly column of smoke drifted lazily toward the sky, marking their grim destination.

As they approached, an acrid, metallic odor began to choke the air, thickening with each step they took. Darien tried to steady his breathing, but the stench of burning wood and blood quickly overwhelmed his senses, forcing him to cover his mouth with the back of his hand.

They crested a small rise, revealing the ruined caravan before them. Wagons lay overturned, splintered wood scattered across the trampled earth. Bodies sprawled in twisted, unnatural angles, their expressions locked in eternal agony. Horses lay motionless, riddled with dark-feathered arrows protruding grotesquely from their lifeless forms. Blood pooled on the ground, dark and glistening beneath the midday sun.

Darien's stomach turned violently, the bitter taste of bile rising in his throat. He barely managed to dismount before vomiting, his breath ragged and trembling. Shame flushed hot through him, but none of the others spared him even a glance. They, too, were pale and subdued, their expressions hardened into careful neutrality.

"Fan out," Evatra ordered sharply, her voice tight but controlled. "Check for survivors and salvage anything useful. Darien—stay with Nardo and Bertryn, and watch the perimeter. If you see anything, anything at all, call out."

Darien nodded, wiping his mouth roughly with the back of his hand, humiliation still burning in his cheeks. He moved away from the caravan, joining two grizzled, grey-skinned trolls as they took up defensive positions near the outer edge of the destruction.

Minutes dragged on with unbearable slowness. Darien scanned the horizon, heart thudding against his ribs. His imagination conjured shadows in the distance, flitting between the sparse trees, darting from one hiding place to another. He tightened his grip on his reins, knuckles whitening.

"Darien," Evatra called suddenly, snapping his attention back to the wreckage. She was crouched beside a large, reinforced chest, her expression focused but strained. "Give me a hand with this."

He hurried over, legs stiff and aching from the ride. Together, they struggled to drag the heavy chest clear of the smoking wagon, wood creaking ominously beneath its weight. Evatra drew her sword and smashed the hilt repeatedly against the heavy lock. The metal refused to yield.

Frustration creasing her brow, she retrieved a heavy broadsword from the discarded weaponry pile and wedged it between the lid and chest, leaning her entire weight against the blade until the lock cracked sharply. The lid sprang open with a heavy thud, revealing a carefully stacked layer of parchment—ledgers, correspondence, documents—seemingly untouched by the violence around them.

Evatra quickly discarded the papers, her movements tense and precise. Beneath the paper lay an array of gold and jewels, necklaces and rings glittering in the harsh sunlight. Yet, rather than relief or triumph, confusion shadowed her expression.

"Something's wrong," she muttered softly, almost to herself.

Darien looked down, puzzled. "What do you mean? Shouldn't we take it?"

Her eyes narrowed, unease tightening her jaw. "No one leaves loot like this behind. Whoever hit the caravan knew exactly what they were after, and it clearly wasn't riches." She glanced around the wreckage again, tension visibly radiating from her. "This wasn't a normal raid—"

She cut herself off abruptly, eyes widening in sudden alarm. "Down!" she shouted, shoving Darien forcefully to the ground just as a piercing horn blast split the air.

Chaos erupted instantly. The earth trembled beneath the sudden rush of hooves, the sharp whistle of arrows slicing through the air. Darien rolled onto his side, heart racing. He crawled desperately behind the heavy chest for cover, eyes wide as he glimpsed the attackers charging toward them—armored figures in dark metal, faces obscured by helmets, moving with unnatural precision and brutal speed.

Evatra had already regained her feet and mounted, bow in hand, firing rapidly into the attacking wave. Her movements were swift, deadly, the calm composure she'd shown earlier replaced by fierce intensity. Yet even she was soon forced from horseback, the rough terrain hampering her mobility. She drew her sword, throwing herself into the melee with fierce determination.

Panic surged, blinding and immediate. Darien spun around, disoriented, searching desperately for safety amid the chaos. The attackers moved with brutal efficiency, cutting down riders before they even fully understood what was happening.

For a brief, frozen instant, Darien considered the palomino nearby—uninjured, unguarded. He could ride away, leave these marauders and the carnage behind. He owed them nothing; they'd captured him, threatened him, used him. He could escape. He could survive.

But his feet wouldn't move. His breathing quickened, chest tightening painfully as his gaze flicked to Evatra, locked in a desperate battle nearby. For all their ruthlessness, these marauders were people—flawed, violent, but still people. Could he truly live with himself, knowing he'd abandoned them to die?

In that brief hesitation, movement at the edge of his vision jolted him back to reality. An armored figure, its helmet dark and menacing, had seen him standing alone, frozen. It charged toward him with deadly purpose, curved sword flashing in the smoke-filled air.

Darien scrambled desperately toward a pile of scattered weapons, heart hammering in frantic terror. He grasped at a sword, but the blade was stuck, wedged beneath a splintered wagon wheel. He tugged harder, panic mounting as he heard the attacker's footsteps pounding closer.

"Move, move, move," he whispered desperately, breath ragged, adrenaline screaming through his veins. The sword refused to budge.

Abandoning it, he snatched the nearest weapon—a heavy, awkwardly balanced lance—and spun clumsily, raising it just as the armored attacker reached him. The enemy's blade arced downward, aiming to cleave Darien in half.

Instinctively, Darien thrust the lance outward. He felt a heavy jolt of impact travel up his arms, wrenching his injured wrist sharply. He gasped in pain, stumbling backward. Before him, the armored figure jerked violently, letting out a strangled, guttural cry.

Darien stared numbly, heart racing, as the attacker collapsed, impaled grotesquely upon the lance's tip by his own momentum. He froze, unable to tear his eyes from the fallen figure, nausea gripping him. He'd never imagined killing like this—no arena rules, no wooden practice swords—just blood, panic, and desperate survival.

Again, the palomino caught Darien's eye, reins loose, freedom and survival just a short sprint away. Every instinct screamed at him to run. But his eyes shot back to the events unfolding around him.

Evatra took a brutal hit—a powerful backhand that sent her reeling to the ground, her sword knocked from her grasp. She barely managed to roll onto her back, dirt smeared across her face as she glared up at her attacker. The armored warrior raised his blade for the killing blow.

Then he froze.

A sword tip jutted from the brutes chest, his body going rigid before collapsing forward, lifeless. Leaving Darien standing where the attacker had been.

Their eyes met briefly, understanding passing silently between them, but there was no time for words or thanks. Behind Darien, another attacker closed in, weapon swinging viciously. Darien ducked, barely evading the deadly arc.

"Don't just stand there!" Evatra shouted, regaining her footing and grabbing her fallen sword. "Fight or we die!"

Darien had no choice but to obey, forced immediately back into the fray as battle roared around him. Fear and adrenaline surged again, blending into a dizzying rush. He tightened his grip on the lance, eyes darting quickly across the chaos unfolding around him. He'd barely had time to process his decision to stay instead of fleeing; now, it was too late to reconsider.

An armored figure charged out from Darien's right flank, emerging from the smoke-filled haze, sword raised aggressively. There was no time to think, only react. Darien pivoted on instinct, his muscles remembering forms drilled endlessly at the Academy. Without conscious thought, he adjusted his stance, bracing for the attack as Master Whyn's voice echoed faintly in his mind: Trust your training, Darien. Let it move you.

The attacker swung high, aiming for his head. Darien reacted instantly, lifting the lance defensively and angling the tip upward. The armored soldier's momentum carried him forward violently, his blade missing Darien by inches. With a jarring, sickening crunch, Darien impaled the man on his sword, his body jerking violently as armor scraped along the length of his blade with a slurp of the creatures' innards.

Darien stumbled backward, almost losing his grip. He watched, stunned, as the enemy fell still, body collapsing heavily to the blood-soaked ground. For a heartbeat, panic surged. What had he done? But the noise of battle left no time to reflect. Another warrior approached rapidly, forcing Darien to snap back into readiness.

The urge to flee resurfaced, desperate and raw, a whisper in the back of his mind: he could leave, find a horse, escape this madness altogether. It wasn't his fight; he owed these people nothing. But as quickly as the thought arose, a flash of Evatra caught his eye, locked in fierce combat, fighting with a determination he couldn't ignore. If he abandoned her now, he'd be condemning her—and possibly himself—to certain death.

He set his jaw, determination hardening his resolve. He'd chosen to stay; now he had to live with the consequences.

Another opponent lunged, and Darien's world narrowed again to the rhythm of battle. His mind emptied, training taking over completely. Master Whyn had always said he fought best when he allowed instinct to guide him—and that's precisely what he did now. Each strike, parry, and dodge flowed without conscious effort, his limbs moving as if they belonged to someone else, someone better trained, someone who had spent a lifetime preparing for this exact moment.

The fear retreated, replaced by calm, precise aggression. He lost track of time, lost track of the chaos surrounding him. He wasn't fighting to prove himself; he wasn't even fighting to win. He fought purely to survive, and somehow, amid the horror of it, his training proved enough—at least for now.

When the last enemy fell, the chaos of battle faded abruptly into eerie silence. Darien stood among the survivors, trembling as exhaustion overcame adrenaline. His gaze flicked involuntarily down to his blood-slicked hands, realizing for the first time how violently they shook. Pain flared suddenly in his injured wrist, fierce and throbbing now that the fight was over. He grimaced, clutching his arm against his chest to steady it, his breath ragged with fatigue.

Nearby, Evatra quickly regained her composure. She wiped blood and grime from her face, already scanning the battlefield, her voice sharp and commanding as she barked orders.

"Drack, Nardo—secure a perimeter. Bertryn, search the fallen. See if you can find any clue who these creatures were, and quickly. We shouldn't linger here."

The others moved swiftly, Evatra's orders galvanizing them into action. Darien stood frozen, staring at the wreckage, uncertainty gripping him again. The adrenaline had faded, replaced by a gnawing ache in his wrist and a deeper ache within him—a sickening realization of what he'd just done.

"Darien," Evatra said sharply, pulling his focus back. She had moved close, eyes narrowed, scanning him from head to toe with sharp scrutiny. Her voice softened a fraction, concern momentarily breaking through her hardened expression. "Are you alright?"

"My wrist," he admitted quietly, voice barely audible as he released a shuddering breath. "I think I hurt it worse in the fight. It's nothing, though."

"It's not nothing," she countered firmly, stepping closer and taking his arm before he could object. She carefully examined his wrist again, frowning at the fresh swelling already visible beneath the skin. "You're lucky you didn't make it worse. A fractured wrist won't kill you, but you'd be useless if we're attacked again."

She released him, glancing up sharply as Bertryn returned, carrying one of the fallen enemy's helmets. He handed it to Evatra wordlessly, though his expression was deeply troubled.

"Have you ever seen armor like this before?" Evatra asked softly, turning the helmet over in her hands with careful scrutiny.

"No," Darien admitted, voice quieter than he'd intended. "Never."

She traced the sharp, angular edges, fingertips lingering briefly on the twisted metal features. A shudder rippled through her frame, though she quickly masked it, expression tightening into practiced neutrality. "Neither have I."

Nearby, Drack approached cautiously, dragging one of the dead warriors behind him. The creature's unsettling features were starkly visible now—blackened, distorted skin stretched taut across a face caught in a perpetual grimace. "They're all like this," Drack muttered, unease evident in his voice. "Whatever they were, they aren't trolls anymore."

Darien glanced toward the other bodies scattered across the battlefield, feeling a chill crawl up his spine. "Were they ever?"

Drack shook his head slowly, eyes narrowing thoughtfully as he studied the corpse at his feet. "Maybe once, but it's like something twisted them. Made them something… different"

Evatra exhaled slowly, exchanging a long glance with Drack before nodding firmly. "Secure this one behind your horse. We'll take it back for Totra-Dal to see." She glanced around the wreckage once more, eyes filled with unspoken regret. "We need to leave quickly."

The others were already mounting up, carrying what little loot they'd salvaged, though their shoulders were slumped, their gazes downcast. Darien's own horse pawed restlessly nearby. He approached slowly, ignoring the pain stabbing through his wrist as he forced himself back into the saddle, feeling every ache magnify as exhaustion began to settle in.

Evatra swung easily onto her horse and scanned the scene a final time. Bodies—friends, allies—lay where they had fallen, their lifeless forms twisted in the grass. There was no time to bury them, no time for words or ceremony. They had fought together, lived together, yet now, in death, the fallen marauders were left abandoned on foreign soil.

"We can't leave them like this," Darien murmured, voice rough with an emotion he didn't fully understand. It was something inborn and primal. His chest ached, guilt and shame settling heavily within him. They deserved better, even if they were marauders.

"We don't have a choice," Evatra said, her voice steady but carrying a heaviness Darien hadn't heard before. "If there are more of these creatures, we can't risk another fight. The dead must find their own peace now."

Darien nodded reluctantly, climbing onto his horse. As the group began to ride out, he stole one last glance at the battlefield, the fallen forms growing smaller with each step, disappearing behind them. He felt a deep, aching sorrow—an unfamiliar grief for people he barely knew and didn't understand. Yet the loss was real, and it pressed upon him in a way he hadn't expected.

They rode in silence, following the same path back toward camp. The trees stretched endlessly before them, shadows lengthening with each passing mile. The mood was heavy, grief mingling with exhaustion, the weight of what had happened settling upon them like an oppressive fog.

No one spoke, and their silence rang louder than any sound.

Chapter 10: The Request

The return ride to camp was mercilessly silent. Darien's wrist burned, the ache amplified by every jolt of his horse's stride, his body sagging under the weight of exhaustion and loss. The survivors moved like shadows through the gates, their battered appearance drawing immediate whispers and uneasy glances from the marauders gathering in curiosity.

At the center of the camp stood Totra-Dal, flanked closely by Kort, whose sneer darkened visibly as his gaze settled on Darien. Far behind them, detached and aloof, Garik observed quietly, his expression impossible to read, the flickering firelight reflecting strangely off his pale skin.

Totra-Dal stepped forward, his thick red mane shining like flame, but the coldness in his eyes extinguished any warmth. "What in Cyprin's name happened?" he demanded, glancing at the corpse Drack had dragged into the camp. His scowl deepened, and suspicion turned swiftly to anger as his gaze snapped to Darien. "You were trusted to join this raid, and this is what happens? What have you done?"

Darien's mouth went dry, uncertainty gripping him tightly, stealing any response he might have managed. Before he could stammer out a defense, Evatra swiftly stepped between them, voice steady but edged with quiet defiance.

"It wasn't his fault," she said firmly. "We were ambushed by something none of us have seen before. He fought beside us—without him, you'd have lost us all."

Totra-Dal's eyebrows rose, incredulity mixing with lingering suspicion as he shifted his attention back to Darien, reassessing. "Is that true, boy?"

Darien hesitated, meeting Totra-Dal's piercing stare. "I just did what anyone would have done," he said cautiously, his voice calm despite the nervous energy coiling tightly in his chest.

Kort snorted dismissively. "More likely he caused it. Maybe they followed him here. Maybe he's part of some elaborate—"

"Quiet," Totra-Dal cut him off sharply, but the doubt lingered in his gaze as it swept back to Darien. "Whatever the truth, we have dead warriors and unknown enemies at our doorstep. That will be addressed soon enough." He gestured toward the two Scillans lingering on the outskirts of the crowd. "Take this body— find out what it is. Quickly."

The Scillans inclined their heads silently and moved forward to collect the corpse, their ghostly figures carrying it away without another word.

Totra-Dal glared pointedly at Darien, the tension thickening until Evatra broke the silence carefully. "We brought it back for study. None of us have ever encountered armor or creatures like that before."

The leader's expression softened slightly, but his suspicion still hung heavy in the air. "Both of you—in my tent. Now."

He turned away sharply, heading toward his tent without another glance. Kort glared venomously at Darien, rage twisting his features, before stalking away into the darkness.

Darien released a breath he hadn't realized he'd been holding. "Did I do something wrong?" he muttered quietly, glancing toward Evatra.

"No," she said softly, shaking her head. "But this is new, even for Totra-Dal. He doesn't handle surprises well."

Darien hesitated, glancing again toward Garik, who watched silently from the shadows. The grey figure's gaze was fixed, intense yet distant, clearly apart from the drama unfolding before him. Garik's presence offered no comfort—only silent curiosity.

"Come," Evatra said, motioning gently. "Better not to keep him waiting."

Darien stepped into Totra-Dal's tent, its warmth immediately wrapping around him, though it offered no comfort. A fire crackled in a small brazier, casting flickering shadows across heavy canvas walls draped with trophies—some clearly valuable, others disturbingly personal. Totra-Dal stood at the center, broad arms folded tightly, eyes narrowed into slits of quiet fury. Kort lurked behind him, arms crossed defiantly.

"Sit," Totra-Dal said sharply, nodding toward a wooden stool. Evatra took a position near the entrance, silent but watchful. Darien moved hesitantly forward, lowering himself onto the seat, every muscle protesting.

The marauder leader regarded him silently for a long moment, his expression unreadable, then finally spoke in a low, controlled voice. "Evatra tells me you fought well today."

Darien hesitated, cautious. "I just did what I had to do."

"Indeed," Totra-Dal said slowly, his eyes narrowing slightly. "And yet Kort claims you might have led these beasts to us. He seems convinced your presence here is a curse. Given that I lost several good people today, I'm inclined to wonder myself."

Darien swallowed thickly, fingers tightening reflexively around the edge of the stool. "I had nothing to do with this," he replied carefully. "I don't even know who—or what—those creatures were."

"That much is clear," Totra-Dal agreed coolly. "Yet somehow trouble seems drawn to you. Explain to me why I shouldn't let Kort deal with you right now. Just to be sure that you're not the focus of it all."

Darien tensed, heart quickening at the threat. Before he could answer, Evatra stepped forward sharply.

"Because Kort is an idiot who'll kill him for sport before we find out anything useful," she interjected firmly. "We don't know what we're facing yet, and until we do, throwing away a fighter—even a novice—is foolish. Besides, had he not stepped in I'd have been gutted myself."

Totra-Dal's eyes flicked toward her, mild surprise registering in the briefest shift of his expression. "You defend him again? Why the sudden loyalty, Evatra?"

"Not loyalty," she retorted immediately. "Common sense. We're already vulnerable. The last thing we need is to weaken ourselves further."

Totra-Dal's mouth twisted thoughtfully before he waved her silent, attention shifting back to Darien. "Tell me again what happened," he demanded. "And spare no details."

Evatra recounted the raid carefully, voice steady despite the growing tiredness that was becoming more and more evident. She described the caravan, the smoke, and wreckage, and the attackers—black-armored figures, fierce and relentless. As she spoke, Totra-Dal's expression darkened further, though he listened intently, saying nothing.

When Evatra finished, the tent filled with heavy silence again. Totra-Dal exhaled slowly, fingers steepled under his chin as he considered. "The armor, their weapons—I've never heard of anything like it."

He turned to Evatra. "What of the corpse?"

"I have no clue. They look almost like trolls and goblins, among others. But twisted somehow," she said. "The Scillans have it now. If anything they'll have the answers. Them or the Peronia. But the Scillans seemed just as troubled as we were."

Totra-Dal rubbed his jaw thoughtfully, considering that carefully. "I trust their judgment, but I still don't like it. Something new is stirring, and I don't enjoy being blindsided." His gaze returned sharply to Darien. "Which brings us back to you."

Darien stiffened slightly, waiting for the next accusation, but Totra-Dal merely narrowed his eyes, assessing him quietly.

"You were found wandering with the centaurs," Totra-Dal mused. "Convenient, perhaps—or perhaps fate playing games. I don't believe in coincidence. Tell me honestly, Darien—do you?"

Darien hesitated, choosing his words carefully. "I believe things happen for reasons we might not understand. But whatever's happening with these…whatever they are, I have no part in it. I was as surprised as anyone by those attackers. They tried to kill me, clearly I'm no ally of theirs."

Totra-Dal exhaled slowly, eyes still probing him for deception, but eventually he nodded, seemingly satisfied—for now. "Very well," he said finally. "For the moment, you've proven useful. I'll grant you that much. But trust is earned, not given." His gaze sharpened. "You will remain under Evatra's command. Prove yourself there, and perhaps you'll earn some measure of respect."

Darien nodded slowly. It wasn't ideal, but it was better than he had dared hope. "Thank you."

"Don't thank me yet," Totra-Dal said dryly.

Darien and Evatra turned to leave together. As he reached the entrance flap he was stopped.

"Darien," Totra-Dal called out softly, voice carrying through the silence of the night. "Come here, boy. I want to continue our conversation."

Darien froze, heart sinking. Gathering what remained of his resolve, he turned and walked towards the big red bearded man.

Totra-Dal studied him carefully, something almost friendly in his expression now, a stark contrast to his earlier cold suspicion. "Sit," he instructed, indicating a stool beside a small table.

Darien obeyed, settling cautiously as Totra-Dal turned and retrieved a bottle filled with amber liquid. He uncorked it and poured generously into two small glasses, sliding one toward Darien.

"Drink," Totra-Dal said gently. "You look like you need it."

Darien hesitated, eyeing the glass suspiciously. "What is it?"

"Freolia," Totra-Dal said proudly. "Made by the fairies in the northwest. They claim it grants flight when consumed in excess—but you'll feel nothing so dramatic from that small amount. Still, it will calm your mind after the day's chaos."

Darien brought the glass cautiously to his lips, wincing as the vapor burned his nostrils. He sipped gingerly, choking back a cough as the liquid burned fiercely down his throat.

Totra-Dal laughed, deep and genuine. "You'll get used to it," he promised, sitting back with his own glass. For a moment, his demeanor was relaxed, almost fatherly, a strange shift from the stern, ruthless leader Darien had seen earlier.

"You know," Totra-Dal mused, swirling the liquid thoughtfully, "I am still trying to puzzle you out. A complete mystery. First, you nearly bring disaster to my camp, then you fight alongside my warriors. And, if Evatra's account is true, you saved her life—something I won't soon forget. Tell me, Darien: why risk your life for people who would gladly see you, and have regularly threatened you to be dead?"

Darien shifted uneasily. "I gave you my word. And," he added quietly, feeling foolish yet compelled to be honest, "I couldn't just watch them die."

Totra-Dal chuckled softly, raising his glass in mock salute. "Honor. Dangerous—and rare in the world these days. And yet you fight as if you've trained your entire life for battle. Do you remember nothing? Not even a name, a place?"

Darien shook his head, feigning greater uncertainty than he felt. "Only bits and pieces," he admitted carefully. "Flashes of memory, but nothing solid."

The troll regarded him silently for several moments, his eyes suddenly sharp again despite his relaxed posture. "A very convenient situation, wouldn't you say?"

Darien felt the implication sink in, knowing denial or explanation would do little good now. Instead, he met Totra-Dal's probing stare with silence, unwilling to trap himself with words.

After a long moment, the troll leader sighed, setting his glass down firmly. "I promised you freedom once you'd earned it. You have, in some ways, done exactly that. But letting you leave now? Kort would see it as weakness." His gaze hardened. "He's eager to test your mortality."

Darien's pulse quickened. "So what happens now?"

Totra-Dal exhaled slowly, leaning forward on his elbows. "For now, you stay here. Until I can determine who—or what—you really are, I cannot let you leave. If Kort sees you as a threat, so be it. He already believes I've grown soft. But understand, boy—I will not lose control of my own people. You remain my guest, under my protection. But a very precarious guest, at best."

"Guest," Darien echoed bitterly. "Your hospitality leaves something to be desired."

Totra-Dal laughed again, louder this time, slapping the table in genuine amusement. "You've grown bold, indeed. Keep that spirit; it will serve you well here."

He waved a dismissive hand, his speech thickening slightly with intoxication. "We will talk more, soon. Go rest."

Darien stood, grateful for the escape from Totra-Dal's oppressive presence. As he stepped outside, the night felt heavy around him, the camp quiet except for the low murmur of dying conversations around distant fires. The air had cooled considerably, carrying the scent of damp earth and smoldering wood. Across the clearing, he noticed the Scillans huddled over the strange, black-armored corpse, their pale faces illuminated intermittently by flickering lanterns. Curiosity pulled at him, urging him closer—but fatigue clawed at him even more fiercely.

Darien stood, grateful for the escape from Totra-Dal's oppressive presence. As he stepped outside, the night felt heavy around him, the camp quiet except for the low murmur of dying conversations around distant fires. The air had cooled considerably, carrying the scent of damp earth and smoldering wood. Across the clearing, he noticed the Scillans huddled over the strange, black-armored corpse, their pale faces illuminated intermittently by flickering lanterns. Curiosity pulled at him, urging him closer—but fatigue clawed at him even more fiercely.

He lingered only a moment, then turned away, making his way toward his tent. Halfway there, he paused, realizing how long it had been since he'd had even a moment to himself. Quietly, he veered off the path into the shelter of the trees, seeking solitude away from the watchful eyes of the marauders.

The shadows swallowed him swiftly, branches scratching lightly against his arms. He took a deep breath, letting the tension ease from his shoulders—but a sudden snap behind him sent adrenaline surging through his veins.

He spun around sharply, hand flying to his sword, but the attacker was faster. A powerful grip slammed him back into a rough-barked tree, pinning him there effortlessly. A cold blade pressed sharply against his throat, stealing his breath. Darien froze, heart pounding wildly, his eyes adjusting to the dim moonlight filtering through the canopy.

"Evatra?" he managed to choke out, recognizing her features in the muted glow. "What—?"

"Quiet," she hissed urgently, pressing the knife just enough to send a sharp warning through his senses. "Walk."

He hesitated, confusion and anger battling within him, but one look at her expression silenced any protest. Something desperate burned in her dark eyes. He moved obediently, feeling the blade's presence at his back as she guided him deeper into the woods, away from the faint glow of the camp.

After several tense minutes, she stopped abruptly. He turned to face her cautiously, relieved to see she had lowered the knife. Still, her posture remained tense, guarded.

"I know who you are," she said finally, voice low and strained.

Darien's pulse quickened. He fought to keep his face neutral, despite the anxiety twisting inside him. "What are you talking about?"

"Don't," she said sharply. Her eyes flashed with frustration and something deeper—something like betrayal. "I heard enough from you and Totra-Dal tonight to confirm it."

Darien took a cautious step backward, raising his hands slowly. "Totra-Dal barely knows anything about me—how could you?"

Evatra shook her head sharply, her voice quiet but intense. "Because he's only seeing you as another puzzle to solve, another pawn to use. He's blinded by drink, suspicion, and pride. But I was there today—I saw you fight."

Darien remained silent, heart hammering in his chest as she took a step closer, her gaze penetrating.

"The way you fought today wasn't just training," she continued, her voice barely above a whisper. "There's a difference between skill and purpose. You didn't fight like a captive desperate to survive. You fought like someone protecting everyone else. No ordinary warrior would risk everything for people who kidnapped and threatened him."

He swallowed hard, struggling to maintain his composure. "That doesn't mean anything—"

"You asked Totra-Dal questions everyone here has known answers to since childhood," Evatra pressed softly, stepping closer still. "Cyprin. The Cycle. Things no one from this world would need explained. You seem completely ignorant, yet you fight as if you've trained your entire life. How does that make sense, Darien?"

He opened his mouth to respond, but words failed him, caught in his throat.

Evatra let out a bitter, humorless laugh. "I've lived through two cycles already. I've seen plenty who claimed to be one of the Eldric—pretenders, charlatans seeking glory. You're the first I've seen who denies it—or maybe doesn't even recognize it yet. Either way, it means something."

Darien clenched his fists at his sides, torn between the need to keep his truth hidden and the burning desire to share his burden. "Even if that's true," he admitted finally, voice strained, "I don't know how to help you. I don't even know how to help myself."

She stared at him silently for a long, tense moment before speaking again, her voice wavering only slightly. "The child possessed by the wraith—her name is Atreya. She's my niece. She's the last family I have left. I begged Totra-Dal to spare her life, to give me a chance to save her. But even he's losing patience. Soon, he'll let Kort have his way."

Her words were edged with quiet desperation, cracking open a vulnerability Darien hadn't imagined existed behind her fierce exterior. His stomach twisted painfully. "I'm sorry, Evatra," he murmured helplessly. "But I don't know how I could possibly—"

"No," she cut him off abruptly, expression shuttering again as her pride resurfaced. "You're right. I thought… maybe someone like you could help. Maybe someone from the stories could do what we couldn't."

Darien shook his head, guilt pressing heavily on his chest. "I never asked for any of this. If I'm one of the Eldric, I don't understand what it means—or what I'm supposed to do. I'm barely surviving here."

Evatra studied him silently, her expression gradually shifting from desperation to quiet disappointment. "Then perhaps I was wrong," she said softly. "I imagined heroes from legend as something more. Maybe you're just a scared kid who can swing a sword."

Her words cut deep, leaving him speechless.

Without another glance, she turned sharply away, disappearing swiftly back toward camp. Darien stood motionless in the shadows, heart heavy with shame and frustration. For the first time since he'd arrived in this world, he felt the crushing weight of expectation—and the unbearable pain of failing to meet it.

When he finally moved again, he finished what he'd come to the woods for, then slowly returned to his tent. Inside, he sat heavily, staring blankly at the fabric walls, thoughts tumbling chaotically through his mind.

Today he'd seen violence unlike anything he'd imagined. He had blood on his hands, lives extinguished because of his blade. He'd earned the trust of people he'd thought were enemies—and had now lost it just as quickly.

The weight of it all crashed upon him suddenly, overwhelming and impossible to bear. Turning away from the tent entrance, he lay down, pulling his pack close, pressing his face into the rough canvas to stifle the sobs he could no longer hold back.

He grieved silently for the lives lost, for the trust broken, and for whatever part of himself had been lost along the way. Exhaustion finally claimed him, pulling him into a restless sleep plagued by dreams of shadowed battles and accusing eyes.

Chapter 11: The Wraith

The next morning, Darien woke to the soft patter of rain against the canvas of his tent. He lay motionless for a moment, feeling the dull ache in his wrist—the raw reminder of yesterday's violence. Rolling onto his side, he stared blankly at the tent wall, memories of the fight mingling with unsettling dreams. He flexed his fingers slowly, wincing at the sharp flare of pain.

Outside, the camp was already awake, filled with hurried activity and low, tense conversations. Darien pulled himself to his feet, stepping out into the gray drizzle. The air was thick with the scent of wet earth and damp smoke. Around him, marauders moved swiftly, securing gear and loading horses. They were preparing for something—and quickly.

At the center of the clearing, Totra-Dal stood in heated discussion with Kort, both of them gesturing sharply. Kort's expression was twisted with barely suppressed fury, his words carrying even from a distance, sharp and accusing. Darien tensed instinctively, but before he could retreat, he caught sight of Garik watching silently from the edge of the camp.

Garik nodded subtly when their eyes met—a small invitation. Darien hesitated only a moment before approaching him, drawn by the troll's calm amid the chaos.

"You seem troubled," Garik observed quietly, his eyes never leaving Totra-Dal and Kort.

Darien followed Garik's gaze, watching Kort's animated anger unfold. "Things don't seem to be going well."

"They rarely do," Garik said with a faint smile. "Kort wants blood. He blames you for what happened, naturally."

Darien stiffened slightly. "Of course he does."

Garik turned his gaze back to Darien, studying him carefully. "And yet, Totra-Dal is uncertain. You've shaken his confidence. He senses you're valuable, but can't quite place why. It makes him uneasy."

Darien sighed, rubbing his forehead tiredly. "None of that makes me feel any better."

Garik tilted his head slightly, amusement glinting in his dark eyes. "Nor should it. Being caught between Kort's suspicion and Totra-Dal's curiosity is a dangerous place to be."

"Why do you even care?" Darien asked sharply, frustration edging his tone. "I'm nobody. I'm not even supposed to be here."

Garik raised an eyebrow, unbothered by Darien's outburst. "That is exactly why I care. You believe yourself lost, but perhaps you're precisely where you need to be."

Darien's breath caught at those words. They echoed inside him, painfully familiar. He'd heard them before—from Chorrun, when he first awoke in Olympus. He shook his head sharply, pushing back the discomfort that surged. "You're not the first to say that," he murmured quietly, avoiding Garik's steady gaze.

Garik's smile widened slightly, as if he had anticipated Darien's reaction. "It seems you've run into more than one person who has a keen mind for insight."

Before Darien could respond, raised voices pulled their attention back toward the center of camp. Kort was storming away, his anger radiating like a storm cloud. Behind him, Totra-Dal rubbed a hand roughly through his thick red beard, visibly troubled. Then Darien saw Evatra, shoulders tense, clearly agitated as she confronted Totra-Dal. Her voice carried faintly across the distance—urgent, pleading, desperate.

Darien watched closely, seeing something in her demeanor he hadn't noticed before: fear. She rarely showed vulnerability, but it was unmistakable now, etched in every tense line of her body. After a few strained words, Evatra turned abruptly, walking away with visible frustration. Totra-Dal simply watched her go, his expression grim.

Darien hesitated only briefly before moving toward Evatra, compelled by the need to understand. "What's happening?" he asked gently, matching her stride.

Evatra spun around sharply, her eyes flashing with barely concealed pain. "Nothing you can fix. Stay out of it."

He flinched slightly at the venom in her voice but held his ground. "Kort wants your niece dead. Is that it?"

She froze, her expression tightening, her voice dropping dangerously low. "Don't speak about things you don't understand."

He took a small step back, raising his hands cautiously. "I just—"

"No," she snapped sharply, cutting him off. Her gaze softened for only an instant before she shut him out again, regaining her composure. "I said stay out of it. There's nothing you can do."

Darien swallowed hard, feeling the sting of her dismissal, but knowing he had no right to push further—not yet. "Fine," he murmured quietly.

Evatra turned sharply, storming off without another word. Darien watched her go, a heavy feeling settling in his chest. He felt helpless and out of place, trapped in a camp full of dangerous strangers, all holding secrets he couldn't fully grasp.

Garik appeared beside him once more, quiet as ever. "She's right, you know," he said softly, his voice gentle but firm. "For now, this isn't your fight. There's nothing you can do for the girl—or for Evatra—until the Scillans understand what we're facing."

Darien nodded slowly, resigned. "Then what am I supposed to do?"

"For now, prepare yourself," Garik said calmly. "We leave within a couple hours."

"Leave?" Darien glanced at him sharply. "Where are we going?"

Garik's expression softened slightly, the amusement fading into a quiet seriousness. "We're moving on. Those soldiers—whatever they were—make our presence here unstable. It isn't wise to linger in one place, especially now that we've caught their attention." He glanced briefly toward the distant glow of the Scillans' lanterns. "We never stay longer than we need to. It's the only way we survive. And for the moment, you're one of us—whether you wish to be or not."

He walked away quietly, leaving Darien alone to grapple with the weight of those words. The camp buzzed around him, busy with preparations, but Darien felt detached, uncertain, adrift. He was caught in the current of events he neither understood nor controlled.

For now, all he could do was move forward—and hope that eventually, somehow, he would find the answers he needed.

Darien spent the rest of the morning loading carts and packing tents alongside the other marauders, the rhythm of the camp around him gradually quickening as the day progressed. The activity was exhausting, every motion sharpening the ache in his injured wrist, but he had little choice except to push through. By early afternoon, most of the smaller tents had been dismantled, supplies bundled and tied into compact bundles ready for travel.

As he paused briefly to catch his breath, Darien noticed Garik lingering at the edge of the clearing, watching silently with his usual inscrutable expression. The troll waited patiently, seemingly indifferent to the commotion of the departing camp, yet clearly paying close attention to Darien.

After several long moments, Garik finally approached. He stopped just a few paces away, eyeing Darien's wrist. "That injury is bothering you more than you're letting on," he remarked quietly.

Darien sighed, dropping a bundle of tent fabric onto a nearby cart. "It's fine. Just a little sore."

Garik raised an eyebrow slightly, faint amusement flickering briefly in his eyes. "No need to lie to me, Darien. You're no use to anyone injured. There's a healer on the far side of camp—older troll woman, good at what she does. Tell her I sent you."

Darien hesitated, glancing at the half-loaded cart. "I've still got work to finish."

Garik waved a dismissive hand. "I'll cover for you. Besides, if Totra-Dal sees you struggling, you'll have more problems than just a sore wrist."

Without another word, Garik turned away, resuming Darien's task seamlessly. With reluctance, Darien made his way toward the edge of the camp, where a small, worn tent stood slightly apart from the others. The healer sat outside, sorting herbs into neat bundles, her wrinkled hands working deftly through each cluster of dried leaves.

She looked up sharply as Darien approached, dark eyes narrowed in suspicion. "What?"

"Garik sent me," Darien said awkwardly, holding up his wrist. "He said you could help."

She eyed him silently for a moment, clearly skeptical, but eventually nodded toward a stool. "Sit."

Darien obeyed, sitting slowly and wincing as the motion jostled his wrist. The healer leaned closer, pressing her rough fingers against the swollen joint, testing his range of movement. He clenched his teeth against the flare of pain but said nothing.

Without another word, she reached into a nearby jar, scooping out a thick, pungent salve that filled the air with its sharp scent. She applied it quickly, spreading it over the swelling before wrapping his wrist tightly with clean cloth. The relief was immediate, the ointment cooling his skin and easing the sharpness of the ache into a dull warmth.

"Thanks," Darien muttered softly.

She merely grunted in response and handed him a small wooden cup. "Drink this."

He eyed it warily, the strong smell burning his nose. "What is it?"

"Medicine," she said bluntly. "Drink."

Reluctantly, Darien lifted the cup and took a sip. It was bitter—far worse than he'd anticipated. He forced it down, gagging slightly as the bitter aftertaste lingered on his tongue. The healer watched him impassively, waiting until he'd finished the entire cup.

When he handed it back empty, she nodded once, returning to her work. "It'll help," she said curtly. "Now go."

Darien thanked her quietly, heading back toward the carts with the bitterness still coating his mouth. By the time he reached his post, midday was fading into afternoon. The camp was nearly dismantled, tents folded and supplies packed securely. At the front, Totra-Dal barked orders as carts were hitched to horses and riders mounted their steeds.

Evatra appeared at the edge of his vision, mounted on her black horse, eyes forward. She deliberately avoided looking in his direction, her posture stiff, unapproachable. Clearly, she was still angry—or at least unwilling to speak to him.

Darien mounted his horse carefully, mindful of his still-aching wrist, and joined the group as they began their slow march northward. The camp was left behind, a scattering of fire pits and flattened grass marking where they'd stayed. As the forest closed in around them again, Darien cast a final glance backward, unease gnawing quietly at his chest.

The caravan traveled at a steady pace, the creaking of carts and muffled hoofbeats forming a rhythmic, monotonous backdrop. The forest had grown dense, trees looming tall around them, casting everything in shifting patterns of shadow and filtered sunlight.

Darien rode toward the rear of the procession, his thoughts restless. The earlier relief from the healer's medicine had faded into a numb ache, a constant reminder that none of this was where he was supposed to be. He didn't belong with these marauders, caught up in their violence and mistrust. His place was elsewhere—with Chorrun, Lotry, and Jodin. Farkland Reach had answers, or at least the promise of them, and he felt a powerful urge to break free, to ride hard and leave it all behind.

His gaze drifted ahead, landing on the pale figure of the Scillan riding quietly along the edge of the caravan. Memories of their earlier interactions tugged at him, mixing curiosity with caution. If anyone here knew something useful—something that might help him escape—it would be the enigmatic Scillan.

Carefully, Darien maneuvered his horse closer, matching pace until they were riding nearly side-by-side. The Scillan glanced at him briefly, its strange black-and-white eyes unreadable.

"You have questions again," the Scillan said quietly, voice measured, neutral.

Darien hesitated, weighing his words. "Yes. But you already knew that."

The Scillan gave a faint, enigmatic smile. "It isn't difficult to guess. You're curious about our destination—and, more importantly, about yours."

Darien tensed slightly, feeling exposed by the accuracy of the Scillan's insight. "I'm just trying to understand. Totra-Dal mentioned the raids, but he never explained why we're moving so suddenly. Why not stay in one place?"

The Scillan turned its gaze ahead, studying the winding road thoughtfully. "Marauders never linger too long, even in times of peace. Settlements that remain stationary are vulnerable. But now, with these new soldiers emerging, staying put becomes suicidal. Totra-Dal recognizes the danger. Until we know who commands these corrupted creatures, it's safer to keep moving. Safety here is always fleeting—merely an illusion."

Darien's throat tightened slightly. "Have you learned anything about the body we brought back? Who—or what—it was?"

The Scillan hesitated, a rare moment of visible uncertainty crossing its pale face. "Some answers, but they bring only greater questions. The body was a twisted amalgamation of races: trolls, goblins, cyclops—even elements resembling my own kind. Whoever created these soldiers did so by corrupting existing beings, binding them to something... darker."

"Cyprin," Darien muttered under his breath, almost without meaning to.

The Scillan's head snapped around sharply, eyes narrowing in sudden interest. "An interesting guess."

Darien felt his pulse quicken slightly, realizing his slip. He chose his next words carefully. "Everyone keeps mentioning him. Totra-Dal, Evatra—they both said the Cycle is beginning again. If these things are appearing now, doesn't it make sense that they're connected to him?"

Darien guided his horse carefully toward the Scillans, who rode in an uneasy silence, each lost in their own thoughts. When he located the one he'd spoken with earlier, he gestured discreetly. After exchanging a cautious glance with their companions, the Scillan rode closer, their face unreadable beneath the pale hood.

"Did you need something?" Their voice remained even, though tinged with caution.

Darien chose his words carefully. "I have questions—about the wraith."

The thought of Atreya's fate had weighed on him heavily, gnawing at him with the desperation of unfinished business.

"Ask," the Scillan replied quietly, guarded yet intrigued.

Darien hesitated, ensuring his voice betrayed nothing of his own identity. "Someone mentioned the Eldric might have the power to free someone possessed by a wraith. Is that true?"

The Scillan's eyes sharpened, scrutinizing Darien's face as if seeking his true intentions beneath the innocent question. After a pause, they responded slowly. "A curious inquiry. The Eldric are indeed said to have influence over the wraiths—if the old stories can be believed. But we do not seek them out for such matters."

"Why not?" Darien pressed, careful to sound merely curious. "If they have the power to help, wouldn't it be worth trying?"

The Scillan's expression hardened, their gaze drifting toward the distant, shadowed mountains. "You misunderstand their purpose. Their duty is to re-imprison Cyprin, not to intervene in the lives of individuals. Every moment spent aiding others distracts from their mission. If word spread that the Eldric were helping people directly, they'd be besieged by endless demands, jeopardizing everything."

Darien frowned, frustration bubbling beneath his surface calm. "But if Cyprin is free, shouldn't things already be falling apart? I haven't seen signs of it yet."

"Because you're looking from too great a distance," the Scillan said darkly. "Closer to the mountain, Cyprin's corruption is surely visible. His darkness is subtle at first, but spreads quickly, devouring everything it touches."

Darien studied their expression, noticing the flicker of uncertainty in their eyes. "What's troubling you?"

The Scillan looked away abruptly. "Just... something I'd rather not dwell upon." They shook their head, clearly dismissing the thought. "The Eldric may have power, but it's a dangerous path. If they were to show themselves openly, chaos would erupt as countless souls sought their favor. The cycle must be completed without distraction."

Darien felt frustration tightening his throat, but maintained his composure. "Hypothetically, if one of the Eldric were here now, how would they help?"

"You're insistent," the Scillan noted thoughtfully. After a brief hesitation, they continued. "Wraiths were once powerful spellcasters. They despise Cyprin above all others. There's a legend of a wraith who fought alongside one of the Eldric against him long ago. Perhaps... perhaps a wraith would listen if one of the Eldric were to speak."

The possibility ignited something within Darien, a flicker of hope immediately shadowed by fear. If this were true, he might be able to help Atreya—but it meant risking everything, including his secret.

"Thank you," he said quietly. "That's helpful."

The Scillan regarded him with cautious suspicion, nodded slowly, and withdrew to join the others in whispered conversation.

Night fell, and Darien lay awake by the fire, thoughts spinning wildly. He knew what he had to do, yet he also knew he couldn't do it alone. Evatra was his only ally here, maybe Garik but who really knew, but she had avoided him for two days now.

By morning, Darien had made his decision. He scanned the camp as the marauders prepared for another day of travel, the air thick with tension and the lingering dread of yesterday's attack. Atreya's fate gnawed at him, her lifeless eyes etched permanently into his mind. The Scillan's words still echoed: if he truly was one of the Eldric, he might be Atreya's only hope.

Darien scanned the ranks anxiously as the marauders began to move out. Finally, he spotted her, riding slightly apart from the rest. Her face was unreadable, the lines around her mouth tight with tension. He maneuvered his horse closer, guiding it alongside hers.

"Evatra," he said cautiously, pitching his voice low. She didn't turn toward him, keeping her eyes fixed stubbornly ahead.

"What do you want?" Her voice was flat, the tension palpable.

"I've decided to help Atreya. But I can't do it without you."

Her eyes narrowed sharply. "Why would you suddenly help now?"

Darien hesitated, then spoke plainly, dropping any pretense. "Because I am exactly who you think I am."

She fell silent, eyes widening slightly in surprise before narrowing again. "Now you admit it? After denying it. You're saying you lied to me?"

Darien shook his head in frustration. "Of course I lied! You're marauders. You captured me. Kort nearly killed me. Did you expect me to tell you everything?"

"So, why now?" Evatra hissed, her voice tight with suspicion. "Why tell me the truth at all?"

Darien exhaled sharply, turning to face her directly. "Because for some reason I can't explain, I trust you," he said firmly. "And because you figured it out on your own, anyway. Maybe I need to prove it to myself as much as to you."

Evatra's jaw tightened, clearly torn. "And you really think you can help her?"

"I don't know. But the Scillan said the wraiths might respond to someone like me," Darien replied, careful to keep his voice steady despite his doubts. "It's worth a try."

She rode in silence beside him, clearly conflicted. When she spoke again, her voice was quieter, strained. "If you're lying to me—"

"I'm not," Darien cut her off gently but firmly.

For a moment, Evatra simply stared at him, visibly wrestling with herself. Finally, she nodded curtly. "Fine. Tonight."

When darkness fell and the marauders' fires dotted the camp, Darien waited anxiously near the wagon, scanning the shadows for Evatra. The goblin guard stationed there, Wret, watched him curiously, leaning casually against the wagon wheel. After several silent minutes, Wret finally cleared his throat, eyes narrowing in curiosity.

"So, you're the one everyone's talking about," the goblin remarked, casually adjusting the belt that held his sword. "The new swordsman, right?"

Darien glanced warily at him, uncertain if the question was sincere or a subtle mockery. "I suppose I am."

Wret grinned broadly, showing uneven teeth. "The whole camp's talking about you after that raid. Kort won't shut up about it—though I reckon he'd rather you hadn't come back at all."

Darien relaxed slightly, recognizing no malice in the goblin's tone. "Kort doesn't seem to like newcomers."

"He doesn't like anyone," Wret snorted, shaking his head. "Anyway, if even half the rumors are true, you're quite the fighter. Think you could teach me a few tricks?"

Darien raised an eyebrow. "You want me to teach you swordplay?"

"Why not?" The goblin shrugged good-naturedly. "Kort won't teach anyone anything, and Evatra's never around."

Before Darien could respond, Evatra arrived, moving swiftly through the shadows toward them. Her expression was guarded, her eyes alert as she briefly glanced toward Wret, who straightened immediately at her approach.

"Oh, Evatra, you gave me a scare," the goblin said quickly, his tone shifting from casual to respectful. "Totra-Dal said you'd be coming by, but he didn't mention you'd have company."

"Relax, Wret," Evatra said calmly, eyes flicking briefly to Darien. "You know who this is. Everyone does by now."

Wret's eyes widened slightly, interest reigniting. "Yeah, the raid—I was just asking him if he could show me a thing or two with the sword."

Darien exhaled, tension easing slightly. "Maybe sometime," he offered carefully, hoping it would be enough to satisfy the goblin's curiosity. "When we're not all exhausted."

Wret chuckled, clearly pleased. "I'll hold you to that."

Evatra rolled her eyes, but a faint smile touched her lips. "Enough of that. I'm here to see Atreya."

Wret's expression sobered instantly. "Of course," he murmured, stepping aside respectfully. "She's inside. Still hasn't moved, poor girl."

Evatra nodded sharply, motioning for Darien to follow. As Darien stepped toward the wagon, Wret lifted a hand uncertainly.

"Evatra," he said, his tone hesitant, "Totra-Dal didn't specifically say anything about him."

She paused, turning back to face him, voice firm. "Totra-Dal told me I could do whatever I thought was necessary. Right now, Darien is necessary."

Wret shifted uncomfortably, clearly reluctant to risk angering either Evatra or Totra-Dal. Finally, he nodded in resignation. "Alright, but if anyone asks—"

"Send them to me," Evatra cut him off smoothly. "I'll handle it."

She didn't wait for another response, stepping up into the wagon. Darien followed closely, the quiet rustle of canvas closing behind them as they stepped into the darkness.

Inside, the dim glow of a small lantern illuminated Atreya's small, motionless form. She sat against the wooden post, wrists still bound. Her face was utterly blank, void of expression or recognition. The sight sent a chill through Darien, reminding him sharply why he was risking this.

Evatra's voice was barely audible, tense with both hope and fear. "Are you sure about this?"

Darien nodded slowly, trying to steady his nerves. "I have to try."

Evatra studied him for a long moment, uncertainty and fear flickering openly across her face. "If you're wrong—"

"I know," he said quietly, his voice steadying. "But you asked me why I would tell you the truth now. It's because of this." He nodded toward Atreya. "This matters to you. You're desperate. So am I. I have no idea if this will work, but I can't just sit by anymore."

Evatra's jaw tightened, emotions warring visibly across her face. "If this goes badly, Darien, it isn't just your life at risk. If you truly are one of the Eldric, and you fail or die here—"

"Then everyone is doomed," he finished softly. "But I can't do nothing."

She exhaled slowly, her rigid posture softening in reluctant acceptance. "Then do it. Quickly."

Darien stepped forward, kneeling carefully in front of Atreya. Her hollow eyes didn't move, didn't blink. He hesitated only a moment before addressing the presence within.

Darien stepped forward, kneeling carefully in front of Atreya. Her small frame remained disturbingly still, hollow eyes fixed on some distant, unknowable point. The girl seemed impossibly fragile, barely breathing, yet beneath that innocence lurked something monstrous.

He steadied his breath, speaking softly into the stillness. "I'm here to talk to the wraith."

For several tense heartbeats, nothing happened. Then Atreya's eyes shifted abruptly, locking onto Darien's with a gaze so filled with loathing it stole his breath away.

"What do you want, outsider?" The voice was cold, sharp, and utterly unnatural coming from a child's lips.

Darien swallowed hard, suppressing the shudder that crawled up his spine. "I want you to release the girl. She's innocent. She's done nothing to deserve this."

A cold, humorless chuckle slipped through the girl's lips. "Innocence?" The word dripped disdain. "None of you living creatures are innocent. Life itself is a crime—one you commit daily, unthinkingly, while we are left to suffer for eternity."

Evatra shifted nervously behind him, her breathing shallow with tension. Darien fought to keep his voice steady. "But why her? Why keep her trapped like this? She's just a child. What use is she to you?"

"Freedom," the wraith hissed bitterly. "This child allows me to roam, to see the stars again, to taste the air. Would you have me return willingly to oblivion? To darkness?" The child's voice lowered to a menacing whisper. "No. She is mine."

Darien's pulse quickened. He forced himself to stay calm, to reason through this carefully. "But she's not truly free," he said, his voice firm but gentle. "Neither of you are. She's trapped, and you're still bound, tethered by fear. Eventually, the marauders will grow tired of waiting. They'll kill you both, and you'll lose whatever small freedom you've gained."

The wraith hesitated, Atreya's expression flickering uncertainly for the first time. "They wouldn't dare."

"You know they would," Evatra cut in softly, her voice trembling slightly. "Totra-Dal's patience is almost gone. Kort wants you dead now. How much longer do you think you have?"

Atreya's eyes snapped toward Evatra, filled with hatred. "Do you threaten me?"

"Not a threat," Darien said quickly. "Just reality. But there might be another way. You don't have to be destroyed."

The wraith fell into tense silence, considering. When it spoke again, the voice was cautious, wary. "Speak."

Darien took a slow breath. Everything hinged on this moment. "Release Atreya, and I promise you safe passage away from here. You can leave unharmed."

Atreya's head tilted unnaturally, black eyes narrowing. "And why would they listen to you? You're nothing here, an outsider without power."

Darien swallowed hard, steeling himself against the risk he was about to take. "Because I'm one of the Eldric."

Atreya's eyes narrowed sharply. "You lie."

"I'm telling you the truth," he insisted. "I was brought here to stop Cyprin. I can promise your freedom, and these people will listen to me."

"Impossible," the wraith snarled, eyes blazing with sudden fury. "I have met others who claimed to be members of the Eldric. All liars, all weak. Why should I believe you?"

Darien hesitated, the weight of doubt suddenly heavy. He glanced briefly toward Evatra, who met his gaze with raw fear. She knew as well as he did that failure now meant death—or worse. Yet, he felt no other option.

"Because I'm not from this world," he admitted quietly. "And if what I've heard about you wraiths is true, that should matter. The Scillans told me you might listen to one of the Eldric."

Atreya stared back at him, expression unreadable. "Words are easy. Truth is not. Allow me inside your mind. Show me you speak truly—or I shall destroy the child now, and everyone else soon after."

Evatra stepped closer, her breath sharp. "Darien, no. Don't."

"I have to," he murmured, feeling the gravity of the moment pressing upon him. He extended a trembling hand toward Atreya. "If this is what you need to believe me, do it."

Atreya's small, cold hand closed around his own. A piercing chill surged instantly through him, a wave of ice crashing through his veins, flooding his mind. He gasped as memories surged unbidden, images of his past, scenes from the Academy, faces of friends he might never see again. His secrets were laid bare, stripped and examined ruthlessly by the entity that now sifted through his thoughts with clinical precision.

He tried to pull away, but his limbs felt locked in place, paralyzed by an invisible force as the presence dug deeper. It probed curiously, almost clinically, yet there was a subtle current of something else beneath—anger, pain, and perhaps even envy.

Interesting... a voice echoed within his mind, cool and analytical. "You truly are not from this world. Your memories are filled with things I've never seen."

Darien shuddered, his breath coming in short, painful gasps. "Get out of my head," he managed to whisper.

"Not yet. I must be sure of your claim."

The sensation intensified, becoming almost unbearable. Darien gritted his teeth against a fresh wave of icy pressure, a presence that dug deeper, searching through him like a knife carving through his thoughts. It was violating, invasive, but there was nothing he could do to stop it.

Then, suddenly, the presence paused.

"You were truthful. You are indeed one of the Eldric."

As abruptly as it had begun, the invasion ceased, replaced by an unsettling calm. The girl's eyes closed briefly, then opened again—no longer hollow, but filled with confusion and fear.

"Auntie E?" Atreya's small voice broke the silence.

Evatra surged forward instantly, kneeling beside her niece, pulling her close. "Atreya," she choked out, holding the girl tightly, relief and disbelief mingling in her voice.

Darien stepped forward, momentarily overwhelmed by the enormity of what had happened, until Evatra's horrified expression drew him back.

"What's wrong?" he asked, his voice still unsteady.

"Your eyes," she whispered, breathless with fear. "Darien—they're black."

Before he could respond, a voice whispered again inside his mind—cold, clear, and impossible to mistake for his own.

"I am here, as we agreed. Take me beyond the edge of your camp, and I will leave you both unharmed."

Darien stiffened, gripping his head instinctively. "What?"

Evatra took a cautious step forward, eyes darting between him and Atreya. "Who are you talking to?"

Darien's pulse quickened. "The wraith," he whispered.

Atreya's gaze was still locked onto Darien, wide with apprehension. Evatra pulled her protectively closer. "Did it possess you?"

Darien shook his head, trying to clear it. "Not exactly. It says it just needs me to take it to the forest's edge, then it'll leave."

Evatra's jaw tightened, the lines of her face growing tense with suspicion. "How do you know it's telling the truth?"

"I don't," Darien admitted. "But what choice do we have?"

The voice in his mind spoke again, clearer now, almost impatient. "Time is short. Take me from this camp, and I promise no harm will come to you."

He swallowed, turning to Evatra. "It's my risk. I have to trust it."

Evatra's expression wavered, torn between desperate hope and bitter frustration. "If something happens to you, Darien, it's not just you who pays the price."

He nodded slowly. "I know. But if I don't do this, what was the point of any of it?"

She studied him for a long, painful moment before finally nodding. "Fine. But be careful."

He gave her a small, forced smile, then stepped out into the darkness of the camp. Wret's voice greeted him softly from the shadows.

"Sad, isn't it? Poor thing."

"Not anymore," Darien replied quietly. "Take a look."

Wret turned toward the wagon, eyes widening as he glimpsed Atreya, now awake and cradled in Evatra's arms. "By the devil himself," he breathed, awestruck. "How——?"

Darien didn't answer. He moved swiftly past, urgency driving his steps, his head throbbing from the wraith's presence. As he reached the edge of camp, voices faded behind him, replaced by the quiet whispers of the forest. It wasn't until he stood completely hidden in the trees that he spoke again.

"How are you going to get out of me?"

"As easily as I entered," the wraith responded. "You need only endure a brief moment more."

Darien tensed, bracing for what he feared would come next.

Pain exploded behind his eyes, white-hot and agonizing, driving him to his knees. His breath caught, his body convulsing briefly as a cloud of inky darkness tore itself from his skin, swirling before him like smoke caught in wind. The ache faded, replaced by an overwhelming emptiness.

The wraith hovered in the air, its form shifting and coiling. "You kept your word, human. For that, I grant you knowledge: you will face Cyprin atop Mount Olympus, and not alone, though that path will be harder than you expect. In addition, when you have need, find my people and ask for their aid."

Darien's breath was ragged. "Wait, what do you mean—"

But the darkness was already dispersing, scattering into nothingness beneath the moonlight.

Chapter 12: The Family

Darien stepped from the shadowed tree line into the waking chaos of the marauder camp. The air was thick with movement—figures emerging groggily from tents while others moved with sharp intent, their boots crunching against the dirt as they made their way toward the wagon. Voices rippled through the camp, low murmurs tinged with curiosity and unease. Word was spreading.

The closer he got, the harder it became to navigate. The crowd thickened, pressing inward as more gathered, drawn by the unseen force of spectacle. Faces turned, whispers spreading like fire through dry brush. At the center of it all stood Evatra, clutching Atreya tightly in her arms. The child buried her face into Evatra's shoulder, small hands gripping fabric as if the world might slip away if she let go.

Evatra's gaze lifted, locking onto him instantly. Relief flickered through the shadows of her expression as she motioned him forward. The crowd hesitated, then parted just enough for him to step through.

"Darien," she breathed, her voice taut with worry. "I didn't see you return. Is it...?" Her eyes searched his face, scanning for any lingering trace of what had taken hold of him.

"Gone," he answered simply.

The tightness in her shoulders eased. A shuddering breath left her as tears, still clinging to her skin, caught the torchlight in streaks of silver. The barest hint of a smile ghosted her lips—a fragile thing, but real.

A voice boomed through the restless crowd.

"What in the blazes is going on here?"

Totra-Dal didn't so much push through the gathering, as it parted by his sheer presence alone. His massive form carved an effortless path as those around him instinctively stepped back. Kort followed in his wake, sneering before he even fully emerged into the torchlight.

"Move aside, move aside," Kort snapped, the sharp edge of his voice slicing through the murmurs.

Totra-Dal's gaze swept the scene before him, taking in Evatra, the child in her arms, then Darien standing just beyond them. His brows furrowed. "How?" he muttered, stepping forward for a closer look. For the first time since Darien had met him, the troll leader seemed at a loss for words.

His voice softened, almost uncertain. "Is she...?"

"She's fine," Evatra whispered, still holding Atreya close. "But she's exhausted. I need to get her somewhere quiet."

Totra-Dal blinked, his lips parting slightly, as if struggling to grasp the reality before him. "But... how?"

"Later," Evatra hissed, her tone leaving no room for argument.

Totra-Dal nodded and gestured for her to move, clearing a path through the gathered marauders so she could carry Atreya away from prying eyes. His gaze lingered after them for a moment before shifting back to Darien, suspicion tightening his features.

"You," he rumbled, his voice low but weighted. "What are you doing here?"

Darien hesitated only for a second. "Evatra asked me to meet her here," he said quickly, unsure how much to reveal.

Totra-Dal's sharp gaze lingered on him, narrowing slightly. "Every time something significant happens, I find you nearby," he muttered before exhaling heavily. "Come along then. I have a feeling you're involved in this somehow."

Without waiting for a response, he turned and strode toward his personal camp. Darien followed, his stomach twisting as Kort fell into step behind him. The goblin's presence at his back made his skin crawl, but he forced himself to keep walking.

As they passed through the thinning crowd, Darien caught sight of the Scillans. The one he had spoken to earlier watched him intently, their expression unreadable. Darien quickly looked away, keeping his gaze to the ground as they moved.

Inside Totra-Dal's camp, the flickering fire cast elongated shadows against the canvas walls. The heat pressed against Darien's skin, the scent of charred wood and aged liquor hanging in the air. A loose semicircle formed around the flames—Totra-Dal, Evatra, Atreya, Kort, and Darien. All eyes inevitably fell upon the sleeping child, her soft breaths the only sound breaking the silence.

Totra-Dal exhaled deeply, rubbing his temples. "I don't even know where to begin," he admitted. "When you asked if you could visit the child, I thought nothing of it. I never imagined..." He trailed off, shaking his head.

Kort's voice cut through the pause, sharp and accusing. "She was never supposed to recover," he sneered. "There was a wraith within her. Those demons never leave willingly. What dark tricks did you use?"

The fire crackled, casting jagged light across their faces. The tension thickened.

Evatra's tone was sharp, unwavering. "I didn't do anything." She turned to Darien. "It was him."

All eyes shifted to him. Darien stood slightly apart from the others, arms crossed against the night's creeping chill.

Totra-Dal's gaze hardened. "Darien?" His tone left no room for evasion.

Darien exhaled slowly. This was it. The moment of no return. Saving Atreya had forced him into a corner, and now there was no more hiding.

"I'm one of the Eldric."

The silence that followed was absolute.

Kort scoffed, breaking it first. "You?" He barked out a laugh, his voice thick with mockery. "You're nothing but a kid who knows some tricks with a sword!"

Evatra spun on him. "It's true! It has to be true! He saved Atreya, and the wraith went into him, but he's not possessed. Look at him! There's no other explanation!"

Totra-Dal held up a hand, cutting off any further arguments. His gaze remained locked on Darien as he considered him carefully. Finally, he turned to Kort. "Go and retrieve the Scillans. I believe we'll have need of them before the night is done."

"But I—" Kort started to protest.

"Go, Kort," Totra-Dal ordered, his tone leaving no room for debate. "We will wait for the rest of this story until you return."

With a frustrated snarl, Kort turned on his heel and stalked off.

For several minutes, no one spoke. Totra-Dal remained standing, his gaze distant, lost in thought. At one point, he walked to a chest near the edge of the fire, opened it, and retrieved a bottle. Darien heard the clink of glasses, but after a pause, the troll seemed to reconsider. Instead of pouring a drink, he returned the bottle to its place and shut the chest.

Kort eventually returned, but he was alone, leading only one of the Scillans into the firelight.

"Where are the others?" Totra-Dal asked, his voice laced with irritation.

"Still with the body of that thing," Kort muttered. "They said only this one had to come." He sneered. "The stench of that corpse is getting unbearable. We should leave it for the beasts."

The Scillan gave a respectful bow before glancing at Darien, recognition flickering in their expression. "How may I be of service?"

Totra-Dal gestured toward Atreya. "The child has been freed from the wraith, as I'm sure you've heard. Evatra says Darien is the reason. Now, he claims to be one of the Eldric. I thought you might offer insight."

The Scillan nodded, making their way to one of the chests positioned around the perimeter of the fire. Settling into a seat, they turned their attention to Totra-Dal, waiting for him to speak.

"Now, Darien," the troll leader said, his bearded face turning toward him. "You make quite the claim. Why didn't you tell me this before?"

Darien exhaled, rubbing the bridge of his nose. "That's kind of hard to explain," he admitted. "It'll probably be better if I just start from the beginning, but it could take a while."

Totra-Dal motioned for him to continue.

Finally freed from half-truths and evasions, Darien spoke. He explained what The Academy was, how he had suddenly transitioned to Olympus, and the journey he had been making to Farkland Reach before his capture. He spoke deliberately, careful not to reveal that he had been completely unaware of the Cycle before arriving or that Evatra had suspected his identity. He wasn't going to get her in trouble—not after everything. Chorrun had warned him to be careful about revealing his ignorance, even to those who were more friendly than the marauders.

When he finished, silence settled over the group. The crackling fire filled the empty space where words had been only moments before.

"It seems," Totra-Dal finally said, a small chuckle escaping him, "that we have become embroiled in one of the stories of old."

"You don't actually believe this nonsense, do you?" Kort scoffed, his face twisting in disbelief.

"I have no reason to doubt him," Totra-Dal replied sharply. "It explains who he is, what he's doing here, and how he fits into this Cycle. And tell me, Kort, how else would you explain Atreya's freedom? Are you suggesting that after all this time, the wraith simply chose to leave?"

"You're a fool!" Kort spat, his voice rising with frustration. "All he's done since the moment I captured him is lie! Why should we trust a pale-skinned child?"

Silence fell like a heavy weight over the group.

Totra-Dal stood, towering over them, his expression dark. "You go too far," he said, his voice quiet but carrying a sharp edge.

Kort remained standing across from him, his breathing heavy. His gaze flickered between Darien and Atreya, his fingers twitching near the hilt of his sword. Darien felt his own muscles tense, his hand unconsciously drifting toward the belt strapped around his waist, though Kort hadn't seemed to notice.

Totra-Dal let out a low, guttural growl. The air became thick with unspoken threats, and Darien felt that any wrong move could set them both off.

Then, after several moments, Kort exhaled sharply, spitting onto the ground before turning and stalking out of the campsite. Darien released a breath he hadn't realized he was holding.

"What happens now?" he asked, unsure of what any of this truly meant.

"Nothing, as far as Kort is concerned," Totra-Dal replied. "He's not the fastest thinker, but once he's had time to consider everything, he'll come around." The troll leader then turned toward the Scillan. "Now, I've asked you here to see if you have any additional insight. Do you believe Darien is telling the truth?"

The pale-faced figure studied Darien for a few seconds before stepping closer into the fire's glow.

"He and I have spoken on two occasions," they said. "Both times, I suspected he was more than he appeared to be. In fact, it was our second conversation that led my fellow Scillans and me to a realization about the creatures that attacked Evatra's party. I had intended to speak with you about this tonight." The Scillan paused, clearing their throat. "But before that, let us settle the matter of Darien."

They turned toward him fully, their expression unreadable. "From everything we know of the Eldric and the Cycle, the timeline is correct, and Darien meets all the requirements. But most importantly, he was able to barter with a wraith—something unheard of in Olympus, except in the histories of the Eldric."

Totra-Dal absorbed the information, nodding slightly before turning back to Darien. "Darien, thank you for finally being honest with me. I wish you had been from the start; it would have saved us all a great deal of trouble. But perhaps this is how it was meant to unfold."

His voice wavered slightly as his gaze drifted toward Evatra, who still clung tightly to the sleeping Atreya. The girl's soft breaths were the only sound in the stillness. Totra-Dal took a steady breath, composing himself before continuing.

"Evatra, did your sister ever tell you who Atreya's father was? Did she ever mention anything about him?"

Evatra's grip on the child tightened slightly. "I... no. I asked her about it years ago, but she refused to say anything."

Totra-Dal nodded as if he had expected that answer. "Evedra was a private woman. She kept many things to herself, including this. But I was the only one she couldn't keep it from." He hesitated, glancing at Atreya. "Nine years ago, she and I were... involved. Atreya is my daughter."

Evatra's face drained of color, shock and disbelief warring across her features.

"She didn't want anyone to know," Totra-Dal continued. "She refused to be seen as the mistress of the camp's leader, so she kept it from everyone. Even you. I doubt Atreya even knows herself."

Atreya slept soundly in Evatra's arms, unaware of the weight of the revelation unfolding around her.

"You and I will have many conversations about what happens next," Totra-Dal said, his voice quieter now. "Now that Evedra is gone, we must decide together what is best for Atreya. But I wanted you to know the truth, and I wanted Darien to know it as well."

Totra-Dal turned his gaze back to Darien, his red beard shifting as he exhaled. "I want you to know the importance of what you've done. I wasn't able to show it, but I loved Evedra dearly. When the wraith took her, and there seemed to be no hope of saving Atreya, I feared that I went mad for a time. I even considered letting Kort kill the child and free the wraith, just so I could face it for what it had done." His voice wavered slightly, and for a brief moment, he seemed smaller, as though the weight of past choices had physically diminished him. He looked down at his hands, then at Evatra, before composing himself.

"And then you, Evatra, convinced me to hold out hope. Thank the seas and skies that you did because otherwise—" His words trailed off, unfinished, heavy with the burden of what might have been.

Silence settled between them as Totra-Dal, the towering figure who commanded a ruthless band of marauders, struggled to contain the emotion trembling just beneath the surface. He inhaled deeply, forcing himself back into control, though the redness in his eyes betrayed the tears he refused to shed.

Finally, he cleared his throat and shifted his attention. "Now, Scillan, you stated that you had news for us to consider?" His voice had returned to its usual strength, steady and authoritative.

The Scillan rose and stepped toward the fire's center. "It concerns the beast that Evatra and Darien brought back after their raid," they began. "We pooled our collective knowledge of the races, consulted the books of history we brought with us, but we were left with more questions than answers." They paced, their pale face unreadable in the flickering firelight.

"Then I spoke with Darien, and I began to suspect something. That suspicion led me to revisit books I had not opened in decades, searching for an answer. And I came to an irrefutable conclusion—this creature is not of our time. It is from the past."

A heavy silence fell over the group.

"We believe this thing is a soldier of Cyprin's dark army, sent down from the mountain," the Scillan continued. "It was likely scouting the area when it came across the caravan, which it and the others destroyed to hide their presence. They must have realized your raiding party was approaching, Evatra, and so they waited. The attack on you was no accident—it was an ambush."

Evatra inhaled sharply. "Cyprin has soldiers?" True fear crept into her voice for the first time. "From everything I knew, they never left the mountain."

The Scillan nodded. "That is true, or at least, it has been in every previous Cycle. Never before have we seen evidence that his forces have ventured beyond the mountain's shadow."

The fire crackled, sending small embers floating into the night sky as the weight of the revelation settled over them. No one spoke for several moments.

Finally, Totra-Dal rose, his eyes sweeping over each of them before settling on Darien. "Well then, my young friend, it seems we need to ensure that you make it to Farkland Reach. That is where the next part of your journey lies. I would be surprised if the others of the Eldric aren't already there."

Darien's heart skipped a beat at the thought. Kara. Philip. Even the ever-skeptical Trey. He hadn't thought about them in days, too consumed by survival. Guilt twisted in his stomach. He could only hope that their journey through this world had been less insane than his own.

"The question is, how do we get you there?" Totra-Dal continued. "Diverting the entire group could take weeks, and you may have noticed—we aren't the quickest when we travel together. No, what you need is something smaller. More than just yourself, but not a full raiding party..." He trailed off, his mind already working through possibilities.

The silence stretched as they all considered the best course of action.

"I'll take him."

Evatra's voice cut through the quiet, firm and unwavering.

Both Darien and Totra-Dal turned to her in unison. "You?"

Totra-Dal frowned. "What about Atreya? She's going to need you to be here."

Darien had already dismissed the idea of Evatra accompanying him, assuming her responsibilities with Atreya would make it impossible. But now, hearing her say it so definitively, a flicker of hope stirred in him. If there was anyone he wanted by his side in the unknown, it was her.

Evatra met Totra-Dal's gaze. "She has family here. Evedra already decided who she should be with."

Something shifted in Totra-Dal's expression—respect, perhaps, or reluctant understanding.

"But you have to give up the drinks," Evatra added, her tone leaving no room for argument. "I can't have you drowning yourself in freolia or whatever concoction you'll find next, instead of taking care of her."

Totra-Dal grimaced, clearly displeased. "I'll..." He hesitated, then sighed. "I'll pass it out to the others tomorrow."

Evatra's arms tightened around Atreya. "No. I want it poured out."

Totra-Dal's jaw tightened, but then his gaze flicked down to the small child resting against her. The tension bled from his shoulders, and after a moment, he nodded. "Fine."

The conversation shifted back to logistics.

"Alright then," Evatra said. "When do we leave?"

Darien turned to Totra-Dal, waiting for the answer.

"As soon as possible," Totra-Dal said, still sulking over the impending loss of his prized liquor. "I think you should take the Scillan with you as well. The knowledge they possess will be invaluable to Aghemnon."

Chapter 13: The Festival

Darien was shaken awake before dawn by the Scillan, their pale face barely visible in the dim morning light.

"Come, it's time for us to leave."

Rising, Darien stretched his tight muscles, wincing as the stiffness from days of hard riding settled into his limbs. He gathered what few belongings he had, adjusting the straps on his pack while shaking off the last remnants of sleep.

The sky was a deep crimson, the sun not yet visible over the horizon, but there was just enough light for them to move comfortably. The four of them—Darien, Evatra, the Scillan and Garik, who had simply shown up as they left without a word—began their trek out of the marauders' camp on foot, sticking close to a line of trees until the camp was out of sight. Only when they could no longer hear the distant sounds of the waking camp did they mount their horses and press westward, riding through the rolling hills they had traveled in the days before.

The scenery was becoming monotonous. What had once been rugged and captivating was now little more than an endless sea of golden grass, broken only by the occasional jagged outcropping of stone. Darien found himself absentmindedly running his fingers along the hilt of his sword as they rode. Totra-Dal had made sure to return it to him before they left.

"You've more than earned this back, Darien," the troll had said, his tone lighter than usual. "By the seas and skies, I never thought I'd meet a member of the El-dric, let alone capture one. You take care of yourself, you hear me? And if you ever need anything, you find me. I'll gladly fight alongside you any day."

Darien had thanked the grey-skinned man, feeling, for the first time, that he had found something close to a friend. Perhaps "trust" was too strong a word, but he understood Totra-Dal well enough to believe that if he ever needed the troll's help, he would come. Unlikely as that might be.

The riders traveled in near silence. Darien refrained from speaking, not wanting to disrupt Evatra's thoughts. She had just regained her niece, only to find out the girls father was a man she barely seemed to tolerate. The decision to leave Atreya behind had clearly weighed on her, though she had made it without hesitation. Darien could see it in the set of her jaw, the tension in her shoulders. She hadn't woken the child before leaving, trusting To-tra-Dal and the other marauders to explain her absence. It was not an unusual situation for Atreya, who had grown up knowing her mother's unpredictable absences as a marauder.

It wasn't until the following day that Evatra spoke about what truly concerned her. "She's such an innocent child," she murmured, almost to herself. "I know she'll blame herself. She needs to know that it wasn't her fault."

Darien listened, responding only when the moment felt right, offering what little reassurance he could. Mostly, he let her talk.

The first day melted away into the next, and they passed in relative silence. Eventually, the feel of the land from uninhabited growth to worn roads and traveled walkways took the place of barely visible trails.

The first sign of Velmark wasn't the buildings, nor the roads leading to them. It was the smell.

Rich spices filled the air, drifting toward them on a gentle breeze that carried hints of roasted nuts, fresh bread, and something smoky and sweet. It was a stark contrast to the empty hills they had been traversing—a sudden intrusion of life, of civilization.

Darien inhaled deeply, the scent coaxing a hunger he hadn't realized he was suppressing. The landscape was beginning to shift, the golden fields giving way to well-worn dirt paths and, eventually, the subtle imprint of wagon wheels hardened into the earth. The occasional wooden post jutted up from the ground, wrapped with colorful strips of fabric, marking the way forward.

Evatra slowed her horse, narrowing her eyes at the horizon. "I don't recognize those banners," she muttered.

"You wouldn't," Garik's voice piped up from behind them, entirely too pleased with himself. He had been riding at a casual pace, as if he had known they would eventually stumble upon something interesting. "They change every year. Velmark isn't loyal to a single banner—it belongs to whoever trades the most."

Darien squinted, following Evatra's gaze. The banners flapped lazily in the wind—some embroidered with unfamiliar symbols, others a patchwork of materials sewn together without rhyme or reason. Beyond them, the vague outline of a town took shape against the horizon.

As they pressed forward, the dirt road hardened beneath their horses' hooves, packed from frequent travel. The edges of the path widened into a proper trade road, and before long, signs of life began to emerge—figures walking, leading carts laden with goods, voices rising in laughter or animated discussion. By the time the town's outskirts became visible, the dull murmur had swelled into a hum of activity.

Velmark was completely unlike Taitron. A clash of styles marked the buildings—stone, wood, and some barely more than tents stretched over sturdy frames. The streets twisted in unpredictable directions, built around what must have once been natural clearings rather than any planned design. Rather than expanding in neat circles, the town sprawled outward, flowing wherever it pleased.

And the people—

Darien slowed his horse, his gaze flickering between the creatures that moved through the streets. A group of centaurs clopped past, their saddlebags weighed down with bundles of cloth. A trio of goblins chattered in rapid, sharp tones, gesturing at a table filled with iridescent trinkets. Further down, a troll with skin the color of wet stone leaned over a stall, inspecting what looked like a collection of shimmering glass vials.

He hadn't seen this side of Olympus before. Until now, his only glimpse of this world had been the quiet, insular village of Taitron and the harsh, cutthroat encampment of the marauders. Those places had felt isolated, each bound by its own rigid way of life. But here, in Velmark, everything spilled together in a chaotic, vibrant tangle. It was messy, loud, full of movement—and it felt undeniably real.

This place was alive.

"Ah, my dear companions," Garik sighed dramatically, swinging off his horse with practiced ease. "Welcome to the Festival of Homonoia."

Evatra gave him a flat look. "You knew we'd arrive in the middle of a festival, didn't you?"

"I had my suspicions," Garik admitted, flashing a charming grin. "But why ruin the surprise?"

Darien was only half-listening. His attention was still on the streets ahead of them, where a procession of figures draped in flowing, multicolored fabrics wound their way through the town square. Music spilled from unseen instruments, the melody light and playful. Overhead, paper lanterns bobbed lazily on unseen currents of air, even though the sun had yet to set.

As they rode deeper into Velmark, the festival's presence became undeniable. What had started as distant murmurs and the faint scent of roasting food now fully engulfed them. The dirt road transitioned into well-worn stone, each piece an irregular shape fitted together as though the town had grown organically rather than by any grand design. Overhead, banners of deep blues, fiery oranges, and golds stretched between buildings, their silken lengths fluttering in the gentle afternoon breeze.

Garik, ever the connoisseur, inhaled deeply and let out a contented sigh. "Ah, the scent of prosperity. Spice, roasted meat, and just the right amount of hedonism. A perfect balance."

Darien ignored him, more focused on the sheer variety of life around them. Every race he had encountered so far—and a few he hadn't—were gathered in this one place. A pair of harpies with shimmering, jewel-toned wings flitted between rooftops, tossing bursts of glittering powder onto the crowd below. A line of centaurs moved in near-perfect unison, their backs draped in bright, festival-patterned cloth as they carried large, woven baskets of goods to the stalls. Small, lithe figures that Darien realized were peronia weaved between legs, slipping unnoticed into the crowd with mischievous grins.

The market itself was a sensory overload. Stalls crowded the narrow streets, packed with exotic wares that Darien had no name for. Fruits that seemed to shift colors in the sunlight sat in woven baskets. A merchant selling thin, glimmering threads wove them into floating patterns above his stall, showing off their magical properties. The scent of freshly baked bread mixed with the tang of something more foreign—perhaps fermented fruit, or some delicacy unique to Olympus.

Evatra, who had remained quiet for much of the journey, surveyed the crowd with a discerning gaze. "It's been a long time since I've been somewhere this crowded without having to watch my back."

Garik gave her an amused glance. "Ah, but here, you don't have to. No one starts trouble in Velmark. The town thrives on trade, and if it's one thing Olympus understands, it's that disrupting commerce benefits no one. The festival is simply an extension of that—business wrapped in celebration."

Darien took in the scene again, this time looking past the colors and spectacle, noticing the flow of the city. The laughter, the bargaining, the performances—everything worked together in an intricate dance of culture and commerce. There was no fear of conflict, no looming threat of war, only the bustling, unspoken agreement that everyone had something to gain by keeping the peace.

Then he noticed something else—people were watching him. It was subtle at first, just lingering glances from passing merchants, a few hushed whispers in unfamiliar tongues. Not suspicion. Not awe. Recognition.

A group of goblins huddled near a merchant cart exchanged words before one of them, draped in layers of fabric and adorned with gold earrings, took a confident step forward. Her sharp, intelligent eyes scanned Darien before she inclined her head. "Travelers, welcome to Velmark. You bring interesting company."

Evatra's hand hovered near her belt, but Garik simply smirked. "We do tend to be a fascinating bunch."

The goblin appraised them for a moment before gesturing toward a shaded street leading away from the central market. "You should come with me. The mayor will want to speak with you."

Evatra exhaled through her nose but nodded, nudging her horse forward. Darien followed suit, his curiosity growing as they moved through the shifting crowds. Garik, ever the conversationalist, kept his tone light. "I assure you, we are not here to cause trouble. Our little band is simply passing through."

The goblin gave him a pointed glance. "You travel with a known marauder and a man few would mistake for a common traveler. Velmark does not tolerate dealings with raiders."

Evatra's jaw tightened. "I am not here as a marauder. I am seeing Darien safely to Farkland Reach. That is all."

The goblin hummed, clearly unconvinced but not outright hostile.

Darien glanced at the Scillan, who remained characteristically silent, observing everything without comment. As they turned onto a quieter street lined with stone buildings, the festival's noise faded slightly, and ahead of them stood a structure taller than the others—ornate but sturdy, built from dark wood and reinforced with iron. The goblin stopped at the base of the steps leading up to its arched entrance.

"Wait here," she said, before disappearing inside.

Darien adjusted his grip on the reins. "That went well."

Garik chuckled. "Oh, I think it went splendidly. At least we weren't thrown out immediately. That's always a promising start."

The doors to the mayor's hall swung open moments later, revealing a broad-shouldered man in festival robes, his sleeves embroidered with looping golden thread. He stepped forward with an expression that could only be described as delightfully overwhelmed. His ruddy cheeks and slightly disheveled hair suggested that he had already indulged in the festivities himself, and he wasted no time in greeting them with a booming voice.

"Ah! Travelers!" he declared, spreading his arms wide as though they were old friends. "And such an interesting assortment of them!"

The goblin who had escorted them gave a small, unimpressed nod. "Mayor Kelric, these travelers arrived in Velmark just now. I thought it best you speak with them first."

Kelric clasped his hands together. "And so you have! Excellent work, truly!" His attention then shifted entirely to Darien. "And you! You look like a man of significance. A noble from Farkland Reach, perhaps? Or a merchant prince looking to establish new ties? Or—" he leaned in conspiratorially, "—simply here to partake in the wonders of Homonoia? Our food, our music, or—perhaps a friendly wager on the festival games?"

Evatra spoke up before Darien could answer. "He is none of those things, Mayor Kelric. Darien is a member of the Eldric, and his journey to Farkland Reach cannot be delayed."

The jovial expression on Kelric's face flickered with surprise, then intrigue. "A member of the Eldric? Here? And at Homonoia?" He let out a booming laugh, clapping his hands together. "Well, that is something! Not for thirty cycles has one of your glorious troop joined us! And you expect me to simply let you pass through without taking part in the festival? Preposterous!"

Darien hesitated, unsure how to navigate the man's infectious enthusiasm. He barely had time to form a response before Kelric's gaze snapped to Evatra and Garik. "Ah, and company, of course! Always good to travel with companions, though..." His smile faltered just slightly as his eyes lingered on Garik. "You do look familiar."

Garik placed a hand over his chest in mock humility. "Mayor Kelric, I assure you, it is merely because I am a man of fine taste, and such men tend to pass through Velmark more than once."

Kelric squinted at him, clearly unconvinced, but Garik pressed on before the mayor could question further. "We are but humble travelers, ensuring that young Darien here reaches Farkland Reach safely. Nothing more, nothing less."

Evatra nodded, her voice steady. "We aren't here for trouble. We won't be staying long."

Kelric let out a deep sigh, rubbing his chin and looking at Evatra's marauder styled garb. "Well, that is a relief. Velmark has no interest in marauder business. We keep our streets safe, and I would hate to see the festival tainted with rumors of outside mischief."

Satisfied with their explanation for now, Kelric's cheerful demeanor returned in full force. "But this is Homonoia, my friends! Not for thirty cycles has a member of the Eldric graced this festival! We must celebrate!"

Darien blinked. "Thirty cycles?"

Kelric nodded eagerly. "Oh, yes! It is rare for one of the chosen to join us. Usually, they are off rushing toward their great quest, ignoring the finer things in life. But not this time! This time, you are here, and you must stay."

Darien glanced at Evatra, who looked ready to refuse outright. "We appreciate the offer, but we can't stay for three days," he said carefully. "Time is against us."

"Time will still be there tomorrow!" Kelric insisted, waving off the concern with a hearty laugh. "You must stay at least one day! What is one day in the grand scheme of history? You will eat, you will drink, you will enjoy!"

Evatra exhaled sharply. "We really should keep moving—"

"Nonsense!" Garik cut in smoothly, slinging an arm around Darien's shoulders. "One day is more than reasonable, wouldn't you say? A meal, some merriment, and we'll be all the better for it. It would be rude to decline such a generous offer, after all."

Darien was about to protest when a warm gust of air carried the unmistakable scent of sizzling meat and spiced honey past them. His stomach growled before he could suppress it.

Kelric grinned, victorious. "Ah-ha! That settles it. You will stay for at least one night. Come, come, there is so much to enjoy!"

As the festival fully unfolded around them, Darien found himself swept up in a world unlike anything he had experienced before. The streets pulsed with energy, laughter echoing against the wooden and stone buildings, the scent of roasted meats and spiced honey clinging to the warm evening air. Lanterns, fueled by an unknown soft-glowing liquid, floated gently overhead, illuminating the vibrant fabrics of festival banners that rippled in the breeze.

The group was quickly enveloped into the revelry. Kelric led them through the bustling avenues, narrating each attraction with theatrical enthusiasm. "Ah, here we have the fire-dancers! Masters of the flame! And there—

the famed Syrin harpies, who sing notes that will melt even the coldest heart! And of course, no festival is complete without—" he dramatically waved toward a long line of people, "—the honeyed spice bread challenge. A fool's errand, but an honorable one!"

Garik, ever the opportunist, raised a brow at that. "Now, that sounds like something worth witnessing. Perhaps even worth competing in."

"I hope you have a strong stomach, traveler," Kelric warned, grinning widely. "Only the bravest attempt it. The spices warm your soul… and possibly ignite it."

Darien, meanwhile, found himself drawn to the sights and sounds around him. A trio of centaurs, their hands clasped in a rhythmic pattern, performed a dance that seemed more ritual than celebration. Goblins worked together on an intricate sand art piece that shifted and reformed on a floating slate, responding to music played by a group of hooded fairies. Children dashed through the streets, their laughter a chorus among the festival's many melodies.

Evatra, at first, remained rigid, her arms crossed as they weaved through the crowd. She was clearly still uneasy in large gatherings, especially those that lacked any sense of danger or control. But the longer they stayed, the more the festival began to work its magic.

It started when a fairy no taller than Darien's waist flitted toward them, her translucent wings glistening under the festival lights. She hovered just in front of Evatra, tilting her head curiously.

"You look far too serious for a festival," the fairy chirped, her voice lilting with amusement.

Evatra's sharp eyes narrowed slightly. "I'm not much for—"

Before she could finish, the fairy reached out, grabbing her hand with surprising strength, and with a quick burst of movement, pulled her into the throng of dancers circling a massive bonfire in the center of the square.

Darien blinked, momentarily stunned, as Evatra—Evatra, who had been nothing but composed, serious, and unreadable since he'd met her—was suddenly caught up in a fast-paced dance, surrounded by laughing strangers. The flickering light of the fire made the moment almost surreal, her hesitation melting away as her movements slowly adjusted to the rhythm. And then—

She laughed.

A real, unguarded laugh.

Darien barely had time to process it before Garik nudged his shoulder. "Now there's something you don't see every day."

Darien shook his head, a slow smile forming. "No, you don't."

The night continued in a blur of experiences. He found himself sampling a fruit that shimmered in the light and changed flavor with each bite—from citrusy and tart to something reminiscent of warm cinnamon. He challenged Garik to the honeyed spice bread contest—a mistake, as he quickly realized—as the heat exploded in his mouth, forcing him to gulp down whatev-er cool liquid he could find. The Scillan watched them all in silence, quietly absorbing the night's events with the air of a scholar documenting a rare cultural event.

For the first time since arriving in Olympus, Darien forgot the weight of the journey and the homesickness that kept bringing his mind back to his friends and the burdens of responsibility he had left behind. The pressure, the uncertainty, the ever-looming destiny that had been thrust upon him since coming to Olympus—it all faded, replaced by the pure, simple joy of the moment.

As the fire burned low and the music softened into something warm and slow, he found himself looking around at the people, at his people—creatures of all shapes and sizes, laughing, celebrating, sharing a peace they all understood was fragile, yet treasured all the same.

For the first time, he saw Olympus not as a place he had been unwillingly brought to—but a world worth saving.

Chapter 14: The Arrival

The morning air was crisp as Darien and his companions rode away from Velmark, the lingering scent of festival spices still clinging to their clothes. He cast one last glance over his shoulder, watching as the colorful banners and warm lantern lights shrank into the distance. The laughter, the music—it all faded, replaced once more by the steady rhythm of hooves against dirt and the vast, empty horizon.

A quieter journey lay ahead. before them the rolling hills stretched endlessly before them, golden in the morning light, occasionally broken by jagged outcroppings of stone. The further they traveled, the more the land began to shift—grasslands giving way to a more structured environment. Fences lined the edges of the path, marking farmland, with scattered cottages in the distance. Smoke curled lazily from chimneys, and Darien could just make out figures moving through the fields, tending to crops or leading beasts of burden.

"This close to Farkland Reach, the land is well maintained," Evatra said, breaking the silence. "Unlike most of Olympus, the trolls believe in shaping the land to suit their needs."

Darien studied the scenery with renewed interest. It was a stark contrast to the wild, unrestrained beauty of Taitron or the bustling, unstructured sprawl of Velmark. Here, everything seemed deliberate—stone roads that grew smoother as they neared the city, irrigation channels running alongside the fields, and watchtowers standing sentinel on the horizon.

The Scillan, ever the silent observer, finally spoke. "Farkland Reach values order. It is one of the few cities built with permanence in mind."

Darien could see that now. The city revealed itself gradually as they crested a large hill, its gray stone walls rising like the bones of the land itself. The keep stood at its heart, its towers jutting upward, built from the same material as the cliffs beyond. Unlike the festive warmth of Velmark, Farkland Reach exuded strength and endurance.

"There it is," Garik mused, his tone light yet unreadable. "A city built to last."

Evatra slowed her horse. "We should stop here for the night."

Darien frowned, glancing at the city that now stood so clearly before them. "But the city is right there!"

"It's farther than it looks," Evatra replied. "The valley makes distances deceiving. We won't reach the gates until midday tomorrow. It's better to enter on our terms, rested and prepared."

Darien exhaled sharply but nodded. He was eager to reach Farkland Reach, to reunite with his friends, but he also knew Evatra was right. There was no sense in rushing in, only to find themselves exhausted and vulnerable.

That night, as they made camp, Darien found his thoughts drifting. Olympus was beginning to feel... vast. No longer just a strange world he had been dropped into, but a place with its own rhythms, its own peoples. Taitron had been peaceful, Velmark lively—Farkland Reach promised something else entirely.

Yet, as he stared into the low-burning fire, a weight pressed against his chest. He had spent so much time focused on surviving, on understanding this world, that he had barely spared a thought for Philip, Kara, or Trey. They were out there somewhere—just as lost, just as alone—and he hadn't even considered what they might be going through. Had they arrived safely? Had they found people who could help them? Or had they, like him, been pulled into something far beyond their understanding?

He thought of Philip first—steadfast, unshakable Philip. If anyone could handle being thrown into a new world, it was him. But Kara... she was different. The idea of her being out there, scared, searching for answers—without him—made his stomach twist. And Trey... well, Trey had always kept to himself, but Darien knew that deep down, he cared more than he let on.

He exhaled slowly, rubbing his hands over his face. He should have thought about them sooner. Should have done more. But there was no changing that now.

Tomorrow, he would reach Farkland Reach. Maybe—just maybe—he would finally have some answers. Maybe his friends were already there, waiting for him.

By dawn, they were on the road again. The closer they drew to the city, the more structured the surroundings became. The road widened into a proper stone path, lined with carefully placed torches. Merchant carts rolled ahead of them, pulled by stout beasts with shaggy coats, their drivers chatting in low tones as they approached the city's outskirts.

Darien took in the details—banners bearing the sigil of a red lion's head against a blue backdrop, mounted ballista lining the walls at precise intervals, archers watching from the ramparts. The city was not just built for trade; it was built for defense.

The gates were massive, reinforced with iron, and stood open—but not unguarded. Troll sentries in polished plate armor flanked the entrance, their expressions unreadable as they surveyed the incoming traffic. Their weapons, halberds with curved silver blades, gleamed in the morning light.

"State your business," one of the guards intoned as they approached.

Chorrun, who had been waiting just beyond the entrance, stepped forward before Darien could respond. "They are with me."

"Chorrun!" Darien called, relieved to see the centaur again.

Chorrun trotted forward, his sharp eyes scanning Darien quickly before nodding in satisfaction. "You're safe. That is more than I dared hope after we were separated. Are you hurt?"

"Nothing permanent," Darien said with a grin. "Where's Jodin? Lotry?"

"I sent them back to Taitron after we arrived," Chorrun said before his gaze flicked toward Darien's companions. His posture stiffened slightly. "And them?"

Darien followed his gaze. "Chorrun, this is Evatra and Garik. And..." He hesitated before gesturing toward the Scillan. "Well, you probably know that they don't have a name."

Chorrun's expression darkened. "But they are...?"

"Marauders," Darien admitted. "But they're not here for that. They're here to see me safely to Farkland Reach. That's all. I'll vouch for them. They've helped me more than I could ever have expected. They deserve a rest in the city."

The sentries exchanged glances before the one who had spoken gave a short nod. "The King has been expecting your arrival. You may proceed."

As they entered, the full scale of the city unfolded before Darien. Where Velmark had been winding and chaotic, Farkland Reach was structured, methodical. Streets ran in neat lines, the buildings sturdy and uniform, each one constructed with a clear purpose. The people moved with purpose too—traders hauling goods toward the inner markets, blacksmiths working in open forges, and soldiers in formation running drills in a designated courtyard.

Despite the imposing nature of the city, it did not feel oppressive. It felt... efficient. Controlled.

Garik let out a low whistle. "Ah, Farkland Reach. Where everything has its place, and nothing is left to chance."

Chorrun smirked. "You sound as though you speak from experience."

Garik's smirk remained, but his eyes flicked toward the nearest watchtower. "I've passed through once or twice."

The road led them toward the massive keep at the city's heart. Darien took in the structure, its pale stone walls rising high above the surrounding buildings. The twin towers flanking the entrance stood slightly uneven, the right one rising higher than the left, giving the fortress an asymmetrical look.

Darien turned to Chorrun, his thoughts shifting back to what lay ahead. "So, what are we doing here now that we've both actually made it?"

Chorrun's ears flicked slightly before he answered. "First, you're going to meet King Aghemnon. He wants to show you his hospitality while you wait for the rest of the Eldric. It's a rare opportunity for him. Normally, the Eldric arrive so close together that he barely has time to entertain them. He's looking forward to it."

Darien's heart kicked up a notch. "Wait—does that mean another one of us is already here?"

Chorrun nodded. "From what I heard last night, yes. They came from the Fairy villages just beyond the mountains."

Darien's pulse quickened. "Do you know who it is? Did you get their name?" He leaned forward in his saddle, unable to contain the urgency in his voice. Was it Kara? Philip? Trey? He was minutes away from seeing someone from home.

Chorrun shook his head. "I don't know. No one mentioned a name. But after you spend your time here, the king will bestow upon you the sword. That will be the first of the Eldric weapons you need to complete the ritual and then you'll decide where to go from there."

As they neared the entrance, the castle gates opened, and a procession of trolls in fine garments emerged. At their head was a tall, broad-shouldered figure, his gray skin lined with age but his dark eyes sharp with intelligence.

Chorrun dismounted. "Darien, I present to you King Aghemnon, ruler of Farkland Reach."

Aghemnon studied Darien carefully before a slow smile spread across his face. "At last, another one of the Eldric stands before me. Welcome, Darien. Your arrival is a moment of great significance."

As they stepped into the castle, a cool breeze funneled through the entryway, offering a welcome relief from the lingering heat of the afternoon. The stone beneath Darien's boots was smooth and cool, polished by centuries of passage. The moment they crossed the threshold, the space before them expanded into a grand hall, its sheer scale leaving Darien momentarily breathless.

The chamber before him was not merely large—it was immense, built on proportions that dwarfed even the towering halls of The Academy. The ceilings arched high above, ribbed with dark beams that had withstood untold centuries, and beneath them, a vast floor of polished black stone stretched outward, reflecting the flickering light of the torches lining the walls. Every inch of this space spoke of history, of permanence.

Portraits and marble busts lined the hall, each depicting regal trolls in solemn poses, their features sharp, their eyes cast downward as though in eternal contemplation. Some held scepters, others blades, their weapons carved in exquisite detail, as if ready to spring to life. The flickering torchlight made their stone visages seem to shift, the shadows playing tricks, making them appear almost watchful.

Tapestries, impossibly old yet still vibrant, hung between the busts, their woven images shifting slightly in the dim light. Some told tales of ancient wars—troll legions clashing against monstrous foes with weapons gleaming under storm-filled skies. Others depicted diplomacy, rulers shaking hands, long feasts held in grand halls much like this one. It was not just history recorded in fabric—it was memory, Olympus itself woven into thread.

As they moved deeper, the soft murmur of unseen voices echoed faintly against the cold stone. Servants bustled about in hushed efficiency, their footsteps swallowed by the weight of the silence, as if even the air itself was reluctant to disturb the stories etched into these walls. The scent of aged parchment, molten wax, and a faint trace of incense curled through the air, thick with the weight of knowledge hoarded over generations.

King Aghemnon motioned for them to follow, leading them through the hall's towering archways. As they moved deeper into the castle, the grandeur gave way to something more functional. Here, the corridors were lined with stone buttresses and iron sconces, built not for beauty, but endurance. The deeper they traveled, the more Darien felt the weight of history pressing down on him.

"This is Fenway Keep," Aghemnon said as they ascended a broad staircase, his voice carrying through the vast hall. "As old as the Cycles themselves, it has stood through the rise and fall of countless generations. Every ruler of Farkland Reach has walked these halls, and every Cycle, at least one of the Eldric has passed through its gates."

The name settled heavily in Darien's mind. Fenway Keep. Not just a castle, not just a stronghold—a monument to the Cycles themselves. A place where the echoes of those before him had lingered, where others had once stood at the precipice of destiny.

From the terrace, the city spread beneath them in rigid symmetry. Farkland Reach had none of Velmark's winding, chaotic streets, none of Taitron's organic, forest-embraced pathways. Here, every building stood in calculated precision, every road planned, every structure designed to endure. This was not a city that had grown—it had been built.

Darien's gaze lingered on the keep's towering walls, tracing the path of the battlements, the reinforced watchtowers that overlooked the city's edges. If Olympus had a spine, this was it.

They entered a vast chamber dominated by a long wooden table, its surface worn with the marks of untold discussions, hands pressed in urgency, maps unfurled, fates decided. The air here was thick with history. Darien could feel it pressing against his skin, the weight of every ruler who had once deliberated within these walls.

"These are the council chambers," Aghemnon explained as he strode forward. "This is where the high council of Farkland Reach meets to determine the course of our people. The council for the coming year has yet to assemble following their election, so for now, it sits empty. We can speak here."

Before anyone could respond, the chamber doors swung open with a quiet creak, and a familiar figure strode inside with his usual casual gait. Garik.

Darien saw King Aghemnon's expression fall. His jovial expression wavered, just for a fraction of a second, before his features smoothed into careful neutrality.

"Garik," Aghemnon said, his tone measured, his voice laced with something unspoken.

Garik flashed his ever-charming smirk and gave a small, theatrical bow. "Your Majesty. A pleasure, as always."

Darien's gaze darted between them. Recognition flickered in Aghemnon's eyes, but whatever connection the two men shared remained unspoken, hovering between them like a ghost. No one in the room dared ask.

The king merely nodded before turning back to the table. "Once again, welcome to Farkland Reach," he said, his voice resuming its warmth. "I want this conversation to be informal, if you're willing. None of this 'Majesty' or 'Highness' business. We have important matters to discuss, and your success is more valuable than courtesy."

Leaning back into the plush cushions of his chair, Aghemnon clasped his hands together. "So tell me, who has been brought to us this Cycle? I know of the worlds you come from, but I do not know you personally. And the history of the Eldric has always been something of a fascination to me—though I suspect Chorrun may rival me in that." He cast a knowing glance at the centaur, who responded with a sheepish smile.

"Come now, let's hear your name."

Darien hesitated briefly before rising to his feet. "My name is Darien Glade, and I'm a human. From... from Earth."

"Splendid!" Aghemnon beamed, though there was a knowing glint in his eye. "I cannot wait to get to know you and the others before you leave. How long will we have the pleasure of keeping you here? I know your journey is only beginning."

"I… I'm not sure," Darien admitted, glancing toward Chorrun for an answer.

The centaur stepped in smoothly. "Once the remaining members of the Eldric arrive, they will need to depart quickly, Your Majesty. In fact, it is a wonder the others have not yet arrived, considering Darien's diversion. That is something we need to discuss."

Before Darien could respond, the chamber doors creaked open once more. A figure entered, their robes drinking in the light, swallowing it like a void. Darien narrowed his eyes, trying to discern the face hidden within the folds of shadow, but it was as if the very air around them refused to reveal it.

Chorrun rose, followed quickly by Evatra and the Scillan. Aghemnon stood as well, his tone taking on a new energy.

"Ah, Darien, allow me to introduce the second member of your party," the King announced. "This is Sir Ristvahkbain, from Taerrun, if I'm not mistaken. He arrived just yesterday."

Darien stiffened. "I'm sorry—I don't understand."

Aghemnon chuckled, clearly enjoying the moment. "Why, he is another of the Eldric, of course!"

Chapter 15: The Sense

"Greetings, I am Ristvahkbain of Taerrun, last of the Eld, member of the Eldric, at your service. That was a kind introduction, Your Highness."

The voice was like a whisper carried by the coldest wind, light and airy yet unsettling, slipping over Darien's skin like a breath from something ancient. It wasn't just the sound of it—it was the way it made him feel, as if he had just glimpsed a predator shifting in the dark, unseen yet all too present.

That's not one of the Eldric. It can't be. Darien's gut twisted. *Where's Philip? Kara? Trey?*

Seated opposite him, the black-robed figure remained unnervingly still. Their hood obscured their face entirely, but the darkness within was too deep, too absolute— as if it wasn't simply hiding something, but refusing to be seen.

Pleasantries were exchanged, but Darien barely registered them. His eyes flicked to Chorrun, searching for something—confirmation, denial, an explanation. Instead, he found something else entirely: fear.

A wave of heat flushed through him, an anger that came too fast, too sharp. His voice cut through the idle conversation like a blade.

"Chorrun. I need to speak with you. Alone."

The entire room shifted at the weight of his words. The warmth of Aghemnon's ever-present smile dimmed slightly.

"With your permission?" Chorrun asked, turning toward the king.

Aghemnon studied Darien, his jovial demeanor carefully measured. "Of course. We will do all we can to accommodate the Eldric. Is there something wrong, Master Darien?"

"No," Darien said quickly—too quickly. "It's just personal. Chorrun was the first person I met when I arrived in Olympus, and I want to speak with him. Just him."

The explanation seemed to ease the tension, if only slightly.

Aghemnon nodded toward a door at the far end of the chamber. "I have a private study just beyond that door. You may have as much time as you need."

Darien murmured a thanks and strode toward the door, barely waiting for Chorrun to follow. The moment it clicked shut behind them, Darien spun around.

Ignoring the interruption, Darien refocused, his frustration rising again. "Who is that?"

Chorrun blinked, caught off guard by the sheer force of his words. "Why, that's one of the Eldric, of course. I know no more of him than you do. That was my first time meeting him."

Darien's jaw tightened. "That is not a member of my team." His voice was sharp, clipped. "I was expecting Philip, Kara, or even Trey. You said my team would be here."

Understanding dawned in Chorrun's face—followed by something else. Something worse. Remorse.

"Oh... oh, my goodness. You—"

"Spit it out already!" Darien snapped, his temper breaking.

Chorrun flinched but held his ground. "You mentioned a team at your school—The Academy. It never occurred to me that it was them you were asking about."

Darien felt the blood drain from his face. "You mean... they're not coming?"

Chorrun hesitated, and for the first time since Darien had met him, the centaur looked... lost.

Darien's stomach twisted. "I have to work with... that? An Eld, or whatever it called itself?" The weight of the realization hit him like a hammer. "I really am alone."

Chorrun exhaled. "Darien, I—"

"Are they coming?!"

Chorrun hesitated, then whispered, "No."

Something inside Darien broke. He sank onto a nearby chair, his hands gripping the edge of the desk as his chest tightened. "I don't believe it," he gasped, struggling to breathe. "This isn't real. None of this is... this isn't happening."

He had endured everything—fear, imprisonment, killing—because he had believed, with absolute certainty, that he would be reunited with his friends.

Chorrun remained silent, giving him the space to process.

When Darien finally spoke again, his voice was quieter. "I want to go home."

A heavy silence filled the room.

Chorrun didn't answer. There was nothing he could say.

A knock at the door shattered the stillness. Chorrun moved to answer it, his large frame momentarily blocking Darien's view. A hushed conversation followed—Aghemnon.

When Chorrun returned, his expression was full of sorrow. "That was the King. They heard your shouting, but I convinced him that everything is fine. If we don't return soon, they'll have questions for both of us."

Darien forced himself upright. The rage had burned away, leaving only emptiness.

Chorrun studied him carefully. "Darien, I warned you once before—do not reveal your ignorance of Olympus.

If the other members of the Eldric realize you are different, it could endanger your purpose here."

Darien barely cared about the Cycle at this moment, but he nodded anyway. "Is there anything else I should know before we go back out there?"

Chorrun hesitated, his gaze flicking toward the tall windows. Something flickered across his expression—something Darien couldn't place.

Then, just as quickly, it was gone.

"Nothing I can think of now," Chorrun said.

Darien didn't believe him.

Steeling himself, he pushed the door open and stepped back into the council chamber.

To his surprise, Garik was still there, lounging in his chair as if he had never left. He was tossing a small dagger between his fingers, catching it effortlessly.

The moment Darien and Chorrun re-entered, Garik looked up, blinking as if noticing them for the first time. "Oh! You're back! Thought you two might've vanished into some secret passageway or something." He smirked. "I was *this* close to leaving, but then I thought—what if they need me? Can't let you lot make important decisions without my expert counsel."

Darien exhaled sharply, rubbing his temples. "Why are you still here?"

Garik raised an eyebrow. "I could ask the same of you. Very dramatic exit, by the way. If you were trying to unsettle everyone in the room, mission accomplished." He leaned back, propping his boots up on the table. "So... what did I miss? Should I be preparing to flee the city or are we all still friends?"

Darien shot him a glare, but the corner of his mouth twitched—just slightly. Even in the worst moments, Garik had a way of making everything seem a little less heavy.

The black-robed form sat patiently, waiting.

"Hello again," the icy voice washed over Darien once more, sending an involuntary shiver down his spine. The hair on his arms stood on end, though Chorrun, standing beside him, seemed entirely unaffected.

"Hello. A pleasure to see you again," Chorrun responded evenly. "Have the others gone—"

"The King and Queen were called away before our meeting could conclude," Ristvahkbain interrupted, the faintest twitch in the depths of the black hood marking his words. "The pale one has yet to share their findings on the beast that attacked Darien and Evatra. They have informed me of your story."

Darien barely heard the last part. His thoughts were elsewhere. "Where is she?" he asked, the worry creeping into his voice before he could stop it.

"She was given quarters for the night," Ristvahkbain replied, his tone unreadable. "You will see her tomorrow at the feast the King has prepared in our honor. He had hoped to time it around the others' arrival, but they appear to be behind schedule."

"I have to find her," Darien said, already moving toward the door.

Chorrun held up a hand. "Darien, I think you and..." he hesitated, turning to Ristvahkbain. "Pardon me, I've forgotten your name?"

"Ristvahkbain."

Chorrun inclined his head. "Ah, yes. I think the two of you should spend some time together. Allow me to speak with Evatra. I have some questions for her about the marauders. That will give you both an opportunity to get acquainted."

Darien hesitated. He wanted to talk to Evatra. She and Chorrun were the only ones he trusted here, and even Chorrun had fallen a few places down that list. More than that, he felt close to her—closer than he should, given the short time they had known each other.

He stopped the thought before it could go any further. It's just a reaction to being alone here.

Realizing that Ristvahkbain would likely find it rude if he left to see someone else, Darien nodded reluctantly. Chorrun left the room, leaving him alone with the dark figure.

"Can we go outside to talk?" Darien asked. "I need to clear my head."

"Of course," Ristvahkbain replied simply.

Something about the answer unsettled Darien. The voice, the presence—it all struck a chord within him, as if he had known, from the very first moment, that this figure was someone to be wary of.

He's worse than Kort.

The two of them left the chamber, moving through the castle halls. With the help of directions from the guards, they found their way into the gardens and stepped into the cool night air. The city had quieted beneath the stars, the bustle of the day replaced by a softer hum of distant conversation and flickering lanterns.

As they walked, Darien noticed something strange—he couldn't hear Ristvahkbain's footsteps.

Every now and then, he tried to catch a glimpse beyond the shifting shadows within the figure's hood, but it was useless. It was as if the darkness itself refused to reveal anything.

Needing to break the silence, Darien introduced himself again. "I'm Darien. From Earth."

"So you've said." The hood turned slightly toward him as they walked. "Hello, Darien of Earth. Tell me, how long have you been in Olympus?"

"About a week, I think."

It felt longer. His mind drifted back to his friends. They were probably terrified by now, thinking he was dead or missing. Would they ever know what had happened to him? Would they ever forgive—

"Your mind is elsewhere," Ristvahkbain noted as they rounded a bend in the garden path. The hedges opened up into a clearing, where topiaries sculpted into the shapes of creatures Darien didn't recognize lined the way. "Are you well?"

Darien hesitated, recalling Chorrun's warning. "I'm fine. Just adjusting."

"You are not fine. But it is good that you say so."

Darien raised a brow. "So, what? You'd rather I lie?"

Rist let out something that might have been a chuckle—though it was cold, mirthless, almost clinical. "I would rather you say what you must to maintain function. Wounds heal. Some take longer. That is all."

Darien frowned but found himself nodding. "Well, that's an odd kind of wisdom. You always talk like that?"

"Yes. Does it bother you?"

Darien thought about it. "Not really. It's different, but at least you don't waste words."

Rist inclined his head slightly. "That is correct. I do not waste words."

A short silence stretched between them before Darien exhaled sharply. "Ristvahkbain," he said, stumbling slightly over the name. "That would be a weird name where I come from. Do you have any nicknames? Something easier to call you?"

"No."

The hood turned away, as if dismissing the thought entirely.

"Well," Darien continued, pressing forward, "Rist-vahkbain is a mouthful. We're going to be traveling together, so something shorter might be a good idea. What about Rist? Or Bain?"

A long silence stretched between them. Darien thought he had offended him, but eventually, the dark figure spoke.

"Rist."

"What?"

"You may call me Rist. Bain is too dark a name, and that word has... meaning. You may therefore call me Rist, as my full name is such a... what did you call it? Ah, a mouthful to say." Rist's voice carried a faint trace of amusement, though it did little to ease Darien's wariness.

Darien hesitated for only a second before offering his arm. Rist mirrored the gesture, gripping Darien's forearm in a firm, measured hold. Even through the fabric of his glove, Rist's touch was cold, an unnatural chill that sent a brief prickle across Darien's skin. His eyes searched the impenetrable void beneath the hood, trying to find something—anything—to connect to.

"Rist it is, then."

There was no warmth, no shift in posture, no hint that Rist cared one way or another, yet Darien felt a strange understanding settle between them. Not quite friendship, not yet, but the beginning of something. A mutual agreement.

They turned back toward the castle, inquiring about their sleeping quarters. Rist had yet to familiarize himself with the twisting passageways, and Darien knew his own limited sense of direction wouldn't help much either. A pair of trolls arrived to assist, one of them beckoning for them to follow.

As they walked, Rist spoke again, his voice softer, but still carrying its natural chill. "I have had many companions over the centuries, Darien of Earth. Some strong, some weak. Some wise, some foolish."

Darien glanced at him. "And what do you think I am?"

"Yet to be determined."

Darien smirked. "I'll take that over weak or foolish."

Rist tilted his head slightly. "I suspect you will make that determination yourself soon enough."

Darien wasn't sure if that was a compliment or a warning, but he decided not to ask.

Their pace steady and movements precise, the trolls guided them through winding stairways and labyrinthine corridors. The deeper they went, the quieter it became. The murmurs of the castle, distant laughter from unseen courtyards, and the faint clatter of distant preparations for the feast faded, leaving only the rhythmic sound of boots and hooves against polished stone.

Darien felt the weight of exhaustion settling into his bones. It had been days since he'd known a moment's peace, and now that the adrenaline had worn off, he felt it in every inch of him.

At last, the procession halted before a row of sturdy wooden doors, each marked with intricate carvings—symbols of the house of Aghemnon, Darien assumed. The trolls moved with effortless synchronicity, pushing open the doors in unison. One gestured for Darien to step inside, bowing slightly.

He barely made it two steps before stopping in his tracks. The quarters were far beyond anything he had imagined.

A magnificent four-poster bed sat in the center of the chamber, its frame dark wood carved with curling patterns of vines and strange creatures. The curtains, tied back, were thick enough to drown out any light, their fabric softer than anything Darien had ever touched. A fire crackled in a large stone hearth, filling the air with warmth, the scent of burning cedar lingering beneath the crisp air of the mountain city.

Wardrobes lined the far wall, their doors slightly ajar to reveal clothes—far too many for a brief stay. Intricate garments woven with silver thread, traveling cloaks lined with fur, thick boots that looked sturdy enough for any terrain. It was as if someone had prepared for him to be here long before he arrived.

Beside them, shelves gleamed with neatly arranged trinkets—ornate bowls, candlesticks of dark metal, a collection of rings and pendants that looked far too valuable for someone like him to wear. Weapons and armor were mounted on mannequins along the far side of the room. Not decorative ones. Real ones. Made for battle.

Darien turned to the troll who had led him. "This is... too much."

The troll, still as a statue, inclined his head slightly. "You are a guest of the King. It is only fitting."

Darien ran a hand through his hair, overwhelmed. "I don't—look, I appreciate it, but I don't need all this."

"Nevertheless, it is yours to use as you see fit." The troll bowed once more. "May I get anything for you, sir?"

Darien hesitated, glancing again at the room—the sheer weight of expectation pressing down on him. He shook his head. "No, thank you."

The troll stepped back, pulling the heavy door closed behind him, leaving Darien alone in the silence.

He exhaled slowly, rubbing his eyes.

It was too much.

The bed called to him, but his mind wouldn't let go of the strangeness of it all. The thought that someone had anticipated his needs, his presence, his stay. That his path had already been laid before him, and he was merely stepping into it.

But exhaustion overpowered his unease. He crossed the room, collapsed onto the bed, and let himself sink into its embrace. The softness swallowed him whole, and within moments, he was asleep—the first restful sleep he had known in days.

He woke to golden sunlight streaming through the tall windows, the warmth spilling over the room in golden streaks. He stretched, blinking against the brightness, momentarily forgetting where he was.

His eyes landed on the foot of his bed.

A fresh set of clothes lay neatly folded there.

His stomach twisted slightly. Someone had been in his room while he slept.

Pushing himself upright, he swung his legs over the edge of the bed and moved to examine the garments. The material was soft, finely woven—similar to the attire Aghemnon had worn the day before. It fit him better than anything he had ever owned, as though it had been tailored specifically for him.

He ran his fingers over the stitching, his thoughts lingering in places they shouldn't. Had his arrival been expected? Were the others given the same treatment?

Stepping into the hallway, he spotted a troll standing at the far end. The moment the guard saw him, he hurried over.

"Did you need something, sir?"

Darien hesitated. "I was wondering if there was somewhere I could clean up?"

"Of course, sir. Right this way."

The troll led him through another maze of corridors before stopping at a door. "You'll find everything you need inside."

Darien stepped in, finding himself in a dimly lit chamber. A large tub rested against one wall, with two cords hanging beside it. He tugged one experimentally, and a stream of steaming water poured from a pipe above the tub. Startled, he let go, and the flow ceased instantly. He tried the other cord, and cool water cascaded down instead.

Fascinated, he played with the controls until the temperature was perfect. Taking what he assumed was soap from a nearby counter, he slipped into the water.

For the first time in over a week, he felt truly clean.

Dressed in the clothes that had been left for him, Darien stepped back into the hallway, where another troll awaited him.

"If I needed to get something or have something made, who would I speak to?"

"That depends, sir. What do you require?"

Darien considered for a moment. "An extra set of travel clothes, better boots, something for cold weather, and a few pieces of armor."

The troll nodded without hesitation. "I will have a messenger brought to you shortly. You may list your needs, and he will visit the shops and smiths on your behalf."

Darien was momentarily taken aback by the lack of questions.

"Th-thanks," he stammered. "Sorry, I'm not used to sending people to get my things. I've always done it myself."

"It is our pleasure, sir. Is there anything else?"

"No, thank you," Darien replied before stepping back into his quarters.

He spent several minutes examining the ornate objects in his room—the carved wardrobe, the delicate metalwork on the candlesticks—until a knock at the door interrupted his thoughts.

Expecting the messenger, he opened the door—only to find Rist standing there.

Without a word, the dark figure strode past him, stopping in the center of the room. His hooded head turned toward Darien, the weight of his presence filling the space.

"Close the door," Rist commanded.

Darien frowned. "What's wro—"

"Close. The. Door."

The hairs on the back of Darien's neck stood up. The voice had returned to its previous chilling tone. His mind raced. Had Rist discovered what he and Chorrun were trying to keep hidden?

Swallowing, Darien obeyed.

For a long moment, they stood in silence, facing each other. Then, finally, Rist spoke.

"What are you wearing?"

Darien blinked. "What?"

"Your clothes. Where did you get them?"

It was the last thing he had expected his cloaked companion to ask.

"They were here when I woke up," he answered cautiously. "I fell asleep, woke up, and they were on the edge of my bed. Look, what are you doing here?"

Rist was still for a moment, then waved a hand dismissively. "We have a problem. Someone in this castle doesn't belong."

Darien stiffened. "What do you mean? With one of us?"

"No." Rist moved toward the window, peering out as if searching for something. "It's someone else. I felt it in the council chamber with Aghemnon and Marenya, and it's only gotten stronger since. But it wasn't anyone in that room." He turned back to Darien. "If we are to work together, we must trust each other completely. That is why I've come to you now."

Darien let out a breath he hadn't realized he was holding. "Oh."

Rist's head tilted slightly. "'Oh?' That's it? I tell you something is wrong, and all you can say is 'Oh?'" His voice carried an edge of irritation, the words drawn out in that same unsettling, deliberate cadence he always used.

Darien ran a hand through his hair, forcing himself to focus. "No, no, sorry. I was distracted." He exhaled sharply. "So, you have a feeling. That doesn't necessarily mean something is wrong. I'm sure Chorrun or the King would have noticed if something was off, too."

"No, you don't understand," Rist said, stepping closer, his presence looming like a shadow given form. "Do you know nothing about my people?"

Darien shook his head. "Not really."

A long pause stretched between them, the air colder now, as if the room itself had recoiled. Then Rist finally spoke.

"I thought not. We keep information about ourselves...private. Emotion is energy. The two are synonymous."

Darien frowned. "I don't follow."

"Just as heat and light are forms of energy, so too is emotion. My people can sense it. It is not metaphorical—it is tangible. A sense, like touch or sight." Rist's voice was calm, measured, but there was something behind it, a depth Darien couldn't quite grasp. "And right now, something in this castle feels... off."

Darien crossed his arms. "Okay, so what do we do?"

Rist was silent for a moment, then finally said, "We watch. There's a feast tonight. We observe, we wait. And if something is wrong, we act."

Darien nodded. "I'll keep my sword close. What do you use?"

Rist let out a rare chuckle, the iciness in his voice momentarily shifting into something unreadable. "I carry what I need."

Darien smirked. "I don't think I want to know what that means."

For the first time since arriving in Farkland Reach, Darien felt like he had found a true ally—though whether that was comforting or terrifying, he couldn't quite decide.

Chapter 16: The Thief

Rist stepped out of Darien's quarters, leaving him alone in the ornate room. For a few moments, silence pressed against him, the weight of everything settling in his chest. Then, restless and unable to sit still, he decided it was time to find Evatra.

After asking a troll for directions, he found himself standing outside her door, suddenly unable to knock.

Get a hold of yourself. It's just Evatra.

Shaking off whatever had come over him, he knocked on the solid wood.

"Come in."

Darien turned the handle and stepped inside, immediately overwhelmed by the room's grandeur. Like his own quarters, it was lined with ornate furnishings, each piece more extravagant than the last. But none of that held his attention.

His breath caught.

Evatra stood near the bed, clad in a vibrant blue dress lined with white lace. The fabric draped around her in soft, flowing layers, making her look nothing like the hardened warrior he had come to know. A slit in the material exposed the smooth length of her leg from the knee down, accentuating the elegance of the ensemble.

Darien was momentarily stunned into silence.

"What are you staring at?" Evatra asked, raising an eyebrow.

"What? Oh—nothing, sorry. I just..." He struggled for words. "I've never thought I'd see you looking so..."

Her scowl deepened. "I know, it's hideous."

"Beautiful."

The word escaped before he could stop it. He immediately felt ridiculous, but it was true.

She paused, watching him carefully as he continued to take in the unfamiliar sight of her. Then, with a small smirk, she snapped her fingers at him. "That's enough of that."

She turned slightly, glancing over her shoulder. "But thank you."

Darien cleared his throat. "No problem."

Evatra sighed, moving to sit on the edge of the elegant bed. "This place is strange, don't you think?"

"It's definitely different from anywhere I've been before." Darien took a seat in the desk chair near a large mirror. He eyed her dress again, then smirked. "So, judging by what you're wearing, I guess that means you're staying for the dinner?"

She let out a sound somewhere between exasperation and resignation. "The King insisted on showing his gratitude for delivering you safely. I'm staying for dinner tonight and leaving first thing in the morning. So is Garik. But I need to get back to Atreya."

Darien nodded, trying—and failing—to ignore the quiet relief that settled in his chest at the thought of having just a little more time with her.

"What did you and the one in the robes talk about?" she asked, crossing her arms. "I don't even want to try pronouncing his name."

"Just call him Rist. It'll be easier." Darien shrugged. "We didn't talk about much. I think we'll get to know each other better later. He seems cool enough, though."

Evatra frowned. "Cool? You mean his voice?"

"No, I mean… 'cool.' Like, interesting. Likeable." He paused. "Huh. I've never had to define that before."

"I wouldn't trust him," Evatra muttered. "But then again, I'm not one of the 'Illustrious Eldric.'" She smirked as she said it, her voice dripping with playful mockery.

She reminded him so much of Kara.

Darien shot her a dirty look, masking the ache of homesickness rising in his chest.

The two fell into easy conversation, talking aimlessly about whatever came to mind. She asked more about his life at The Academy, and he asked more about what it had been like growing up among the marauders. Time slipped by unnoticed, the weight of the past few days momentarily forgotten.

Eventually, Darien stretched his arms, noticing how low the sun had fallen in the sky.

"Whoa. Between you and Rist, I've talked the whole day away." He stood, rubbing his neck. "I gotta get back and get ready for this dinner."

Evatra nodded, watching him as he stepped toward the door.

"Darien?"

He paused just outside the threshold, turning back.

She glided across the smooth stone floor, stopping close enough that he could see his reflection in the deep black of her eyes.

"I don't know when I'll get the chance to say this," she said softly, her voice quieter than he had ever heard it. "I just want to thank you. For everything. You saved my life. You saved Atreya. And soon, you're going to save the whole world, and..." She exhaled sharply. "I'm not good at this, but... thank you."

Then, before he could respond, she stood on her toes and placed a gentle, lingering kiss on his cheek.

Darien's mind went completely blank.

By the time he regained himself, Evatra had already stepped back, smiling softly before closing the door.

He stood outside for what felt like hours, his hand unconsciously pressing against the still-warm spot on his cheek. Then, realizing where his thoughts were going, he shook himself out of it.

Good thing Kara wasn't here to see that.

Shortly after returning to his room, there was a knock at the door. When he answered, an elegantly dressed troll woman stood in the doorway.

"Good evening, sir," she said, bowing slightly. "His Royal Highness, King Aghemnon, requests your presence in the dining hall."

Darien fastened his sword belt beneath the cloak that had come with his new clothes, ensuring the weapon remained concealed. The troll's expression didn't change as she observed him.

Stepping into the hallway, he found the others already waiting.

Rist stood in his same stark black robes, the Scillan was dressed in a fine tunic similar to Darien's, and Chorrun wore a black vest of richly woven fabric. Then, of course, there was Evatra, still in that stunning blue dress. And Garik—who somehow managed to look entirely at home in a deep emerald jacket embroidered with silver filigree, leaning lazily against the wall as if he had been waiting for this his whole life.

Darien forced himself not to stare.

The group walked together, following their guide through the winding corridors until they reached a massive set of wooden doors. Two guards stepped forward, gripping the ornate handles and pulling them open.

The room beyond was vast, rivaling even the entrance hall in grandeur. A long table stretched down the center, already filled with elegantly dressed trolls. Torches flickered along the walls, casting deep shadows that shifted and danced as though vying for dominance.

At the far end of the room, Aghemnon stood, his booming voice filling the space.

"Trolls of Farkland Reach!" Aghemnon's voice thundered across the great hall, amplified by the high ceilings and resonating through the stone walls. "I present to you two members of the Eldric from our sister worlds—the heroes of this Cycle who will save us from Cyprin and his tyranny. Rise with me and give them welcome!"

The room erupted with applause as Darien and the others approached the long dining table. The trolls stood, clapping and cheering, their voices rising in an overwhelming wave of sound. At the head of the table, Queen Marenya sat beside Aghemnon, offering a measured but warm applause. Their host motioned to the empty seats at their end of the table, and the group took their places. The sheer size of the table made Darien uneasy; at least forty trolls sat along its length, each elegantly dressed and eyeing the newcomers with curiosity and reverence.

As the room settled, Darien found himself seated between Rist and Chorrun, a placement he welcomed. These two, despite everything, had begun to feel like allies, even friends. Well, Chorrun at least. Across from him, Evatra sat next to the Scillan, her blue dress catching the warm candlelight. When their eyes met, she smiled. An unexpected feeling stirred in Darien's chest—uncomfortable, unfamiliar, but not entirely unpleasant.

Garik, meanwhile, had already slipped seamlessly into conversation with a group of nobles seated to his left. Darien couldn't help but overhear snippets of their discussion—something about maritime trade routes along the southern coast, the political turmoil brewing between distant provinces. It was spoken in the casual, knowing manner of men who had seen and done more than they let on.

Darien's brow furrowed. How in the world does a supposed marauder know so much about economics?

Aghemnon lifted his goblet high. "Now that the guests of honor have arrived, let the feast begin!"

Platters of steaming food were brought forth, filling the room with the rich scent of roasted meats, spiced vegetables, and freshly baked bread. The meal was one of the most lavish Darien had ever experienced, each dish cooked to perfection. The drinks, sweet and smooth, left a pleasant warmth in his stomach, though he was careful to avoid them in excess, recalling his experience with Totra-Dal's freolia. Music played as trolls danced around the table, their laughter and voices creating an atmosphere that was almost intoxicating in its joy.

But amid the revelry came questions—too many questions. Nobles leaned in eagerly, bombarding them with inquiries about their journey. Some introduced themselves as thanes or magistrates, expressing their honor in meeting members of the Eldric before shaking hands and hurrying along. The sheer volume of attention was overwhelming, but Darien forced himself to remain engaged, answering as best as he could while keeping Rist's warning in the back of his mind.

At one point, Garik turned to Darien, raising his goblet in a knowing salute. "Enjoying yourself, young hero?"

Darien smirked, shaking his head. "I wasn't prepared for an interrogation."

Garik chuckled, setting his goblet down with a quiet clink. "Ah, but you must remember, to them you are history in the making. These moments—the feasts, the meetings, the questions—this is how the stories begin."

"Is that how your story began?" Darien asked, watching Garik carefully.

Garik merely smiled, lifting his drink once more. "Oh, I think my story began long before I ever sat at a table like this. But I do so love a good meal."

The night stretched on, and one by one, guests began excusing themselves. The Scillan was among the first to leave, followed by several nobles. Soon, only Darien, Rist, Evatra, Chorrun, the King and Queen, and a few servants remained.

Marenya, her voice softened by the effects of the evening's drinks, smiled as she spoke. "I do hope you have enjoyed your night."

Evatra returned the smile with a small nod. "We have. Thank you."

Aghemnon stretched and rose from his chair. "Come now, let us retire for the night." The others followed his lead, pushing back their chairs and making their way toward the guest quarters.

The halls were eerily quiet as they walked. Darien glanced at Rist several times, but the hooded figure remained as still as ever, not once turning to acknowledge him. The night had settled heavily over the castle, the remnants of celebration fading into a peaceful stillness.

Then, from below, the sound of crashing wood shattered the quiet.

A door slammed open, followed by the unmistakable sound of hurried footsteps.

"A thief! A thief!" A panicked voice rang through the halls. "He has stolen the sword!"

They all froze.

Darien barely had time to register what was happening before Rist vaulted over the railing, dropping a full fifteen feet to the floor below. He landed in a controlled crouch before springing into a full sprint toward the fleeing figure.

Darien's heart pounded as he shrugged off his cloak, sprinting for the stairs. He barely caught a glimpse of Rist's boots vanishing around the castle's outer wall as he burst through the doors into the cool night air.

In the distance, he spotted Rist already in pursuit, his dark robes flowing behind him as he chased the thief through the streets. Darien's eyes flicked to a parallel road. If he moved fast enough, he could cut the thief off. Without a second thought, he took off, his feet pounding against the stone as shouts echoed from behind him. Guards were stirring, but he didn't wait for them.

The roads converged, and Darien pushed himself harder. He spotted the thief ahead—tall, broad-shouldered, and fast, but tiring. They weaved through narrow alleyways, dodging past carts and vendor stalls, until they reached a gate.

The thief threw his shoulder against it, breaking the lock, forcing it open with brute strength.

"Darien, wait!" Rist's voice rang out from somewhere behind, but Darien ignored him.

He wouldn't let this thief escape with the sword. It was the first key to unlocking the mountain—the key to his way home.

Darien charged through the broken gate and found himself in an open market square. The night's chill had settled into the stone, the air thick with the remnants of the evening feast—burnt embers, distant laughter, the scent of roasted meat still clinging to the wind. But here, in this abandoned pocket of the city, there was only silence.

The thief had come to a stop at the far side, hemmed in by buildings and a large stone fountain. The only exits were a barred tunnel, the locked doors of various shops, or the way they had come.

Darien skidded to a halt, chest heaving, sweat cooling against his skin because of the cold. His eyes locked onto the figure in front of him.

The thief turned to face him.

Even in the dim light, Darien recognized him as a troll. The mask concealed his features, but his posture was calm despite his ragged breathing. Not a hint of fear, not even urgency. As though he had been waiting for this.

Without a word, the thief reached for the curved blade at his waist, letting the stolen sword fall to the ground behind him. The metal clattered against the stone with a deliberate finality.

Darien tensed, gripping his own sword tighter. This wasn't a sparring match. There was no instructor to call it off, no wooden practice blades to soften the blows. This was a fight for something real. If he won, he'd recover the weapon. If he lost…

The troll stepped forward, his voice thick with malice. "Leave, human. This sword is no longer meant for you."

Darien stayed silent, steadying his breath, clearing his mind.

The thief's grip tightened on his blade. "I won't say it again. Leave now, or this city will be your grave."

Darien met his gaze and advanced, sword raised. The thief wasted no more words.

He attacked.

The first strike came so fast Darien barely registered it. A blur of silver and shadow, the whistle of steel slicing through air. He barely managed to bring his blade up in time, the impact sending a shock through his arms. The force of it pushed him back, boots skidding over the stone.

The thief didn't relent.

He was fast—unnaturally fast.

Darien barely caught the next strike, a downward slash that nearly wrenched his sword from his grip. He twisted, attempting to counter, but the troll was already gone, moving like a shadow slipping through cracks in the light. A flash of motion—

Pain lanced across Darien's ribs. He hissed, stumbling as the edge of the thief's blade nicked through his tunic, a shallow but burning cut. He had never fought something like this before.

The troll struck low, aiming for his ankle, then feinted, slashing high toward his shoulder. Darien barely ducked in time, feeling the wind of the blade as it passed inches from his throat.

The relentlessness of the assault was overwhelming.

Darien swung wide, forcing distance between them, trying to find his footing, trying to breathe. But the thief gave him no time. The troll moved with a predator's efficiency, reading him, toying with him.

Their blades clashed again—Darien's heavier, built for defense, but the thief's blade was like liquid silver, moving faster than his eyes could follow. Sparks flickered as metal scraped against metal. Darien parried, twisting to counter, but his opponent was already moving, anticipating every shift, every intention.

He's reading me.

The realization sank in just as a boot slammed into Darien's chest. The world tilted, his back hit the stone, the air knocked from his lungs in a gasp. His sword slipped from his fingers, skidding away into the shadows.

The thief loomed over him, pressing a heavy boot against his chest to pin him down. Darien struggled, but the weight was solid, final.

"You are weaker than I thought." The thief's voice dripped with venom. "You have no place here, human."

Darien gritted his teeth, clawing at the boot, but the troll pressed down harder, cutting off his air.

He lunged—a desperate move, grabbing for his fallen sword—but the thief was faster.

Pain flared through his side as the troll's blade sliced through flesh. A shallow cut, but enough to remind him that mercy was not coming.

"Pathetic," the troll sneered. "You aren't even worth the magic it took to bring you to this world. If you can't beat me, then you are no match for Cyprin. My master gave me only the smallest bit of magic and look at you. Fallen before your journey could even begin."

Darien gasped, his head spinning, the weight on his chest unbearable. He could hear the blood pounding in his ears, his vision blurring at the edges.

The thief raised his blade. Darien threw up his arm, knowing it was useless. He braced for the strike.

It never came.

A whistling hiss cracked through the air before a sharp thunk rang out, the unmistakable sound of steel piercing flesh.

Darien barely managed to lift his head in time to see the glint of a thin blade lodged cleanly between the thief's eyes.

For the first time, the troll faltered. His arms went slack, his sword slipping from his grasp. His body staggered backward, foot lifting from Darien's throat as he crumpled to the ground.

Darien gasped, rolling onto his side, coughing against the cold stone as air rushed back into his lungs. His hands trembled as he pressed them against the wound on his arm warmth seeping through his fingers.

From the direction of the gate, footsteps approached swiftly, the echo of boots against stone a steady rhythm.

A dark figure knelt beside him. Darien caught a glimpse of Rist's hood before everything faded to black.

Chapter 17: The Hope

"How can we let him continue?"

"You don't have a choice."

"He couldn't even defeat one of them!"

"No one has faced an opponent like that in nearly three millennia! Who knows who could have won that fight?"

Darien's eyes fluttered open. The voices hovered at the edges of his consciousness, their words coming in fragmented bursts, distant but sharp. The room around him remained blurry, a haze of dim candlelight and the flickering silhouettes of figures moving beyond his vision.

"We will not be held responsible for what happens to him from here on out," a voice growled.

"No one is asking you to," came Rist's calm response.

As his vision cleared, Darien found himself in a small circular room. Stone walls, lined with tapestries, enclosed him in a quiet space that smelled of dried herbs and melted wax. A bed of thick furs had been placed beneath him, and as he moved, a dull, deep ache coursed through his limbs. He sat up, grimacing as pain shot through his upper arm. Bandages were wrapped tightly around the injury. He tested the movement—it stung, but it was nothing more than a scratch. His muscles ached, but nothing was limiting his mobility.

Twice I've gotten lucky.

With some hesitation, Darien swung his legs off the bed, his body momentarily light-headed. The soreness settled into his bones like lead, his head throbbing with every beat of his heart. He took a steadying breath, forcing the dizziness to pass. When he felt strong enough, he moved toward the door.

"He's reckless. Running off like that was foolish and immature!" The voice was shrill, laced with frustration.

"He and I both ran from the castle. Do I appear immature or foolish to you?" Rist's voice cut through the tension, calm but edged with authority.

"Well… no, but—"

"If not for Darien, we would have lost the sword, and our chance to end this Cycle," Rist interrupted sharply. "You do not make decisions for the Eldric."

The sound of footsteps retreating signaled the end of the argument. Darien stepped quietly to the door and opened it, only to find himself face-to-face with Rist.

"I know you heard the end of that conversation, and I apologize," Rist said, his voice soft but guarded.

"Who was that?" Darien asked, confused but curious.

"It doesn't matter. Just someone who can't see beyond their own fear," Rist said dismissively, his eyes darting to the door again.

"But he's right, Rist," Darien said, his voice resigned.

Rist turned fully to face him, the hooded figure's expression unreadable. "There may be some truth in his concerns," he said, moving past Darien and sitting in a chair next to the bed. "But what matters is the whole truth, not just bits and pieces."

Darien crossed the room, brushing past the dust-filled sunlight filtering through a narrow window, and sat at the edge of the bed, his arm still aching.

"What do you mean?" he asked, his voice quiet with confusion.

Rist was silent for a moment, studying him. "You're part of the Eldric. A group with a mission we must finish. Because of the spell cast after the Civil War, we are bound to complete it. If one of us falls, the worlds will fall with us. Cyprin's rule will return."

Darien felt the weight of his words sink in. "You're not making me feel any better, Rist." His voice was quiet, heavy with worry.

"What the others don't see," Rist continued, "is that even one member's failure could mean the end of us all. The people here are so focused on the end goal that they forget the steps it takes to get there. The Cycle is sacred to them—almost like a religion. And gods don't fail."

"So, I did fail?" Darien asked, a hollow ache in his chest.

"In a way," Rist said with a nonchalant shrug. "You didn't defeat him, but you stopped him from escaping. In that sense, you succeeded."

"I guess there's something to be said for the bigger picture," Darien muttered, sarcasm barely veiled in his voice.

Rist gave a small nod, seemingly unaware of the sarcasm. "What happened to you after you blacked out?" Rist's voice softened. "What do you remember?"

Darien paused, thinking back. "I remember seeing the sword sticking out of the troll's head… then you. Then everything went dark. What happened to everyone? Are they alright?"

Rist's mood shifted, and the room seemed to dim with the change. After a long pause, he spoke again, his voice low. "King Aghemnon is dead."

Darien froze, the words reverberating in his mind. "What?" His voice cracked, and his stomach turned. "How is that possible? Evatra, Garik, and Chorrun were with him, not to mention the guards…"

Rist didn't meet his eyes. "Tahmer wasn't alone. He had others under his influence. He worked in the kitchens for twenty years, plotting this." Rist's voice turned colder. "The sword was stolen, and the attack happened soon after. The King's guards betrayed him. Chorrun and Evatra fought their way to him, but the King was mortally wounded before they could save him."

Darien couldn't process it. The people who had shown him kindness—real, good people—were gone. The weight of it hit him hard. "I think I'm going to be sick," Darien muttered, rushing to a bucket beside the bed as his stomach churned. The pain from his head and arm seemed distant now, compared to the heaviness of his grief.

Rist said nothing as Darien retched, his body trembling from the shock.

"What happens now?" Darien asked once the nausea had passed. His voice was raw, and he felt more vulnerable than ever.

Rist stood and adjusted his cloak, his expression unreadable. "We meet with the others. We need to hear your version of events. While we have ideas, you're the sole person who's spoken with Tahmer. We need your account."

Darien stood slowly, feeling the weight of the room pressing down on him. He nodded, though his stomach still churned. Every inch of him felt heavier than before. The loss, the failure, the expectation—it was all pulling him into something deep, dark, and inescapable.

He followed Rist out the door and into the darkened hall of the castle, the walls heavy with the grief of the King's death. The torches flickered dimly in their iron sconces, casting long shadows that made the corridors feel like endless tunnels. The scent of old parchment, melting wax, and stone damp from the cold mountain air clung to everything, a stark contrast to the warmth of the feast the night before. Their footsteps echoed, swallowed by the vast silence that had settled over Fenway Keep.

The castle felt different now. Before, it had been a place of power, of ancient strength—but now, it felt hollow, a tomb that hadn't yet realized it had lost its king.

They walked in silence until they reached the council chamber.

Inside, Marenya sat at the head of the table, her posture stiff but dignified. The light from the high windows cast harsh lines across her face, making her look older than she had the night before. Chorrun stood by her side, his arms crossed, his equine form unmoving. Evatra leaned against the stone table, her fingers curled into fists, looking as if she were physically holding the weight of the world on her shoulders. A few guards stood in the corners of the room, their gazes flickering between each other, as though unsure how to process the weight of the moment.

The stolen sword lay in the center of the table, wrapped in thick cloth. No one dared to look at it directly, as if it might rise and claim another life the moment they acknowledged its presence.

Marenya spoke first. Her voice was exhausted, yet it held strength. "Darien, I have to thank you. Without your efforts, we may have never caught the one behind the attack. We mourn the loss of the King, but our people are grateful to you for stopping his killers."

Darien blinked. Grateful? The word barely registered. He had expected blame, anger—not thanks. His throat tightened, but he forced a response. "I… you're welcome," he muttered, his voice barely above a whisper. He glanced at Evatra, but her expression remained unreadable.

Marenya continued. "The sword will remain safe in our vaults until the Eldric leave the city. Now, you spoke with Tahmer before the duel. We hope you can shed light on who he was, how he managed to steal the sword, and what he hoped to gain by doing so."

The weight of their gazes pressed into him. He was the last person to speak with the assassin. The last one to see him alive.

Darien took a breath and spoke quietly, recounting everything he could: the chase through the streets, the encounter in the market, how he had cornered the troll alone. He explained the desperation in Tahmer's voice, the conviction behind his words, the way he spoke of Cyprin as though he had already won. Rist filled in details of his own, explaining his attempt to cut ahead, unaware that Darien had gotten there first. Darien repeated everything Tahmer had said—his strength, his command over others, his unwavering allegiance to Cyprin.

At the mention of Cyprin's name, the room fell silent. The air itself seemed to tighten.

One of the guards erupted in disbelief. "That's impossible! Cyprin hasn't sent anyone into Olympus in three thousand years!"

Rist's voice was chilling. "Times have changed."

Marenya turned to Chorrun. "Is he correct? Has Cyprin sent agents into our lands before?"

Chorrun hesitated before answering. "No, not beyond Zanarchin. Cyprin has never reached this far from everything I've studied. We don't know how long it would take him to regain full strength."

The Scillan spoke then, their voice calm and sure. "If Cyprin has sent one agent, it's likely more are coming, or are already in place. This is a shift. In previous Cycles, there was time for the Eldric to complete their journey."

"True," Chorrun agreed. "But it appears things have changed."

The Scillan continued, "This is an escalation. If Cyprin can send one, he could send many. His attempt at stealth has failed. He may make his next move more directly."

Chorrun added, "Tahmer didn't just infiltrate Farkland Reach. He killed the King. This puts the entire city at risk."

Silence stretched thin, thick with unspoken fear. If Cyprin was rising again, Farkland Reach would be his first target.

Garik, who had been lounging at the far end of the table, feet propped up on a chair, finally spoke. "War has a way of arriving, whether you're prepared for it or not. Best to start thinking about the inevitable."

Darien looked at him sharply. Garik never seemed to be where he was expected, yet always seemed to be where things of importance were taking place. He wasn't smiling now, though. His usual mischief had been replaced by something else. Something colder.

Marenya let out a breath, her exhaustion weighing her down. "What many of you don't yet know is that we sent scouts to monitor the mountain's base. They returned with reports of mobilization activity. We had hoped to not reveal this in an effort to keep things calm. To keep the cycles moving. This was two months past."

An air of unsettled emotion fell on the room as the implications of her words took hold. Before anyone could voice concerns or protest at the fact that this information had been hidden until now, she continued.

"I'll send scouts. I'll also request aid from the surrounding cities. If this was the first thrust at an attempt to destabilize the peoples…"

Darien tuned out the rest. He didn't belong in this conversation. The longer it went on, the heavier the air became, suffocating him. They were talking about war—real war—and he was standing in a room with warriors and rulers, people who had spent their lives preparing for this. What did he know?

He wasn't a leader. He wasn't even a real fighter. He had been defeated so easily.

He slipped out of the council chamber doors and walked down the hallway, his breath uneven.

"Darien!"

He turned to see Evatra calling after him.

"We need you in there. There's a lot to do," she said, watching him with concern.

"No, you don't," Darien shook his head, frustration boiling beneath his skin. "I don't know anything that's useful. Besides, after last night I…" His words trailed off as the humiliation settled deeper.

"Last night doesn't matter, Darien. It wasn't your fault," Evatra reassured him.

"Yes, it was, Evatra," Darien's voice cracked. "It was my job to stop him, and I failed. I couldn't even beat one guy. One. If there's an army coming—full of soldiers like him. I'd just be getting in the way." He couldn't carry the weight of his failure any longer. He had to get out of the castle.

"Please, come back in. I know you can—"

"Enough, Evatra, okay?" Darien cut her off, voice sharp. "Just… enough."

He turned away, leaving her standing alone in the hallway, her hurt gaze following him as he walked out of the castle.

Darien wandered through the city, the mix of sad, curious, and excited looks from the people around him only deepening his sense of isolation. The once-lively streets of Farkland Reach now felt oppressive, each whisper and stolen glance a reminder of what he wasn't. He had failed. And they all knew it.

The city felt different tonight—or maybe he was different.

The glow of lanterns hung low over the streets, their warm light doing little to thaw the cold sinking into his chest. Vendors still lined the market, but their voices were quieter, their enthusiasm muted by the weight of the king's death. Somewhere in the distance, the sound of metal being worked rang through the air—a smith, perhaps, preparing for a war that had only just begun.

Eventually, Darien found himself back in the market, at the very place where the thief had bested him. He stood there, staring at the worn cobblestones, as if they might hold answers he had missed the first time. He'd never lost a fight like that before. The weight of it pressed against his chest, suffocating him. If he couldn't even beat one opponent, how could he possibly be part of the Eldric? Rist was wrong. He didn't belong here.

They'd have better chances without me.

Sighing, Darien turned to leave. He barely noticed the small figure sprinting toward him until tiny arms wrapped around his leg. Surprised, he looked down to find a young troll, her bright eyes full of something he hadn't seen in a long time—hope.

"Aren?" a woman's voice called out, frantic. "Aren, what are you doing? Come back here!"

The woman rushed forward, pulling the child off Darien's leg with a quick, apologetic bow. "I'm sorry! I don't know what's gotten into him."

Darien shook his head, forcing a weak smile. "It's okay." He turned back toward the gate, ready to disappear into the city.

"You're going to protect us, aren't you?" The child's voice rang through the quiet street, piercing through Darien like a blade. "You're going to stop the bad guys from coming out of the mountain?"

Darien flinched at the question, the weight of it sinking deep into his chest. He looked around, noticing the silence that had fallen over the small crowd. The other trolls had stopped moving, their eyes heavy with expectation. They had lost their king, their protector, and now they were looking to him for answers.

He didn't know what to do. How could he carry their confidence when he couldn't even shoulder his own?

He knelt down to meet the young troll's eyes, forcing a calmness he didn't feel. "We're going to do everything we can," Darien promised, his voice more steady than he felt.

The child beamed, throwing their arms around him again. Darien staggered back, almost losing his balance, and winced at the pain in his arm. He embraced the young troll, giving what comfort he could. In that moment, he tried to take whatever hope he could from the child's innocence, even as he unknowingly took some of his own in return.

Aren pulled away and ran back to her mother. Darien waved, watching the child glance back at him before disappearing into the crowd.

A voice interrupted his thoughts.

"The people here need us."

Darien spun to find Rist, his figure looming around the corner, watching the scene unfold. The hooded figure was still as a statue, unreadable, but there was something different in his presence tonight. Something softer.

"Are you my babysitter today?" Darien shot back, irritation flaring. "Aren't you supposed to be inside?"

"Even if we face impossible odds, we are still heroes to them. They need hope," Rist replied, ignoring Darien's comment. "We have to give them that hope."

"Can we, though?" Darien's doubt slipped into his voice as they began walking back toward the castle. "What if we fail?"

Rist's voice remained steady. "Then we fail. But that hasn't happened yet."

Darien let out a breath, shaking his head. "That's not exactly reassuring."

"Reassurance is meaningless," Rist said simply. "Action is everything."

For once, Darien didn't argue.

They walked in silence for a few more moments, the sounds of the city fading behind them as the castle loomed closer. The torches at the gates flickered in the wind, casting long, stretching shadows against the towering stone.

Then, just before they reached the entrance, Darien hesitated. He looked up at Rist, something raw in his voice when he finally spoke.

"Rist, can I ask you something?"

Rist gave a short nod under his hood.

"What if I'm no good here?" Darien swallowed, his throat dry. "What if you all have to protect me, and I'm just… baggage? What if I'm not strong enough to face Cyprin? Tahmer barely had any magic, and I couldn't even beat him. If I can't handle him, how am I supposed to stand against Cyprin?"

Darien stopped halfway through the castle gates, looking up at Rist, waiting for an answer. The other man stood still for several moments, silent.

Then, finally, he spoke.

"First, you say this as if you are the only person this cycle relies upon. Since coming to Olympus, you've done nothing but gather allies. Why do you seem to believe that you face this alone?"

Rist let a small silence pass between them before continuing.

"Second, from what little I've seen of you, the only way that you will fail is if you choose to."

Without another word, Rist turned and walked the rest of the way into the castle, leaving Darien standing alone on the steps, the weight of the conversation pressing down on him.

Chapter 18: The Plan

The next few days blurred together in a haze of relentless preparation. What had once been a city of commerce and conversation had become something else entirely—a fortress under siege, even though the enemy had yet to arrive.

Darien walked through the streets, his boots crunching over displaced earth as trenches deepened around the city's perimeter. The scent of sweat, damp soil, and burning oil hung thick in the air. It reeked of desperation.

The transformation wasn't just physical. It was in the way the people moved. Merchants, whose hands were once used for counting coins and sealing deals, now struggled under the weight of lumber and stone. Fishermen's nets were replaced with bows. Mothers hurried their children inside at the first hint of dusk, their voices hushed in fearful murmurs.

Near the southern wall, a group of inexperienced recruits trained under the harsh bark of their instructors. Darien paused, watching them struggle through drills. Their swords wavered, grips unsteady, feet unsure. They were farmers, bakers, merchants—people who had never fought a day in their lives. And now, they would be expected to hold a city.

Darien clenched his jaw. This wasn't what war was supposed to be.

He passed a forge where blacksmiths hammered out crude spears from scavenged iron, their faces smeared with soot and exhaustion. Supplies were stretched thin. Even with Chorrun's reinforcements arriving soon, it wouldn't be enough.

A conversation drifted toward him from the gates. Two sentries, their voices low but edged with anxiety.

"They say there's a force twice the size of our city."

"They also said the last Cycle ended before Cyprin could send an army, yet here we are."

Darien swallowed hard. Was this how every Cycle felt? The creeping dread, the uncertainty?

Darien lost himself in the work. Anything to distract from the gnawing doubt in his chest. His arm still ached, a constant reminder of his loss, but he pushed through it, forcing himself to be useful. If he wasn't fighting, if he wasn't leading, at least he could build. At least he could help.

He spent hours alongside the workers reinforcing the castle walls, hammering iron supports into place, dragging stones into position. The physical labor burned through his frustration, but it never fully silenced it.

By midday, his shirt clung to his back with sweat, his hands raw from gripping the worn wooden handles of a pickaxe. He gritted his teeth as he drove it into the hard-packed earth, digging another trench along the outskirts of the city.

"You're holding it wrong," came a smooth, amused voice from behind him.

Darien turned, already knowing who it was. Garik.

The self-proclaimed marauder stood at the edge of the trench, arms crossed, looking infuriatingly clean compared to the rest of them. He raised an eyebrow at Darien's grip on the pickaxe.

"You're wasting energy," Garik continued, stepping down into the trench like he had all the time in the world. "Swing too low, and you lose power. Swing too high, and you wear yourself out. It's about rhythm."

Darien scowled. "I don't remember asking for your expertise in excavation."

Garik grinned. "I have many talents, my dear friend. Though, I suppose watching you struggle is more entertaining than helping."

Darien exhaled sharply and wiped the sweat from his brow. "Shouldn't you be doing something important?"

"I am," Garik said, adjusting his sleeves. "Observing. A highly undervalued skill."

Darien rolled his eyes and swung the pickaxe again. He half-expected Garik to disappear like he always did, slipping away to whatever shadowy dealings he occupied himself with. But, to his surprise, the man crouched down and picked up a shovel, shoving it into the ground.

"Well," Garik mused, eyeing the deepening trench. "Might as well see if I remember how to do honest work."

Darien smirked despite himself. "Doubtful."

Garik laughed. "Very."

As the city transformed from a trade hub to a fortress, Darien watched the landscape change. Trenches were dug around the perimeter, creating barriers from the displaced earth. Fallen trees from the nearby forests were felled and used to strengthen the defenses. The branches had been sharpened into deadly points, creating an impenetrable ring. The battlements, once humble, began to take the shape of a funnel, directing any attacking force exactly where the defenders wanted them.

The sun had just begun its slow descent when Darien climbed one of the archery towers, surveying the land beyond the castle walls. The world outside Farkland Reach stretched out in eerie stillness. What had once been rolling green fields now bore the scars of their preparations—trenches, wooden spikes, and makeshift fortifications meant to delay an inevitable attack.

But delay wasn't enough.

As he scanned the horizon, a flicker of movement caught his eye—a lone figure, small against the vast expanse of the eastern road, riding hard toward the city. His heart thudded in his chest. A scout.

Darien didn't wait. He scrambled down the tower's ladder, nearly losing his footing as he landed, then took off running. He pushed past workers hauling stones, past weary soldiers drilling formations, past the haunted faces of citizens trying to hold onto normalcy in a world that was rapidly unraveling.

By the time he reached the council chamber, his lungs burned, and his legs ached. He shoved open the heavy wooden doors, nearly stumbling as he entered.

Marenya, Chorrun, the Scillan, Rist, Evatra and Oratrin, the queens top commander and leader of her personal guard, all turned sharply at his entrance.

"Darien? What is it?" Marenya asked, concern flickering in her tired eyes.

"It's... the scouts..." Darien panted, hands braced on his knees. "One of them... came back."

Silence gripped the room.

"Are you sure?" Oratrin asked, his voice tight.

Darien nodded, chest still heaving. "I saw him. He's back."

Marenya was already moving, stepping past him, and the others followed suit. Darien barely had time to catch his breath before he was running again, this time toward the castle gates.

The city's defenders had already gathered, forming a loose semi-circle near the entrance. The tension was thick, unspoken fears lingering in every hesitant step, every shared glance. Then, hooves thundered against the cobblestones, and the gate swung open just in time for a lone horseman to ride through.

The scout, a young troll named Poltin, barely managed to slow his mount before dismounting in one fluid motion. His horse was lathered in sweat, nostrils flaring, its sides heaving. Poltin himself wasn't much better—his cloak torn, his face smeared with dirt and exhaustion.

"Your Majesty," he gasped, his voice raw. "I have word."

Marenya stepped forward, every inch the queen, though Darien could see the tension tightening her jaw. "Tell us."

Poltin swallowed, struggling to steady himself. "It's true, my lady. A force gathers in the east. We were spotted, but I managed to slip away. The others I rode with..." He faltered, his throat bobbing as he fought back emotion. "They didn't make it."

The weight of his words settled over them like a shroud.

"How far?" Oratrin demanded, his voice like steel.

"Seven, maybe eight days' ride from here," Poltin answered, his hands curling into fists. "But I can't be sure how fast they'll move. There's a massive force, twice the size of Farkland Reach."

Darien saw Marenya's face pale, the reality of it sinking in. They weren't just unprepared. They were hopelessly outnumbered.

"Thank you, Poltin," Marenya said, forcing her voice to remain steady. "You've done your duty well. Rest. We will see to your needs."

Poltin nodded weakly, barely managing a bow before stumbling toward the castle.

Inside the war room, the council gathered again. The large wooden table was covered with maps, hastily drawn battle plans, and scrawled messages from surrounding villages. Darien stood near the edge of the room, listening as the discussion unfolded, but feeling more like an outsider than ever.

Chorrun broke the silence. "Your Majesty, I sent word three days ago to Taitron. Forces should be arriving here in two days. They'll have informed the surrounding villages. We can offer you the support of over two hundred cavalry."

Marenya sighed. "Thank you, Chorrun. But I fear it won't be enough."

Darien's eyes traced the map, the winding roads, the mountains looming to the east. They weren't prepared for a siege. The trenches, the barricades—they would slow an army, but they wouldn't stop one. His mind flickered back to his studies at the Academy, where they had analyzed historical battles, dissecting the mistakes of commanders long dead. He had studied fortifications, siegecraft, even the tactics of famous generals. Their plans weren't enough, they needed something else. Some advantage Cyprin wouldn't expect. They needed an enemy that would fight him to the last.

Darien traced his journey across the map, starting from Taitron. His finger followed the winding roads, recalling the days spent traveling with Chorrun, the vast plains that had once felt open and freeing, now feeling like choke points waiting to trap them. He followed the inked routes north, remembering what Chorrun had said about the caves in passing—how even the marauders avoided them, how the land itself rejected trespassers.

As his fingers moved across the map, they stopped on something that made his pulse quicken. He couldn't read the script. The transition magic had only done so much, leaving him fluent in spoken language but still unable to decipher the intricate script of Olveery. Yet, even without understanding the letters, he recognized the symbol.

A mark of warning, carved into the parchment like a scar. Stay away. Death, or worse awaits you here.

A place no one dared to tread. That was what he was looking for.

His eyes sharpened as he pointed at the location. "How long would it take to get here?"

The conversation at the table was already deep in debate. Marenya and Chorrun were discussing the possible reinforcement strategies, while Rist and Oratrin argued the merits of a preemptive strike versus a defensive stand. The Scillan remained silent, observing but unreadable. Darien waited, listening, feeling the weight of the discussion press down on him. These were rulers, warriors—people who had been making decisions like this their entire lives.

His eyes drifted down to the map again. The roads and rivers, the trade routes and strongholds. He recognized Taitron's placement, traced the route he had taken with Chorrun, following the inked lines north. What had Chorrun said about the caves? Even the marauders avoid them. The land itself rejects trespassers.

He spoke again, cutting through the ongoing conversation. "Hey! How long would it take to get here?"

The room paused their debate of tactics and strategy to look at the map splayed on the table.

Oratrin's gaze followed his finger, then narrowed. "The Mist Caves? Why in the depths would you want to go there?"

Darien's mind was racing now. He could still hear the wraith's voice, distant and whispering at the edge of memory, curling around him like smoke. It had spoken to him before; it had made a promise. That had to mean something, didn't it? Could he trust it? He surprised even himself at the idea of walking into the mouth of the unknown, wagering not just his life, but the fate of this city and the world on a gamble. But maybe that was all they had left—a gamble.

"I have to go talk to them," he said.

The silence in the room was heavy.

"Are you mad?" Oratrin scoffed.

"Probably," Darien admitted. "But I've spoken with a wraith before. It promised to help me if I needed it. This seems as good a time as any to collect on that debt."

Chorrun frowned. "Wraiths do not keep their promises. They twist them."

Darien shrugged. "Maybe. But we just got word that we're outnumbered at least four to one. The trolls and people here haven't fought in a war for the last three thousand years, and we have proof that Cyprin is sending agents into at least this city, if not more. If ever there was a time for desperate measures, I'd say this was it."

His words were met with immediate resistance.

"You would risk everything on a conversation with a wraith?" Oratrin snapped, his voice thick with disbelief. "You're gambling with lives, Darien. With all of our lives."

"And doing nothing isn't?" Darien shot back, his frustration boiling over. "You're missing the forest for the trees! We're talking in circles about fortifications and formations when none of it is going to matter if that army reaches us! You think walls are going to hold back an enemy like this? You think we have enough soldiers? If you do, you're lying to yourself!"

His voice had risen before he even realized it. The silence that followed was heavy, pressing down on him, suffocating. His heart pounded in his chest as he registered the stunned faces around the table.

These were his friends. Marenya, who had shown him kindness despite her own grief. Chorrun, who had brought him here, guided him. Evatra, who had stood by him when no one else did. And here he was, yelling at them.

Darien swallowed hard, forcing himself to take a deep breath. When he spoke again, his voice was quieter, but no less firm.

"I know it's insane. I know trusting a wraith sounds like the worst possible plan. But we don't have the luxury of safe options anymore. This is our best chance to turn the odds in our favor, and I have to try."

He met Oratrin's gaze, holding it. "Let me try."

The room remained silent, tension thick between them. Darien could feel their doubt pressing in from all sides. Chorrun shifted uncomfortably, Marenya's lips were pressed into a thin line, and Oratrin looked ready to argue again.

Then Evatra stepped forward. "Then I'm going with you."

Darien blinked, caught off guard. She had intended to leave after the King's dinner, but Marenya had convinced her to stay after Aghemnon's sudden passing. Now, she was choosing to stay longer. Choosing to go with him.

Oratrin let out a frustrated breath, turning to Marenya. "Your Majesty, this is absurd. A marauder leading one of the Eldric into wraith territory? Do you not see the risk?"

Marenya's sharp gaze flicked to him, her tone cold and unwavering. "Enough, Oratrin. Evatra has proven her loyalty to this city more than once. I will not hear another word against her."

Oratrin scowled but fell silent, clearly unhappy but unwilling to challenge his queen further.

Evatra crossed her arms, glancing between them. "I should be heading back to Atreya. That's what I told myself. That's what I wanted. But if Cyprin comes back, if we lose this fight, then none of that matters. There is no future for Atreya or anyone else if we fail."

Darien nodded, the finality in her words settling deep within him. "We'll leave now. We can't waste time if we're going to get back before the army arrives.

Rist's voice was sharp. "If anyone should ride with Darien, it's me."

"No, Rist," Darien said, careful but firm. "They need you here. You're more valuable helping with the defense. If something goes wrong, it should only happen to one of the Eldric, not two."

Evatra spoke up, looking at Rist. "I was with the marauders when the wraith first attacked Atreya. I know the area."

For a moment, Rist didn't speak. Then he nodded reluctantly. "Fine. But take the fastest horses, and waste as little time as possible. We need you both here when the battle begins."

The decision was made.

Within the hour, Darien and Evatra were mounted, their horses restless beneath them. As they rode through the city gates, Darien cast one last glance back at the castle, its high walls illuminated by torchlight. He wasn't sure what he was riding toward. But he knew what he was leaving behind.

And for the first time in days, he felt like he was moving toward something rather than running away.

Chapter 19: The Caves

The ride out of the city was faster than the journey in, but it wasn't easier.

Darien gritted his teeth as the horse beneath him lurched forward with a force he wasn't prepared for. His grip on the reins tightened instinctively, his fingers aching from the tension. Despite the time he had spent riding in Olympus, it hadn't come naturally to him. The Academy had never taught horsemanship—not to anyone. Now, as his mount galloped across the open fields, he was paying for that oversight.

Evatra rode a few strides ahead, her posture relaxed, her form fluid. She was completely at home in the saddle. She didn't need to jerk at the reins or shift uncomfortably every time the horse adjusted its pace. Darien, on the other hand, felt like he was one wrong movement away from toppling off entirely.

His thighs burned from gripping the saddle too tightly, his arms strained from holding himself steady, and every time they hit uneven ground, his stomach lurched. It took everything he had to keep from cursing aloud.

It had been embarrassing enough the first time he had tried to gallop. That had ended with him in the dirt, staring at the sky while Kort and come up and captured him. He wasn't about to fall off again. There was too much at stake.

They rode for hours without speaking, the tension between them stretching taut like a wire that neither dared to snap. Darien wasn't sure if it was exhaustion, or if Evatra simply didn't want to talk. Maybe both.

By the time the sun dipped low on the horizon, they had reached the edges of the mountains. The air was cooler here, the green of the meadows giving way to jagged gray rock and narrow winding paths. The land itself seemed to grow harsher, like it knew what lay ahead and wanted to warn them.

Evatra finally slowed her horse to a stop. Darien followed suit, grateful for the reprieve as he adjusted his sore legs.

"We'll camp here for the night," she said, dismounting in one smooth motion. Darien swung his leg over to follow, but his foot caught in the stirrup, and he nearly went down. He barely managed to catch himself before hitting the dirt.

Evatra didn't comment. Which somehow made it worse.

They set up camp in silence. The stew they made was simple—nothing more than dried meat, root vegetables, and water boiled over the small fire. The kind of meal that did its job and nothing more. Darien stirred his portion absently, watching as the fire flickered in the growing darkness.

Before he could summon the courage to break the silence, Evatra turned away and lay down, pulling her cloak over her shoulders.

Darien sighed and did the same.

The morning air was sharp, biting through Darien's cloak as he tightened it around his shoulders. The fire had long since died, leaving only the cold and the fading scent of smoke clinging to the air. He rubbed the sleep from his eyes, shifting stiffly in his bedroll. His body still ached from the previous day's ride, the soreness settling into his bones like a weight he couldn't shake.

Evatra was already awake, crouched near her horse, adjusting the straps on her saddle. She hadn't said a word to him since waking, her focus entirely on the task at hand.

Darien rolled to his feet, stretching out the tightness in his back. "We heading out?"

Evatra gave a single nod, tugging the last strap tight. "We need to make the foothills by midday if we want to reach the caves before dark."

He sighed, brushing dirt from his cloak before moving to saddle his own horse. The animal snorted, shifting slightly under his touch as if sensing his inexperience. It was a mutual distrust at this point. He performed the daily ritual of brushing and cleaning the beast as he had been shown and then climbed into the saddle, adjusting his grip on the reins, determined not to embarrass himself further.

The ride started in silence, only the rhythmic thud of hooves against dirt filling the space between them. The landscape around them began to shift—the grassy plains thinning out, giving way to dry, uneven terrain. The towering peaks in the distance grew larger with each passing hour, their jagged edges cutting into the pale blue sky.

Darien squinted at them, trying to gauge the distance, but he wasn't confident in his ability to estimate it. Maps had never been his strong suit. He had spent years studying war strategy, but maps meant nothing without context.

"How close are the mountains?" he finally asked, breaking the silence.

Evatra didn't answer immediately, her gaze fixed ahead. She briefly glanced up at the peaks before returning her focus to the road.

"We'll be in the foothills by midday, and at the caves before nightfall," she replied flatly, her tone devoid of emotion. "We're making good time."

Darien nodded, though he wasn't sure why. He felt the tension between them pressing against his chest like a weight, heavy and unyielding. He needed to break it.

"I'm glad you decided to stay," he said carefully.

Evatra turned her head slightly, her gaze flicking to him. "I wouldn't have thought so," she said, her words blunt, almost like a jab.

Darien sighed. "Look, I didn't handle things well back at the castle. I know that. There was a lot going on. I was—" He hesitated, then forced himself to say it. "I'm sorry."

Evatra's grip on her reins tightened. "You disappeared for three days, Darien."

He winced. That was fair.

She let out a frustrated breath, her voice rising slightly. "Where were you?"

Darien fiddled with the leather bindings on his saddle, avoiding her gaze. "I was working on repairs and fortifying the city's defenses."

"I needed you back with us," Evatra said, her tone softening but carrying a deep intensity. "We had a lot to do. We could have used you."

Darien met her eyes, the sincerity in her face impossible to miss. "You needed me?" he repeated, unsure if he had heard her correctly.

Evatra looked away, and Darien, still processing her words, took a moment before she finally stammered out, "I meant—we did. Everyone in there did. We could've used your help with planning the city's defense. Oh, never mind, just forget it. Let's get to the mountains and finish this."

The silence grew again, this time heavier, as they continued to ride in uneasy quiet. Darien felt the weight of her words settle over him, pressing into the space between them like an unspoken truth. She had needed him. Not just as another warrior or strategist, but as someone she could rely on. And he had been absent. It was a strange thing, realizing how much his presence had mattered to her. He had spent so much time doubting himself, questioning whether he belonged in this world, whether his presence even made a difference. But Evatra had just given him an answer, even if she hadn't meant to.

He exhaled, the cold air sharp against his lungs. He wanted to say something—to tell her that he hadn't meant to disappear, that he hadn't known anyone was counting on him. But the words caught in his throat, tangled in the weight of everything else. Instead, he pressed his heels into his horse's sides, urging it forward, letting the quiet stretch on. Some conversations weren't meant to be finished in a single moment.

By midday, they reached the foothills, the rugged terrain ahead of them still daunting. Darien tried to push away the growing anxiety. This, at least, was something he could contribute to—speaking to the wraiths, convincing them to fight for them. That was the promise he'd been given. He had to make it happen.

As the mountains rose higher, Darien found himself pushing harder to summon his courage. The air grew cooler as they entered the shadow of the cliffs. The meadows faded into rocky gray, a stark reminder of

Farkland Reach, and Darien realized this stone might have been the same material used to build the castle walls.

Evatra stopped suddenly, pulling her horse to a halt. Darien followed suit, peering ahead.

"Just beyond those trees," she said, pointing toward a distant line of gnarled branches. "There's a cave. Atreya was playing near it when one of the wraiths came out and attacked her."

Darien strained to listen, but there was only silence— the rustling of leaves in the wind, the distant cry of some unseen bird. No movement. No sign of life.

"Is this it, then?" he asked, trying to steady himself.

Evatra looked at him, her expression unreadable. "It is," she said, sounding almost melancholic—or was it anxiety? Darien couldn't tell.

The air between them thickened again.

"Look," Evatra spoke, her voice softer than before. "Darien, I'm sorry I've been harsh with you. It's just... after living with the marauders for so long, there's no one you can trust. But with you, that's different. I can trust you, and... that scares me."

Darien frowned. "Scares you? Why? Wouldn't that be... I don't know, refreshing after everything you've been through?"

"It should be," she admitted, giving him a small, sad smile. "But it isn't."

She looked away again, as if suddenly regretting saying anything at all. Then, with a quiet sigh, she dismounted, turning her focus to setting up camp. "I'm going to stay here. I don't think it's a good idea for me to go into the cave with you."

Darien studied her for a long moment before nodding. "You're probably right. This is something I have to do on my own."

He hesitated, glancing at the mouth of the cave in the distance. "Have a fire ready when I come out, okay? I don't know how long this will take, but we need to rest tonight before heading back tomorrow."

Evatra nodded, her expression unreadable. "It'll be ready."

Darien dismounted, rolling his shoulders before taking a few cautious steps toward the cave. Evatra handed him a torch, its flame flickering wildly in the cool mountain air. They shared a final look before she turned back toward the campsite.

Darien turned toward the cave, exhaling slowly. The darkness waited for him.

The darkness swallowed him whole, thick and suffocating, as if the cave had devoured him and refused to let him go.

Darien took slow, cautious steps, holding the torch high. The flame flickered wildly, barely piercing the thick blackness pressing in from all sides. Each step forward made the air colder, not just a physical chill but a creeping, unnatural cold that gnawed at his bones. It felt wrong. Not like the bite of a mountain wind or the damp chill of a storm—but like something watching, waiting.

The walls of the cave were slick with moisture, the scent of damp earth and decay clinging to the stale air. A place untouched by time, undisturbed until now. Water dripped from the ceiling in slow, deliberate beats, the rhythm unsettling, like an unfamiliar heartbeat.

He had expected something—movement, sound, a presence. But there was only silence, thick and unyielding.

Another step forward. Then another.

His boots slipped slightly on the wet stone beneath him, and he caught himself against the wall, steadying his breath. There was something deeply unnatural about this place.

He ventured deeper, the oppressive quiet pressing against his ears. He stopped and called out, his voice cutting through the emptiness.

"Hello?"

His voice echoed unnaturally, stretching, distorting, as if the cave itself was deciding whether to acknowledge him.

Then, nothing.

Darien's grip tightened around the torch. What if this wasn't the right place? What if the wraith had lied? What if he had led them here for nothing?

Pressing forward, he counted his steps. Fifty paces, then another fifty. The torchlight revealed the far end of the cavern—a smooth, unbroken wall of stone.

His heart pounded. A dead end.

"No," he muttered, his pulse quickening. That couldn't be right. They had to be here.

Turning sharply, his boots scraped against the slick floor. He was about to retrace his steps when he noticed how distant the entrance felt. The light from outside was barely a sliver, swallowed by the shadows. The cave had consumed it, just as it had consumed him.

A wave of unease slithered up his spine.

A screech split the silence.

Darien flinched, ducking instinctively, his pulse hammering in his ears. The sound didn't just echo—it multiplied, bouncing off the walls in unnatural ways, as though the cave itself was screaming back at him.

The torch slipped from his fingers, clattering to the ground, rolling across the slick stone. Its flame flickered, casting erratic shadows along the walls, twisting and contorting into figures that weren't there.

Then the ground shuddered.

A massive stone fell from the cave's roof, slamming into the ground behind him with a deafening boom.

Darien spun, his breath catching. The entrance— gone.

Trapped.

He stumbled forward, pressing his hands against the fallen stone, shoving with all the strength he had left. Nothing. His palms scraped against the wet rock, searching for any crevice, any weakness. It was sealed.

A whisper, layered and hollow, slithered through the air.

"Do not touch your fire."

Darien froze. The words didn't echo as they should have. Instead, they came from everywhere at once.

He swallowed hard. He wasn't alone.

"Where are you?" he called, forcing his voice to steady.

"We are here."

A presence pressed against him, unseen but undeniable. A weight. A force.

"I don't understand," he said, his throat dry. "Why are you doing this?"

"You came into our caves. You disturbed our home. You walk the lands, free to be in the world. You were free to go anywhere, and you chose here. You were not invited. For that, you will die."

Darien's stomach twisted. "No! I came to ask for your help!" His voice cracked, but he pushed forward. "I need you—Olympus needs you!"

Silence. Then a low scurrying, as if a thousand unseen limbs were moving at once.

"I'm one of the Eldric," Darien continued, his voice desperate. "I helped save one of you, a wraith. It went inside me, looked at my memories. I let it stay with me. It said to come find you when I needed help. That's why I'm here! I need your help!"

A pause.

Then—

"You lie. None here have touched you before."

Darien's breath hitched. No. No, no, no.

Had the wraith lied to him? Had it been alone? Were these wraiths different?

"No! I promise, it's true!" he shouted. Panic clawed at his chest, rising faster than he could suppress it. Had he miscalculated everything? Had he doomed himself?

The whispers turned sharper.

"We tire of this talk. We will not help one of your kind. This is pointless."

Darien clenched his fists. One chance. Think. Think.

"Wait," he said, his voice hoarse but firm. "What if I'm not lying? What if another wraith made a promise, based on what they saw when they were inside my mind? Can you afford to ignore that?"

The whispers swelled, louder, layered, merging into something inhuman. A decision was being made.

Then, finally—

"What do you propose?"

Darien exhaled shakily. This was it. His only shot.

"You possess people, right? I'm giving you permission. Go inside me, see if what I'm telling you is true. I am one of the Eldric. You'll find what the other wraith saw."

A pause. Then the scurrying grew deafening.

"It is... agreed."

A wave of relief washed over him—but it shattered the moment the cold returned.

This time, the invasion was violent. Unrelenting. A force tore into him, invading every fiber of his being, burrowing into the recesses of his mind. It wasn't searching—it was ripping him apart.

It was worse than before. Deeper. Crueler.

Memories surfaced—some his, some not. Faces blurred together—Kara. Chorrun. Philip. Evatra. Trey. But then—Master Whyn. The image of him lingered, stretched, as though something was holding onto it longer than the rest. Sifting through Darien's memories, the wraiths paused at Whyn. The sensation turned from a passive search to a sharp, digging intrusion, as if they were peeling back layers, looking for something deeper.

The moment stretched too long, and then the wraiths tore past it, moving on.

Images that didn't belong to him flashed across his mind in rapid succession, like flickers of lives he had never lived. The pain was unbearable. He wanted to scream, but he couldn't. As suddenly as it had begun, it stopped.

Darien collapsed to the ground, gasping, his limbs shaking, his mind a swirling mess of fractured thoughts. He had never felt so violated, so completely undone.

The voice returned, quieter, but final.

"You are not lying. And something is... different."

The voice did not carry the same chilling certainty as before. There was hesitation, something Darien hadn't heard in them until now. The presence that had invaded his mind did not immediately withdraw. Instead, it lingered, brushing against his thoughts as if searching for something it did not expect to find.

"This Cycle turns in a new way."

The cave seemed to contract around him, the air growing heavier. The wraiths were murmuring, whispering among themselves in a language that Darien could not decipher. It sent an unnatural shiver down his spine.

Then, the voice returned, slower, more deliberate. "There was a name in your thoughts. A man not of this world. You know him."

Darien blinked, his breath still unsteady from the invasion of his mind. "Who?"

"Whyn."

The name sent a jolt through him. Of all the faces they had seen in his memories—his friends, his past, the people he loved—why him? Why Whyn?

Darien forced himself to sit upright, still shaking from the ordeal. "He was my instructor. Back at the Academy. He taught strategy and war theory."

The whispers surged again, no longer disjointed but deliberate, spoken with purpose. He could not understand them, but he could feel them.

"Who is he to you?"

Darien's fingers curled into the damp stone beneath him. "I told you—my instructor. A teacher." He narrowed his eyes, scanning the void. "Why? What do you know about him?"

Silence. Then, the voice returned, but not with an answer. "Your memories of him are strong. They hold weight."

Darien's jaw clenched. "And?"

A long pause, then, "We will not answer you."

Frustration flared hot in his chest. "You're avoiding the question."

The voice ignored him. The cold air thickened again, pressing down on him, suffocating in its indifference.

"However, this battle you must fight, we cannot join."

Darien's stomach dropped. No. No, they had to help.

His exhaustion turned into desperation. "Why not? You exist outside the physical world, don't you? You could turn the tide of this war in an instant. Why refuse?"

A slow, crawling dread settled into his chest as the voice responded, "We cannot."

Darien's head snapped up. "That's not an answer."

"It is the truth. We are bound. We have always been bound."

A realization crept into his mind, but he refused to accept it. "You're trapped."

The voices did not answer immediately. The air around him vibrated, as though the wraiths themselves were shifting, unsettled. Then, finally, a whisper.

"Yes."

"Well, then we need to find a way," he rasped, his throat raw.

"We must find a way to leave these caves. Until we find that answer, we will be unable to help you."

Darien's shoulders sagged in defeat. He had come all this way for nothing. The weight of the realization pressed into him, heavy and suffocating. He had risked everything, pushed himself beyond exhaustion, and yet the wraiths, these beings who existed beyond the limitations of mortal bodies, were as powerless as he felt.

"Then what am I supposed to do?" His voice was hoarse, raw from the lingering pain of their intrusion into his mind. "I came here because I believed you could help us. That you would help us. You owe Olympus more than silence."

The whispers stirred again, an uneasy, shifting presence around him. "Owe?" The word twisted in the air, as if being weighed, dissected. "You do not understand the prison we exist in."

Darien clenched his fists, forcing himself to stand, even as his body trembled from the aftershocks of their presence. "Then help me understand."

A longer silence. Then, for the first time, the voice hesitated. "We remember a name like his."

The air shifted, the cold pressing against him like unseen hands. "Leave. This Cycle has already turned beyond what we foresaw. Your presence disrupts it further. We must watch. We must listen."

Darien swallowed hard, gripping his torch as he backed away. "You said you'd join us when you find a way out. Don't forget that."

"We do not forget."

A deep, shuddering rumble shook the cavern as the massive stone blocking the entrance slowly slid aside.

Darien hesitated one last time, staring into the darkness that still loomed behind him. Out of ideas, and not wanting to push his luck more than he had already, he turned and stepped into the open night air. The cold wind hit his face like a slap, and the weight in his chest only deepened as he made his way back to Evatra and the dying firelight waiting beyond the trees.

Outside, the night air felt colder than before, as if the cave had leached the warmth from his body along with whatever fragile hope he had carried in. The two moons of Olympus hung low in the sky, casting an eerie glow over the jagged cliffs. Darien guessed it had been at least six hours since he and Evatra had parted, though it felt like much longer. His muscles were weak from the wraiths' assault, his body trembling as he made his way down the winding mountain path. Every step sent fresh pain lancing through his limbs, but he pressed on.

He finally spotted a faint light ahead—Evatra's campfire. She had stayed behind, waiting for him, just as she had promised. The sight of it sent a strange mix of relief and shame washing over him. He had gone in search of salvation and returned empty-handed.

Evatra must have heard his approach because she turned sharply, her hand already drifting toward the hilt of her dagger. The moment she saw him, her features softened, and she rushed forward, catching him by the arm just as his legs nearly gave out beneath him.

"You're freezing," she muttered, her brow creasing. "What happened?"

Darien let out a shaky breath, allowing her to guide him the last few steps to the fire. He sank down beside it, stretching his hands toward the flames, though their warmth barely reached the deep cold settled inside him.

"I failed," he admitted, his voice barely above a whisper.

Evatra's eyes widened. "Failed? But how? The wraith promised—"

"That wraith wasn't there," Darien said, shaking his head wearily. "They examined my memories, and... they were thorough. They agreed to help us, but—"

Evatra gripped his hands in hers, her touch grounding. "But you got them to agree to help!"

Darien took a deep breath, closing his eyes for a moment before speaking again. "They don't know how to leave the caves. Not without possessing someone. I can't think of anyone who would willingly let a wraith use their body, can you?"

Evatra released his hands slowly, the weight of his words settling between them. "No," she said softly, her shoulders sagging in resignation. "No, I can't."

They sat in silence for a long moment; the fire crackling between them. It was the only sound, save for the occasional gust of wind rolling through the mountains. Darien stared into the flames, watching the embers flicker and fade.

"They asked about my teacher," he said suddenly.

Evatra turned her head slightly, frowning. "What?"

"The wraiths," Darien murmured. "When they searched my mind, they lingered on him longer than anyone else. And then they asked about him." He hesitated. "It seemed like more than just curiosity."

Evatra's brow furrowed. "Why would they care about an instructor from your world?"

Darien let out a bitter laugh, shaking his head. "I asked them the same thing. They didn't really explain.'"

Evatra was quiet for a moment before leaning back against her pack. "That's cryptic."

"Yeah," Darien muttered. He didn't like it.

Evatra shifted, watching him carefully. "You look like you're trying to solve a puzzle with half the pieces missing."

"That's what it feels like," Darien admitted. "But I don't think we have time to figure it out."

Evatra sighed. "Then I guess we focus on what we can do."

Darien nodded. He was exhausted, his mind barely holding on, but one thing was clear—the wraiths were not their answer. At least, not yet.

After a moment, Evatra reached out and gently cupped his face in her hands, her fingers cool against his skin. Darien barely had time to process it before she leaned forward, pressing her lips to his in a soft, lingering kiss. It wasn't desperate or hurried—just a quiet, personal moment in the middle of everything unraveling around them.

When she pulled away, she studied him, searching for something in his face. Darien exhaled, still caught in the moment, still trying to understand what it meant.

"Why did you—"

"Because I wanted to," Evatra interrupted simply, but there was something guarded in her eyes. "And because tomorrow, we go back to war."

Darien nodded slowly. He didn't know what this meant for them. Maybe neither of them did. But he did know one thing: they were out of time.

Evatra turned away, settling onto her bedroll, and Darien followed suit. The fire burned low, casting long shadows over the rocky ground. He closed his eyes, listening to the wind.

"Well then," Evatra murmured, barely audible over the crackling embers. "I guess we go back?"

Darien nodded, taking another drink of water, avoiding her eyes. "We go back. And we hope that Farkland Reach and the centaurs will be enough."

Chapter 20: The Duel

The journey back north felt longer than the ride south. The adrenaline that had pushed them forward before had faded, leaving only exhaustion in its place. Darien and Evatra rode at a steady pace, their horses slower now, the wear of travel clear in their movements. Even the animals seemed to understand the weight of failure that clung to their riders.

Darien was grateful for the slower pace. His body still ached from the wraiths' intrusion, his muscles sluggish, his thoughts heavier than they should be. Whatever the wraiths had done to him, it lingered. It wasn't like before. This time, it was as though something had been taken from him—some part of himself stripped away, leaving him exposed.

They traveled in silence, avoiding the topic neither of them wanted to discuss. The kiss. It had been unspoken between them since that night, a moment neither had acknowledged. Darien wasn't sure if it had meant something or if it had simply been a moment stolen in the face of uncertainty. Either way, neither of them seemed ready to face it.

After several hours of quiet, Evatra finally broke the silence.

"Are you sure one of them didn't stick around in your head like last time?" she asked, her voice level but edged with curiosity.

"No, you know when they're there," Darien replied, rubbing the weariness from his eyes. "It's like knowing there's a dream you want to remember, but you can't recall the exact details once you wake up. I'm just tired. I'll be fine."

Evatra didn't respond, but she didn't look convinced either.

They continued on, the land passing by in a blur of ashen fields and jagged ridges. The weight of what lay ahead was heavier than either of them admitted. They were returning empty-handed.

Cyprin's army was only five days from Farkland Reach. Even at their best speed, they would arrive in three. That left them barely enough time to prepare for the battle before it began.

Darien tried to distract himself. Though he had fought before, had bloodied his hands in combat, he had never stood in an open war. The thought of it filled him with a creeping terror he couldn't quite suppress. It wasn't the death that frightened him—it was what would be left if they lost.

That night, they ate in near silence, the fire between them offering only the illusion of warmth. Darien told Evatra more about Earth—about his life before Olympus, about the Academy, about how war had become nothing but history in his world. She listened, intrigued, asking more than a few questions about battles long forgotten by his people. He gave her the best answers he could, though history had never been his strongest subject.

The next morning, Darien woke with a renewed sense of urgency. "We need to push harder today," he told Evatra. "We can't afford to waste time."

She didn't argue. They rode with more determination, but even so, by midday, Evatra suddenly slowed her horse, eyes scanning the ground ahead.

"Wait here," she ordered, dismounting.

Darien pulled on the reins of his horse, watching as she moved carefully across the trail. She studied the earth intently, moving in slow circles, scanning for something he couldn't see.

"What is it?" Darien asked, impatience creeping into his tone.

"Tracks. Marauder Tracks," Evatra said, her voice tight with focus. She crouched low, brushing her fingers across the dirt.

Darien, growing increasingly frustrated with the delay, pressed again. "Why would they have come through here?"

Evatra waved him off, still concentrating. "I don't know. Last I knew, they were heading down the eastern coast toward Veritrium. But they must have changed direction after we left." She pointed westward. "They came this way right after we left."

Darien's heart began to race. "We have to go get them!" His mind was already moving ahead, new possibilities forming.

"Huh?" Evatra blinked, caught off guard by his sudden excitement.

"Think about it! If anyone can help us fight Cyprin's army, it's the marauders. Can you think of anyone better suited for this job?" Darien's voice took on a note of urgency. "Besides, Totra-Dal promised me before we left. If I ever asked, he'd help. We have to go to him."

Evatra's face shifted, worry creeping into her eyes. "I don't want Atreya to go to Farkland Reach," she murmured. "If Totra-Dal helps us, he'll send everyone there."

Darien thought for a few seconds before an idea hit him. He knew he had to sell it to her.

"What if not everyone goes?" Darien suggested. "The wagons are too slow to make it to the city before Cyprin's army does. Totra-Dal can send the bulk of the marauders with us. The rest can follow a few days later, after the battle is either won or lost."

Evatra stood still for several heartbeats, considering his words. Finally, she sighed, nodding reluctantly. "You're right," she said, though doubt still lingered in her eyes.

Darien thanked her, and together they rode west, following the tracks left by the marauders. By the end of the day, Darien spotted the caravan and, as night fell, they were almost upon it.

The sky had deepened into an ink-black canvas by the time they neared the camp, the only light coming from the scattered fires flickering like distant beacons. Smoke coiled lazily into the air, mingling with the earthy scent of dampened soil and the unmistakable tang of sweat and cooked meat. The landscape ahead pulsed with the quiet energy of an army at rest—a temporary stillness before inevitable chaos.

Darien and Evatra slowed their pace, their horses' labored breaths echoing their own exhaustion. Their mounts moved sluggishly, muscles tight from the relentless pace they had kept. Even the animals seemed to recognize the weight of the moment, stepping hesitantly as though they knew they were no longer in neutral territory.

Closer now, Darien saw movement—figures hunched over grindstones, sharpening weapons; others tending to battered armor. Fires flickered against weatherworn faces, casting shifting shadows over the hardened expressions of marauders who had spent their lives surviving on the fringes. They weren't soldiers. They weren't disciplined. But they were dangerous.

As they approached the perimeter, a sharp voice rang out. "Ho there! Turn back, you'll find nothing but trouble."

Darien's grip on the reins tightened, his body already reacting before his mind caught up. He recognized that voice. "Drack?"

A pause. Then, out of the firelight, a figure stepped forward. Torchlight illuminated a familiar, rugged face lined with years of rough living. Drack's eyes flicked between Darien and Evatra, his expression unreadable before breaking into a smirk. "Evatra? Darien? What in the depths are you two doing here? Thought we'd never see you again. Didn't you have a grand journey to finish?"

Evatra rode forward, her posture tense, unreadable. "We need to speak with Totra-Dal. It's urgent."

Drack studied her for a beat longer than necessary, then sighed, waving them through. "You'd better be quick. He's got his hands full tonight."

As they rode into the camp, Darien felt the weight of stares. Some were familiar faces, others were strangers, but they all carried the same expression—suspicion. Recognition. Unease. The further they rode, the more the camp unfolded before them—rows of wagons, tattered tents, the scent of burning wood thick in the air. This wasn't just a camp. This was a gathering before something bigger.

The walled-off section near the center stood out. That was where Totra-Dal would be. Two guards flanked the entrance, their hands resting on their weapons, watching as Evatra and Darien dismounted. They didn't speak, didn't need to. One of them nodded, stepping aside.

Inside, Totra-Dal's gruff voice carried through the tent. "I couldn't give two boar tusks about that. Just keep the peace out there. If you can't keep your group in line—"

He stopped mid-sentence, his sharp gaze snapping toward them, his face unreadable in the firelight.

"Evatra! What's going on? What took you so long? Darien, what are you doing here?"

Darien forced a smile despite the tension weighing on the room. "Hello, Totra-Dal. I've come to collect on the promise you made."

Totra-Dal's brow furrowed. "Promise? What promise?"

Darien stepped forward. "The one you made, that if I ever came asking, you'd help."

The low murmur in the tent stilled. Several marauders exchanged glances, their eyes flitting between Totra-Dal and Darien.

"Help?" a sneering voice cut through before Totra-Dal could respond. "What is he talking about?"

Darien stiffened before he even turned. He knew that voice. Kort. The goblin sauntered forward, arms crossed over his chest, his ever-present smirk stretching across his face.

Darien ignored him, focusing on Totra-Dal. "Farkland Reach is in danger. The King is dead. Cyprin has raised an army, and it's nearly at the city's gates. I need your help."

A murmur rippled through the camp. Darien could feel the shift in energy, the undercurrent of something unspoken among the gathered marauders. But Kort only laughed, shaking his head. "What's Farkland Reach to us? Let the Eldric handle it. We're not their soldiers."

Evatra's head snapped toward him. "You don't understand, Kort! This isn't just another war. This isn't another kingdom falling, or a city changing hands. If Cyprin wins, there won't be a world left to fight over."

Kort scoffed. "I'll not fight for anyone but myself."

Totra-Dal exhaled, rubbing a hand over his face before finally speaking. "We're taking the marauders north. We'll ride for Farkland Reach."

Kort's face twisted in fury. "You'll do what you want, but I'm not going."

Totra-Dal's patience thinned. "Then stay here with the children and tend to them."

The insult landed like a slap. Kort didn't hesitate.

With a swift motion, he lunged, drawing a dagger from his belt and driving it deep into Totra-Dal's back.

Chaos erupted.

Evatra and Darien both shouted as Totra-Dal staggered forward, clutching at the wound. The gathered marauders leapt to their feet, hands on weapons, but Kort was already moving, his dagger glistening in the firelight.

Darien barely had time to react before Kort was on him. The fight was immediate, brutal, and exhausting.

Kort was fast—faster than Darien expected. His strikes came sharp and relentless, forcing Darien on the defensive. But Darien was tired. Slower than he should be. The fight in the cave, the days of travel, the sleepless nights—they all crashed down on him at once.

Steel rang against steel, the sound filling the air as they circled each other. Kort's smirk was gone, replaced with something cold, something real. He was fighting to kill.

Darien shifted, trying to predict the goblin's movements. Kort was smaller, more agile—he needed to turn that against him. But before he could fully form a plan, Kort feinted left, then struck low.

Darien saw it too late. The goblin's blade flicked out, knocking Darien's sword from his grip. Panic surged.

Darien lunged, grabbing for Kort's wrist, dragging them both down into the dirt. They rolled, fists connecting in frantic blows, neither of them able to reach their weapons.

Kort twisted, managing to get the upper hand, his dagger hovering inches from Darien's throat. Darien's muscles screamed in protest, but he pushed back, forcing all his weight into Kort's arm.

The blade shifted—

And then it sank deep into Kort's own chest.

For a moment, neither of them moved. Kort's eyes widened, his lips parting in shock.

"You think you've won?" Kort's final words were spoken so silently that only Darien heard them.

Then he slumped, the firelight flickering over his still form.

Darien gasped for air, rolling off him, hands shaking as he pushed himself up. His heart thundered. His body ached. But he was alive.

The camp had fallen into silence after the fight, but the weight of the moment had not lifted. The only sound was the distant crackle of flames and the muffled voices of marauders speaking in hushed tones beyond the firelight. Kort's body lay motionless, his own dagger buried in his chest, his lifeless eyes reflecting the flickering light. The dirt beneath him was dark and wet with blood, soaking into the earth.

Darien's breath was still ragged, his arms trembling from the sheer effort it had taken to survive. He wasn't sure if it was exhaustion or shock that left him feeling numb, but the reality of what had happened was slowly sinking in. He had killed Kort.

Evatra knelt beside Totra-Dal, her hands pressed firmly against the wound in his back. His breathing was shallow, his massive frame unnaturally still. The surrounding marauders watched, their faces unreadable, their eyes darting between Darien and Evatra, waiting.

One of the older marauders finally spoke, his voice rough. "By rite of combat, leadership passed to Kort when he struck Totra-Dal. Until he lived or died, Kort was in command." He looked down at the body, his expression unreadable. "And now that you've killed him, Darien... the right of leadership falls to you."

The words rang in Darien's ears, but he barely registered them. He felt the weight of every eye on him, the quiet expectation of the marauders waiting for his response. He swallowed hard, his exhaustion momentarily forgotten.

"No," he said firmly, shaking his head. "I can't lead you."

The murmurs in the crowd grew louder. Some looked confused, others irritated.

Evatra finally stood, her face unreadable. "If you don't, someone else will. And that someone won't take you to Farkland Reach. They won't care about your fight. They'll care about power."

Darien turned to her, desperate. "Then it has to be you."

Evatra's expression hardened. "No. I can't."

"You can," Darien countered, stepping closer. "You know these people. You understand them. You can lead them. I can't."

She looked away, jaw tightening. "You think they'll follow me? After I left them?"

Darien exhaled sharply, frustrated. "Evatra, you're the only one who can do this. I don't know their ways. I don't know their rules. And if I try to lead them, we all lose."

A heavy silence stretched between them. The marauders watched, waiting for a decision. Totra-Dal remained unconscious, his breathing shallow but steady, as the Scillans worked quietly to stabilize him.

One of the older marauders, a grizzled man with deep scars across his arms, stepped forward. "You know how this works, Evatra. Totra-Dal won't wake for days, maybe longer. Leadership has passed. If you don't take it, someone else will."

She turned away sharply, exhaling through her nose, trying to contain her emotions.

"They need you," Darien pressed. "Farkland Reach needs you. Olympus needs you. And Atreya—she needs a world where she can be safe. That won't happen if Cyprin wins."

Evatra closed her eyes briefly, then turned back to the waiting marauders. She scanned their faces, reading their expressions. Some skeptical, some wary, some waiting for her to prove herself.

Finally, she inhaled deeply and squared her shoulders. "Gather everyone. We're calling a meeting."

Her words stirred the camp, whispers growing into movement as the call spread. The marauders gathered near the fire, some standing, some sitting on overturned crates, all of them watching Evatra expectantly. Deep shadows, cast by the firelight, obscured their faces, highlighting the uncertainty in their eyes.

She took a breath and stepped forward, her gaze sweeping over the gathered marauders. "Kort betrayed us all," she began, her voice steady but carrying the weight of anger. "He struck down Totra-Dal, not for our survival, not for the good of the camp, but for his own ambition. And in doing so, he challenged for leadership. By our own laws, he was in command until he either proved himself worthy or fell. And tonight, he fell. Darien avenged Totra-Dal's attack, and by rite, leadership passed to him."

A murmur rippled through the crowd, some nodding in agreement, others exchanging uncertain glances.

Evatra exhaled slowly, steadying herself before continuing. "But Darien is not one of us. He is not a marauder, and he never will be. His destiny lies in something greater. He knows that, and I know that. And that's why he has given that right to me. I will lead us." She paused, letting the weight of her words sink in. "Not back to the life we had, but forward—to something greater."

The murmurs grew louder. Some nodded. Others remained motionless. She continued.

"We have a choice. We can keep running, keep raid-ing, keep living as shadows on the edge of the world. Or we can stand. We can fight. Not as thieves. Not as ma-rauders. But as something more."

A hush fell over the group.

"Farkland Reach is about to face an army unlike any-thing we've ever seen. If we don't stop them, the world we know is gone. Everything. Gone. Our way of life, our freedom, our families—all of it. Cyprin doesn't care who we are or what we've done. He'll burn it all. Unless we stop him."

She took a step forward, her voice steady. "I'm not asking you to be heroes. I'm asking you to survive. And the only way we do that is by fighting."

Another silence stretched out. Then, slowly, one voice called out.

"What would you have us do?"

Evatra straightened. "We ride for Farkland Reach. We take the fight to Cyprin's army before they take it to us. We stop being ghosts and become warriors. We become the ones who stand when no one else will."

Another pause. Then, a low murmur of agreement. It grew, voices joining together, the energy shifting from uncertainty to something sharper—something deter-mined.

Evatra nodded. "Then we ride. At first light, we ride."

The murmurs turned to shouts of agreement. Weapons were drawn, fists were raised. Evatra looked at Darien and he gave her an encouraging smile. The fate of the marauders was now in her hands.

They turned back to the rest of the camp, the rest of their journey ahead uncertain, but one thing was clear: they weren't returning to Farkland Reach empty-handed.

Chapter 21: The Enemy

The march north was relentless. Driven by urgency, the marauders rode, their horses strained to the limit, riders hardened by years of surviving on the world's edges. The wind carried the scent of damp earth and the distant promise of war, mingling with the sweat of exhaustion that clung to them all.

Darien felt every mile in his bones. The wraiths had left him drained, his body sluggish, his mind clouded with lingering unease. Evatra rode beside him, her expression unreadable, her gaze always fixed ahead. The unspoken tension between them stretched thin, fragile but unbroken. They had no time for words that wouldn't change what lay ahead.

The horizon darkened as they approached Farkland Reach. Smoke curled from the city's chimneys, torches lining the battlements like watchful eyes. As they neared, a scouting party rode out to meet them. At its head, clad in polished mail that gleamed under the fading sun, was Chorrun.

"Darien!" the centaur called, his voice carrying over the open field.

Darien raised an arm in greeting before sweeping it behind him, gesturing toward the riders at his back. "We brought help."

Chorrun's gaze flicked over the assembled marauders, his expression shifting from relief to hesitation. It was one thing to accept ragged bands of volunteers—another to welcome the very people his kind had spent centuries defending their lands against.

"Is the city ready for battle?" Darien asked, his eyes locking onto the centaur's armor, the chainmail draped over his torso flowing seamlessly into the protective plating on his back. He had never seen Chorrun fully armored before.

Chorrun exhaled sharply. "Almost. Your timing couldn't be more perfect. The enemy is less than a day away from our outer defenses. We expect them tomorrow afternoon."

Evatra shifted in her saddle, her fingers tightening around the reins. "So soon."

Chorrun nodded grimly before his gaze slid past Darien to the marauders behind them. He hesitated, then asked, "Are those…?"

Darien had nearly forgotten. When they left the castle, they had been searching for the wraiths. "No, that didn't go as planned. These are the marauders."

Chorrun's expression darkened slightly, his posture stiffening. This wasn't the kind of reinforcement he had hoped for.

"They're here to fight with us, Chorrun," Evatra reassured him, a smirk tugging at her lips. "Don't look so frightened."

Chorrun huffed, shaking his head. "I suppose you have another story to tell, then?"

Darien forced a smile, though tension coiled in his chest. "You won't believe this one," he admitted. "Or maybe you will. Who knows what to believe anymore?"

The group rode on, pushing past Chorrun's questions for the time being. The centaur eventually relented, instead filling them in on the final preparations.

"It sounds like we might just have a shot, then?" Evatra asked, hope edging her voice.

Chorrun's expression remained grim. "Based on our scouting reports, Cyprin's forces outnumber us four to one."

Darien swallowed. Four to one.

Chorrun continued. "However, it doesn't appear that Cyprin himself is among them. If he were, we wouldn't stand a chance. The only question is whether or not he's imbued any of his soldiers with magic. That's what we suspect happened with Tahmer."

That didn't bring him much comfort. If Cyprin had given any of his soldiers magic, even a handful, their already overwhelming numbers would become an unstoppable tide.

When they reached the city gates, Chorrun turned to Evatra.

"The best place for the marauders would be alongside the forces stationed at the eastern gates," he suggested. "Give them some space, though. They won't look favorably on marauders near their city."

Evatra rolled her eyes. "We're not here to steal anything, Chorrun."

"You know that, and I might even believe it," Chorrun replied with a wry smile. "But that doesn't mean they will."

Evatra led the riders toward their assigned position, though not before casting a glance over her shoulder at Darien. Chorrun noticed but said nothing.

Inside the city, Darien and Chorrun made their way through the castle, up to the council chamber. Marenya and Oratrin were there, the room dimly lit by the evening sun filtering through narrow windows. Marenya greeted them both, eager for news, but agreed to wait until Rist arrived before beginning.

A servant brought food, which Darien gratefully accepted. He ate without hesitation, barely tasting the meal, realizing he no longer cared what it was. He wasn't going to be getting food from home anytime soon—he had to adapt.

When Evatra entered, she wordlessly sat across from him. Without a second thought, Darien slid the rest of his food toward her. She hesitated only briefly before taking it, eating with the same quiet urgency.

Good thing I was finished.

By the time Rist arrived, apologizing for his lateness, Darien was already bracing himself for the conversation ahead. No one asked where the hooded figure had been—no one really wanted to know.

Darien finally recounted everything. The failed attempt with the wraiths. The decision to seek out the marauders. The attack on Totra-Dal. Kort's betrayal. The duel. Evatra's rise to leadership.

He carefully omitted anything personal between him and Evatra—that part of the story was only theirs.

Marenya listened, shaking her head. "Master Darien," she murmured, "adventure follows you wherever you go. I wish I could say I'm not disappointed about the wraiths, but their aid was never a certainty. What you have brought us, however, is an army. For that, you have my thanks."

She turned to Evatra. "How do you think it best to use them in the coming battle?"

Talk turned to war plans. Darien and Evatra were briefed on the final defenses, the enemy's expected movements, and where they themselves would be stationed. They were too valuable to be lost early in the fight. Their role wasn't to be in the thick of battle—it was to survive.

The conversation stretched late into the evening. When they were dismissed, Darien expected to speak with Evatra, but she left before he had the chance, choosing to spend the night with her people.

Darien tried to sleep, but rest eluded him. Every time he closed his eyes, he saw the enemy marching. Saw hulking figures clad in black armor. Felt the impact of steel against steel, the weight of an enemy blade bearing down on him.

He woke several times, reaching for a sword that wasn't there.

Finally, as dawn approached, he gave up. There was no use pretending anymore.

Dressing quickly, he opened his door to find a pile of armor waiting for him—a gift from the Queen. A note sat atop it, but he couldn't read it. Still, the message was clear.

He examined the craftsmanship. The armor was perfect, measured precisely to his frame, its design both elegant and lethal. He ran his fingers over the crest of Farkland Reach emblazoned on the shield, letting the weight of it settle.

When Darien was fully armored, he pulled himself in front of the mirror and examined the image. He thought he looked silly, but trying to look past that, he supposed he looked somewhat fierce. The perimeter of the helm surrounding his face was engraved in the shape of a falcon, making him look pointed and severe. Darien decided to stop watching himself in the mirror and find where he was to be stationed. Exiting the room, he found his way back to the castle doors, by memory this time, and made his way toward the eastern walls. Climbing to the top, he was astonished by what he saw.

The ramparts under construction when he left had since doubled in number, and the spiked branches of the trees had more than tripled. Soldiers in various different armors milled about below, all of it matching the quality of the armor he wore himself. Their weapons were of equally high quality, outstripping even his own sword. For a peaceful people, they made perfectly crafted tools of war. When offered one of the troll blades, he had declined. This sword was his last link to home. He wouldn't use anything else.

The trolls made up the bulk of the force, with the odd goblin or other race mixed in among their number. Every man of fighting age had been asked, though not pressed, into service. All of the citizens who had refrained from volunteering to defend the city were ordered into the medical wings to care for soldiers who would be wounded during the fighting. The only exceptions were mothers of young children, those expecting a child, and the children themselves.

Those of this last group were given the option of staying in the city or being escorted by a small group through the mountain passes. The group that had left had been sent along with official notes from Queen Marenya, detailing their plight and asking that the surrounding cities send what aid they could should Farkland Reach stave off the oncoming army. At the northern end of the force amassed before him, he saw the centaurs—maybe two hundred in number. He saw Chorrun walking among his people, stopping to talk with them every few moments. A few of them wore armor similar to Chorrun's—finely woven mail and arm guards similar to Darien's own vambraces—but most were in simple leather armor, as it befitted their natural way of life in the forests. To the south, Darien saw the marauders, seemingly unorganized, but something about their movements suggested order amidst the chaos. Looking out on the horizon, Darien could make out a black line, the first he had spotted of the enemy soldiers. He couldn't discern much detail, but he could see them marching forward.

Darien climbed down from the wall, his boots striking the stone with a hollow finality. The city hummed with nervous energy, an undercurrent of tension threading through the streets. The scent of damp earth, sweat, and the acrid tang of oil filled the air. Somewhere, the rhythmic clang of hammer against steel rang out, final adjustments being made to weapons that would taste blood before the sun set again. Fires burned low in the forges, their embers dancing against the pre-dawn darkness. The mood in the streets was somber as he walked toward the eastern gates, and once outside, he turned north to find Chorrun.

As he entered the camp, he saw Jodin and Lotry, both of whom nodded as he passed. Darien returned the greeting, but then he saw someone he hadn't expected.

"Torin?!" Darien exclaimed, incredulously. "What are you doing here?"

Torin looked up in surprise.

"Oh, Darien! It's good to see you!" the young centaur called back.

The two shook hands and embraced, one arm over the other's shoulder, their hands squeezing.

"It's good to see you, too. But what are you doing here?" Darien asked, still surprised to see the young centaur. "Shouldn't you be back in Taitron?"

"No," Torin shook his head, his expression turning serious. "They needed everyone they could get here, and I wasn't turning away. I'm here to fight with you and everyone else."

Darien examined the young centaur's armor. It was sparse, hardly even armor at all—nothing more than a leather covering to protect his chest from the elements.

"Listen," Darien began carefully, "you could get killed out there, and you don't have much to protect you. Do me a favor, okay? Stay back and fight with a bow. Find cover and shoot from there. Anything else, and you'll just make yourself a target, understand?"

"But—"

"'But nothing,'" Darien cut into Torin's protest. "I'm going to talk to Chorrun about it, too. Please, don't argue—just do as I say."

Darien felt himself slipping back into his role as a leader. He supposed it was probably the best mindset for the day ahead. Chaos would likely spread through the ranks, and calm, composed voices would be a rare commodity.

"Fine," Torin said sullenly.

"Listen," Darien said, his voice full of genuine concern, "I want you to survive this. That's all. I don't doubt your heart or your abilities, but this is your first time in something like this, and you're young. You don't need it to be your last day."

"Thanks, Darien. I appreciate it," Torin said, his mood lifting slightly.

Darien slapped Torin's shoulder and moved on to speak with Chorrun. The elder centaur was busy coordinating their plan of attack. Darien stood back, listening as Chorrun addressed the leaders of the various groups. When Chorrun finished, he turned and spotted Darien for the first time.

"Oh, Darien. I didn't see you there. Can I do something for you?"

"Nothing really, I'm just wandering back and forth, killing time," Darien answered, grimacing at his choice of words. "Listen, I want to talk to you about Torin."

Darien explained his desire to protect the young centaur. Chorrun eyed him curiously, and Darien thought he might refuse, but he agreed. Darien thanked him and made his way toward the marauders to find Evatra. He wandered through their camp for several minutes, nodding at those who greeted him. But Darien couldn't find her, and no one seemed to know where she might be. Deciding he'd find her later, Darien turned toward the barracks when a shadow peeled away from the wall. He froze, fingers twitching toward his sword, but the movement was fluid, familiar.

"You look like a man about to walk into his own funeral," Garik's voice was smooth, touched with amusement. Darien turned to see the rogue standing there, arms folded, his ever-present smirk in place. But something was different. Garik looked tired. Not physically—he moved with the same coiled ease as always—but there was something darker beneath his usual bravado.

"Maybe I am. Where the hell have you been?" Darien asked, his eyes narrowing.

Garik chuckled, stepping forward. The smell of blood clung to him. Not fresh, but not old either. "Working. Preparing. Ensuring that when this starts, our enemies will already be fewer."

Darien frowned. "What does that mean?"

Garik tilted his head, his smirk widening. "It means, my dear friend, that I've been out among the shadows. Let's just say... not all of Cyprin's spies made it back to him."

Darien stiffened. "You've been hunting them?"

Garik shrugged. "Hunting is such a vulgar word. I prefer cleaning up loose ends. Farkland Reach has enough to worry about without traitors feeding the enemy information."

Darien let out a slow breath. "How many?"

Garik's smile didn't waver. "Enough."

His gloved hand drifted to his belt, where an unusual weapon hung. A pair of curved, narrow blades, their hilts bound in dark leather, rested against his hip. The metal gleamed with an unnatural black sheen. They looked too thin to be practical, yet something about them was undeniably lethal.

Darien gestured at them. "New?"

Garik unsheathed one effortlessly, twirling it in his fingers. "I had them made before you left. A little something special, forged with obsidian dust and troll steel—quick, light, deadly. They call them Theron's Fangs, named after a story from long ago. It's said that a powerful man, Theron, punished those who walked the world when they shouldn't have. Seems fitting, doesn't it?"

Darien swallowed. Garik had been busy.

"And where were you planning to be during the battle?" Darien asked, watching as Garik spun the blade between his fingers with practiced ease.

Garik sheathed the weapon and dusted off his hands. "Oh, don't worry about me. I'll be exactly where I'm needed. And when the time comes, the enemy won't even know I was there."

Darien wasn't sure if that was reassuring or terrifying. Something in the way Garik talked always left him uneasy. He decided to perform his sword forms just to make sure he still had full range of motion.

Darien ducked into a secluded courtyard inside the walls of Fenway Castle, letting the weight of his armor settle into his body. He exhaled, drawing his sword in a slow, deliberate motion. The blade caught the torchlight, gleaming with a sharp finality. The courtyard smelled of damp stone and oil, the whispers of past warriors lingering in the stillness. He let memory take over, his body effortlessly flowing from one position to the next, just as he had when he last practiced in Taitron. He decided then that he would have to continue his discipline to maintain his skill. Assuming he survived the battle, Darien resolved to keep up his routine at least three times a week, as he had back at The Academy.

Satisfied, Darien made his way back toward the gates, climbing to the walkway above the giant wooden doors. He waited, sitting on the edge of the city's gates. There wasn't much left to do for the time being. The wait was excruciating. Darien thought he would welcome the battle when it finally arrived—anything to break the monotony. No, he wouldn't. That wasn't a good place for his mind to go.

Darien stood atop the eastern walls of Farkland Reach, his fingers gripping the stone parapet as the cold wind curled around him. The sky had shifted into a bruised palette of purples and grays, the last vestiges of daylight being swallowed by the encroaching night. He should have been used to the waiting by now, but it gnawed at him, stretched the tension in his muscles tighter with every passing second. The weight of his armor pressed against his shoulders, a constant reminder of the role he had stepped into—one he had never asked for.

He forced himself to focus, letting his eyes drift over the battlefield. Below, the last of the preparations were being finalized. Soldiers moved like pieces on a well-rehearsed board, their formations set, their nerves barely concealed beneath forced expressions of resolve. Fires crackled, casting flickering shadows against the sharpened stakes lining the trenches. The air was thick with the scent of damp soil, burning pitch, and sweat.

A voice sliced through the quiet. "Are you ready?"

Rist's presence still had the uncanny ability to make the hair on Darien's arms stand on end. Even now, knowing him as well as he did, there was something unsettling about the man—or whatever he was.

Darien exhaled slowly. "As best as I can be," he admitted. "Are our guard units in position?"

Rist inclined his head, the hood casting his face in deeper shadow. "Waiting just behind the outer barricades. Oratrin handpicked them. If nothing else, they'll hold the line."

They fell into silence, the weight of what was coming settling between them. Darien shifted his grip along the stone, his fingers tingling from the cold.

"How much longer?" he asked, trying to sound unaffected.

Rist tilted his head, his gaze drifting toward the horizon. "More than an hour, less than two. They're moving slowly, letting the dread sink in." His voice carried something between amusement and calculation, like he was observing an inevitable conclusion rather than preparing to fight for his life.

Another stretch of silence. Then Rist turned to him, his voice softer this time. "Do you think we'll win?"

Darien considered the question, his mind drifting to the past days—to Aren, to Atreya, to the people at Velmark and their festivals, to every life that hung in the balance. He thought of the men and women in the city below, sharpening blades, donning armor, saying quiet goodbyes to their loved ones.

The wind shifted, carrying with it a distant sound—a rhythmic, measured thunder.

Rist turned his head slightly, listening. "They're closer."

Darien followed his gaze. Far along the horizon, the dark tide was approaching. At this distance, they were a smudge against the land, an inky mass of moving shapes, unnatural in their unity.

His stomach twisted. They were too many.

His fingers curled into a fist against the stone. Was this what the first war had felt like? Knowing the enemy was coming, knowing their numbers, yet standing against them anyway?

Behind him, the city was eerily quiet. They had all seen it. And they knew.

"They're waiting for something," Darien murmured.

"A signal," Rist corrected. "They won't break into a charge until the order is given."

Darien forced himself to breathe through the tension building in his chest. "Then let's not waste time."

Rist's tone changed into something that gave his voice the sound of a smirk. "Would you like to let Cyprin's army know, or should I?"

Darien actually laughed—harder than he had in days. It bubbled up unexpectedly, spilling over before he could contain it. It was too much, too absurd. He clutched the parapet, trying to steady himself, but the laughter just kept coming, wild and unrestrained.

Rist simply watched, amused.

Darien finally wiped at his eyes, the laughter fading into something else—a resolve he hadn't expected. "Thanks, Rist. I needed that." He straightened, rolling his shoulders. "Come on. Let's go meet our babysitters."

They descended from the wall, moving toward the soldiers waiting at their positions. The groups assigned to Darien and Rist were hand-picked by Oratrin—five trolls per unit, their armor reinforced, their expressions grim. These weren't common foot soldiers. These were the best Farkland Reach had to offer, warriors chosen for their skill and resolve.

Darien exchanged nods with the captain of his guard before taking his place at the rightmost flank. Rist positioned himself on the opposite side. From this vantage point, Darien could see everything. The city behind them, the soldiers waiting, the battalions prepared to meet the enemy head-on.

And the enemy itself.

The dark army had finally emerged in full view. They moved in near-perfect unison, black-clad figures stretching as far as the eye could see. Their armor was seamless, their movements unnatural. Where their armor parted, glimpses of shadow-touched flesh peeked through— dark skin stretched over sinewy limbs, tufts of black hair jutting out at unnatural angles.

Darien scanned their ranks, noting the strange, grotesque variations among them. Some had elongated, angular faces, features twisted into something nearly human but not quite. Others bore the hooked noses of goblins, but their proportions were wrong, stretched too tall, too thin. Some had cyclopean eyes glaring forward, unblinking, as if seeing something beyond the battlefield itself.

Darien stared at the twisted forms in front of them, nearly identical to the ones he and Evatra had faced down during their raid.

He let out a slow breath. "Being imprisoned for three thousand years has to take a toll on you, I guess."

The dark humor wasn't lost on his guard, but it didn't lessen the tension in the air.

Darien's mind whirled. These weren't just soldiers. They were remnants. The last surviving members of Cyprin's forces, twisted by time and imprisonment. This wasn't a new army—it was an old one, waiting for its revenge.

A horn blast shattered the silence.

Darien barely had time to react before the enemy surged forward, a wall of black metal and glinting weapons, rushing toward the gates with a deafening roar.

The battle had begun.

Chapter 22: The Promise

The sun dipped low behind the jagged peaks beyond Farkland Reach, casting a golden glow over the battlefield. The light danced off thousands of armored figures, a sea of gleaming steel and dark banners rippling under the wind.

The enemy surged forward, a tide of shadows rushing toward the city walls. The ground quivered beneath their charge, a rhythmic drumbeat of boots and hooves thundering against the earth. A moment later, another horn answered—this one from the defenders of Farkland Reach. It was not a call of fear, but of defiance.

"Archers, nock!"

Oratrin's voice rang over the walls, sharp as steel. Hundreds of bows rose as one, string pulled taut, waiting. The breath of the battlefield held for one more instant.

"Loose!"

A wave of arrows soared through the sky, their black tips vanishing into the deepening dusk. The front lines of the enemy faltered as the deadly rain struck home. A second volley followed, then a third. But the dark army did not slow. They climbed over their fallen, undeterred, pressing forward like a storm tide crashing against the shore.

"Brace the gates! Hold the lines!"

Darien stood at the vanguard, his sword drawn, his breath steady despite the chaos unfolding around him. The city's warriors lined up beside him, shields locked, their faces set in grim determination. Trolls loomed over their allies, their massive war clubs and axes ready to strike. Darien could hear the ragged breathing of the men around him, smell the sweat and steel that filled the air. He tightened his grip on his sword.

Then the enemy was upon them.

The first impact sent a tremor through the ranks as the two forces collided with a deafening crash. Shields splintered, blades clashed, and the air filled with the cries of warriors locked in deadly combat. Darien parried a wild strike from a snarling soldier, driving his sword into the man's side before spinning to block another attacker. The weight of the battle pressed down on him, relentless and unyielding.

A roar erupted to his left. A towering brute wielding a spiked mace bore down on a troll warrior, the weapon swinging in a vicious arc. Darien barely had time to react before the troll countered, catching the blow on his massive shield and driving his axe into the enemy's chest. The brute staggered, then collapsed, but another took his place.

Darien cut through another soldier, his movements quick and precise. His training had been relentless, but nothing had prepared him for this—the raw brutality of war, the ceaseless tide of enemies. He could feel the exhaustion creeping in, but he pushed it aside. There was no room for weakness here.

From above, a barrage of flaming ballista bolts streaked toward the enemy ranks, each impact sending up plumes of dirt and fire. The battlefield became a shifting landscape of shadows and flame, figures darting between bursts of light as the battle raged on. The city walls loomed behind them, but Darien knew they wouldn't hold forever.

A sudden cry from the eastern flank caught his attention. The enemy had breached a section of the outer defenses, pouring through like a flood. If they weren't stopped now, the city itself would be lost.

Darien turned, his pulse pounding. "Reinforce the right side! We can't let them break through!"

His guard moved with him, cutting through the enemy ranks as they pushed toward the collapsing line. A young soldier beside him staggered, an enemy blade slipping through his armor. Darien caught him before he fell completely, his grip tight.

"Stay with me!" he commanded, dragging the soldier back even as he struck down another enemy with his free hand.

The soldier coughed, blood on his lips, but managed a nod. "We have to—" His voice cut off in a sharp gasp as another enemy blade found its mark.

Darien barely had time to react before the enemy was on him again, forcing him to let the young man slip to the ground. His chest burned with exertion, but he kept fighting. There was no time to grieve—not yet.

A guttural horn blast echoed across the battlefield, deeper and more menacing than before. From the distance, the second wave of the dark army appeared over the ridge, their banners whipping against the wind. And behind them, monstrous figures loomed, their twisted forms barely recognizable as men.

Darien's stomach clenched. The battle was far from over.

And if they faltered now, it would never end.

The sky turned from gold to crimson, then to deep purple as the sun dipped below the horizon. The battle had raged for hours, and exhaustion weighed heavy on the defenders. The city walls were slick with sweat and dust, the air thick with the acrid scent of burning wood and iron.

Yet the enemy did not falter.

For every fallen soldier, another took his place. For every line of warriors who gave their last breath to hold the defense, a fresh tide of dark-clad foes surged forward. Darien's arms ached from swinging his sword, his breath came in ragged gasps, but there was no time to stop. No time to rest.

Garik fought beside him, his twin blades flashing in the dimming light. He moved with a brutal efficiency, carving through enemy after enemy, his large frame a wall of muscle and fury. "We're being pushed back!" he shouted over the din of battle. "We can't hold much longer!"

Darien knew it was true. The defenders had been forced back, inch by inch, step by step, retreating toward the inner gates. The streets of Farkland Reach were only a few dozen yards away now. If the enemy broke through completely, the battle would become a slaughter inside the city.

Rist darted between warriors, his daggers flashing as he struck from the shadows. He had abandoned any attempt at defense, relying on speed and precision instead. He leaped onto an enemy's back, driving both blades into his neck before rolling away and slicing another's legs out from under him.

"Darien!" Rist's voice was urgent. "They're moving archers into position! We won't last long under a hail of arrows!"

Before Darien could respond, another voice called his name—sharp, urgent.

He turned to see Evatra astride her horse, her bowstring snapping as she loosed an arrow into the fray. She wheeled the horse around, dodging an enemy spear as she galloped toward him.

"I couldn't find you before it started!" she shouted, breathless. "The Queen needs you and Rist back at the command post—now!"

Darien's pulse hammered. He took in the battle-field—the bodies, the burning wreckage, the crumbling defenses. The enemy had driven them back nearly to the gates. They were losing ground, losing men.

"Understood," he said. "Rist, let's go!"

Evatra extended her hand. Without hesitation, Dari-en grabbed it, pulling himself up behind her as she turned the horse toward the city. Rist sprinted ahead, slipping through the chaos like a ghost. They rode hard, dodging wounded soldiers and flaming debris as they sped toward the inner defenses.

As they neared the command post, Darien cast one last glance over his shoulder. The battle was slipping away from them. Unless they found a way to change it, the city would fall before dawn.

Darien surveyed the battlefield from atop the walls, his breath heavy in his chest. What had once been an orderly defense had descended into chaos. The enemy moved like an unrelenting tide, surging forward no mat-ter how many fell. They had already lost nearly a third of their forces, and the defenders had been pushed back dangerously close to the city walls. The once-stable line had fractured, with isolated groups fighting desperately to hold their ground.

Evatra stood beside him, her bow still in hand, her knuckles white from gripping it too tightly. Sweat matted her hair to her face, but her green eyes burned with an intensity that mirrored Darien's own. Behind her, the sky had deepened into a dark crimson, the last vestiges of daylight washing over the blood-soaked battlefield.

"The Queen needs us," she said, her voice urgent but steady. "We need to go now."

Darien exhaled sharply, his frustration mounting. He wanted to stay. To fight. To push back. But he knew she was right. He sheathed his sword, nodding once before turning toward the gates.

"Climb up," Evatra instructed, extending a hand.

Without hesitation, Darien placed his foot in the stirrup and swung himself onto the horse behind her. He barely had time to secure his grip around her waist before she spurred the horse into motion. The animal thundered through the open gates, dodging wounded soldiers as they streamed into the city, seeking shelter in hastily converted homes and makeshift medical tents.

The scent of iron and burning wood filled the air as they veered left, taking the narrow stone staircase that led up to the city walls. Darien could hear the muffled cries of the wounded, the desperate orders of medics trying to keep them alive, and the roar of the ongoing battle behind them. He forced himself not to look back. Not yet.

At the summit, they dismounted in a rush. Marenya, Oratrin, and Rist were waiting, their faces grim. Rist's fingers clenched the stone railing so tightly that Darien thought they might break under the pressure. The

Queen stood tall, but the exhaustion in her posture was evident. Her royal garb was disheveled, her hair damp with sweat. She turned as Darien and Evatra approached, her expression unreadable.

"Darien, thank the gods," Marenya breathed, though her relief was overshadowed by the dire situation. "We lost track of you. We feared…" She let the sentence die on her lips.

"I'm here," Darien said, cutting through the tension. "But the battle isn't going well."

Oratrin exhaled, rubbing a hand down his face. "It's worse than we thought." He gestured to the field below. "They just keep coming. We strike them down, and they climb over their dead. We don't have the numbers to hold much longer."

Darien stepped forward, gripping the railing as he looked over the battlefield. His stomach twisted. The enemy forces were still massive. His earlier estimates had been wrong—badly wrong. Nearly two-thirds of their forces remained unbroken. The trolls, the human warriors, the archers on the walls—all of them were being overwhelmed.

"We've tried to hold," Oratrin continued, his voice tight with frustration. "But our warnings came too late. We weren't ready for this."

A shadow crossed Rist's face as he finally spoke. "If we stay, we die."

Darien slammed his fist against the railing. "Then what do we do? Run? Surrender?" The thought made his blood boil. He turned back to them, his eyes blazing with defiance. "There has to be another way."

Evatra stepped beside him, placing a hand on his shoulder. "Darien... it's over."

Her voice was calm, almost too calm, as if she had already accepted the reality of their situation. Darien, however, refused to. He looked around at them, searching for an answer, for anything that could turn the tide. But there was nothing. Only exhaustion, defeat, and grim resignation in their faces.

The sun had fully set now, leaving only a blanket of stars overhead. As Darien stared up at the night sky, a strange feeling settled over him. An unease. A silence that shouldn't have been there.

Then the scream came.

A high-pitched, piercing shriek that ripped through the air like a blade.

Darien's breath caught. A ripple of panic spread across the battlefield. Even the enemy forces halted, their monstrous, twisted forms stiffening at the sound. Trolls clamped their hands over their ears, warriors staggered back, and for a moment—just a moment—the battle stopped.

Then the silence fell again.

Darien felt it before he heard it. Cold. A creeping, unnatural frost that coiled through his veins like ice. He flexed his fingers, and they felt numb, distant. A whisper brushed against his thoughts—both distant and intimate all at once.

We have come.

His heart slammed against his ribs. He turned sharply to Evatra, and his breath caught when he saw her expression—her lips slightly parted, eyes wide in shock.

"Your eyes," she whispered.

Darien swallowed, feeling something shift within him. He turned back to Marenya, Oratrin, and Rist. They, too, were staring at him, confusion and uncertainty flickering in their gazes.

He knew what had happened before they even spoke the words.

"The wraiths are here," Darien said, his voice steady, a grin curling at the edges of his lips.

He turned his gaze back to the battlefield, now illuminated by the eerie, flickering torchlight of the trolls and the distant fires along the city walls. In the shifting light, he saw chaos.

The enemy ranks were breaking.

Will you fight with us? Darien thought, addressing the presence now undeniably woven into his own consciousness.

I will fight, the wraith's voice echoed in his mind. *But I wish to remain within you. I can amplify your abilities, sharpen your senses beyond human limits. With me, you will not falter.*

Darien hesitated. *What's the cost?*

Nothing you do not already carry, the wraith whispered. *I do not seek to control you, only to exist within you as an ally.*

He flexed his fingers, feeling the unnatural energy coursing through them. It was unlike anything he had ever known—his body thrumming with untapped strength, the weight of exhaustion momentarily lifted.

Then let's finish this, Darien thought.

The wraith's presence pulsed in response. *As one.*

Darien unsheathed his sword, the metal gleaming with unnatural sharpness.

"For Farkland Reach!" he roared. "For your homes! For your King!"

Then, he leapt from the horse into the fray, his blade flashing under the wraith's guiding hand, cutting through the enemy with inhuman precision.

Darien fought like a man possessed, and in many ways, he was. The wraith coursed through his veins, its presence sharpening every movement, every strike. His sword felt weightless in his grip, a natural extension of himself. The battlefield slowed before his eyes, enemies moving sluggishly as he danced between them, his blade cutting through flesh and armor alike with terrifying precision.

A hulking warrior swung a massive hammer toward his head. Darien ducked, stepping to the side and driving his sword into the man's exposed flank. He barely had time to withdraw before another attacker lunged at him. He moved on instinct, his body shifting effortlessly, as if the wraith already knew where the next blow would come from.

All around him, the tide was shifting. Chorrun and the centaurs charged from the northern flank, their powerful bodies smashing through the disoriented enemy. The trolls rallied, forcing back the dark army step by step. For the first time since the battle had begun, victory felt within reach.

Darien turned in time to see a familiar figure weaving through the chaos, his shield raised high. Torin. The young centaur had disobeyed orders, thrusting himself into the thick of the fight, his youthful determination burning in his eyes.

"Darien! Hey, Darien!" Torin called, breathless but grinning, his hooves kicking up dirt as he cut down an enemy soldier.

Darien lifted his shield in greeting, pride swelling in his chest—

Then his world shattered.

A black blade sliced through the air, silent and merciless. It struck Torin's chest with sickening finality, cutting through flesh and bone. The young centaur gasped, his sword slipping from his grasp. His body staggered, his expression frozen in shock.

Darien watched, helpless, as Torin fell to his knees. The light in his eyes flickered, his hands gripping weakly at the wound as if trying to hold himself together. A choked breath escaped his lips, barely audible over the din of battle.

Darien ran. "No—NO! Torin!"

He dropped to his knees, cradling the centaur's trembling form. Torin's breathing was ragged, his body quivering with the effort to cling to life. His blood pooled beneath him, dark against the churned earth.

Torin's eyes met Darien's, wide and unfocused. He coughed, his voice barely a whisper. "Did... we win?"

Darien swallowed, his throat thick with emotion. He gripped Torin's hand tightly. "Hold on. Just—just hold on."

Torin's lips twitched, a weak attempt at a smile. "I... fought well?"

Darien's vision blurred. "You were incredible."

Torin exhaled slowly, his grip on Darien's arm weakening. "That's... good," he murmured, his voice drifting.

Darien's chest constricted as he turned inward, his mind screaming. *Wraith—help him. Save him!*

Silence.

Damn you, DO SOMETHING!

The wraith's voice was calm, final. The soul has already left the body.

Torin let out one last, shaky breath.

And then—stillness.

Darien froze. The battlefield, the battle itself, felt impossibly distant. All he could hear was the dull ringing in his ears, all he could feel was the lifeless weight in his arms.

Torin was gone.

A scream built in Darien's chest, but it never escaped. Instead, something inside him cracked, splintering into something raw and unforgiving. He lowered Torin's body gently, his hands trembling as he brushed his fingers over the centaur's lifeless face, closing his unseeing eyes.

Then he stood.

His grip tightened around his sword. His body vibrated with fury, grief turning into something sharper, more dangerous. The wraith inside him stirred, feeding off his rage.

If we can't save him... Darien thought, his hands trembling. *Then we'll kill every last one of them.*

His vision tunneled, his breath steadying. Then, with an inhuman roar, he threw himself into the fray, his sword carving through the enemy with brutal efficiency.

Torin was gone.

But the fight wasn't just for him. It was for all of them.

For the people of Farkland Reach, who had once welcomed him into their city, celebrating in the streets, laughing and drinking under golden lanterns. For the children who had watched him with wide eyes, hanging on his every word, dreaming of their own heroics. For Aren, the boy who had stood at his side, innocent and full of hope, waiting for a world worth growing up in.

This had to stop.

Darien's blade became an extension of his fury, his grief, his unrelenting purpose. He was no longer just fighting—he was ending this. His movements became a blur, every cut more precise, every thrust more merciless. The enemy fell before him like dry leaves in the wind, their numbers thinning, their will breaking.

His armor was becoming caked with gore, but he didn't care.

Every strike, every movement, was a promise. They would pay.

Chapter 23: The Eldric

When the sun rose the next morning, the battlefield lay silent. The echoes of war had faded into the cold dawn, leaving only the still bodies of the fallen as grim reminders of the battle that had raged through the night.

Darien walked alone among the dead, the damp morning air thick with the scent of blood and scorched earth. The bodies of trolls, centaurs, and fallen defenders were scattered across the crimson-stained ground, mingling with the monstrous forms of the enemy. His boots felt heavy, every step a reminder of the cost of their victory.

Victory. The word felt hollow.

He knelt beside a fallen soldier, turning him over gently. No breath, no flicker of life. Darien swallowed hard, moving to the next body, and then the next. The outcome was the same. None of them had survived.

Over half of the troll forces had been lost. The defenders had fought until the last moment, until their weapons shattered and their bodies gave out. And yet, even in their sacrifice, they had only won because of the wraiths.

Darien turned his gaze toward the southern edge of Farkland Reach, where the wraiths still lingered. They remained in the bodies they had stolen from Cyprin's army, monstrous forms now animated with something new—freedom.

For centuries, they had been cursed, confined to the darkness, unable to walk the world of the living. Now, for the first time, they were free. Even if it was temporary.

Darien's wraith had left him the moment the battle was won, retreating to aid its own. It had found a new form—an enormous cyclops, one of the last creatures to fall before the wraiths had turned the tide. When Darien approached that morning, the wraith had looked down at him with its massive, unblinking eye, giving only a nod before turning away.

No words were needed. They understood each other now.

Darien exhaled, shaking off the weight of his thoughts, and turned back toward the city gates.

The streets of Farkland Reach were lined with the wounded. Trolls, men, centaurs—those who had survived, but not without cost.

Makeshift beds were spread through the halls of the castle, the city's houses no longer enough to contain the injured. He walked past rows of those too weak to stand, their eyes weary but watching him. Some nodded as he passed. Others called to him, pleading for promises that he would finish this. That he would stop Cyprin.

Darien didn't answer them. He only carried their faces with him.

Eventually, he reached the council chamber, stepping inside to find it empty. He was early. For the first time in what felt like weeks, he allowed himself to sit.

The chair beneath him was cold, his limbs aching as exhaustion finally settled in. The quiet was welcome. No war cries. No battle. Just silence.

His head pounded, a lingering ache left in the wake of the wraith's possession. He leaned forward, rubbing his temples, trying to will the pain away.

A firm hand shook his shoulder.

Darien jerked upright, eyes bleary. Rist stood before him, arms crossed.

"Oh. Sorry," Darien muttered, pressing his fingers into his eyes. "I must have drifted off."

"You haven't slept since the battle," Rist noted, his voice unreadable.

Darien groaned as sunlight cut through the chamber windows, the brightness splitting his headache wide open.

"Are you well?" Rist asked.

"Yeah, just my head," Darien replied. "Ever since the wraith left, it's been getting worse. But it'll pass. I just need—"

"You should see the healers."

"I said I'm fine, Rist."

The sharpness in his voice surprised even himself. Darien exhaled, shaking his head. "I'm sorry. I just—yesterday was…" He trailed off. There were no words for what yesterday was.

Rist didn't press further. Instead, he took a seat across from Darien, allowing the silence to settle between them.

For the first time in hours, Darien let his eyes close. Not to rest, but to grieve.

Marenya, Chorrun, Evatra, and Oratrin entered the chamber soon after, their faces marked with exhaustion. The last to step inside was the wraith—its new cyclops body looming over them all.

"I need to thank you all for what you've done for this city," Marenya said, her voice steady despite the weariness in her eyes. "I believed we would fall. We would have, if not for you. And most of all, for you, sir wraith." She turned toward the creature. "Without your kind, we would have lost."

Oratrin tensed, his hand resting on his sword. "We shouldn't be allowing this thing into our halls."

Marenya shot him a sharp glance. "Enough. We owe them our lives."

Oratrin said nothing more, but his glare toward the wraith remained.

"What happens now?" Rist asked.

Marenya sighed. "Scouts have been sent out. But they won't return for days. Until then, we need a plan."

Silence.

Then, all eyes turned to Darien.

His head pounded, the pain flaring behind his skull. Before he could answer, before he could even think, a sharp, blinding agony ripped through his mind.

A scream tore from his throat before he slumped forward.

Then—darkness.

When Darien awoke, he felt… normal.

The pain was gone, his body no longer heavy with exhaustion. His vision cleared, and he found himself in his quarters. A male troll in white robes stood nearby, mixing something into a goblet.

"What happened?" Darien asked, his voice hoarse.

The troll glanced at him. "I think that's best answered by the healers." He turned toward the door, speaking briefly to someone outside before returning.

Darien sat up, rubbing his temples. "Who are you?"

"The doctor's assistant," the troll replied. He shoved the goblet toward Darien. "Drink this."

Darien wrinkled his nose. "It smells awful."

"So my nephew said when I made it for him," the troll muttered impatiently. "Drink."

"What is it?"

"A tonic to keep the headaches from coming back."

Darien hesitated, then took a sip. It tasted like metal and old roots. He grimaced but forced it down.

A tall, older troll in white robes entered the room, followed closely by Rist and Evatra. His face was lined with deep creases, his weary eyes carrying the weight of too many years spent tending to the wounded.

Darien forced a weak smile, suddenly aware of how ridiculous he must have looked—laid up in bed after collapsing in front of everyone. "Hi."

Rist gave him a silent nod, but Evatra's concern was evident. She stood slightly behind the doctor, arms crossed, watching him closely.

Darien swallowed. "What happened?" He needed answers—real answers.

The doctor sat on the edge of the bed, his robe shifting as he leaned forward. "We believe this, the headaches and your being unconscious for two days, is a side effect of the wraith's possession," he said. "Nothing quite like this has ever been recorded in our histories."

Darien frowned. "I've been out for two days?"

"Nothing we did could wake you," the doctor confirmed. "We've consulted the wraiths, and even they don't fully understand what has happened. But we do know one thing—it may happen again."

Darien's stomach tightened. "Again?" The word came out sharper than he intended. "I—I don't think I can take that again."

"We can't know for certain," the doctor admitted, his voice measured, calm. "But we've made an educated guess. The wraith didn't fully possess you. Your mind created a space for it to exist without complete domination—a shield against its influence. But in doing so, it may have damaged itself."

Darien let out a slow breath. Damaged. The word dug into him, heavier than the weight of his own exhaustion.

Had he done this to himself?

"If the wraith had taken full control," the doctor continued, "it would have subdued your consciousness entirely. The way it was... coexisting with you was unnatural—neither full possession nor complete separation. We believe that left a scar."

"So what does that mean?" Darien asked, his fingers gripping the sheets beneath him.

The doctor hesitated. "It means that if another wraith tries to take hold of you again... it will kill you."

A silence fell over the room, thick and suffocating. Darien stared at the doctor, willing himself to breathe, to think, but his mind felt like it had hit a wall.

"So I'm stuck with this," he murmured. "Forever."

"We don't know," the doctor said gently. "But your mind has already changed. What's done is done."

Darien clenched his fists beneath the blankets. He had worked for control—of his thoughts, his emotions, his body. Discipline had defined him. And now? Now he had no control over his own mind.

"I'll leave you to rest," the doctor said, rising to his feet. "If you need anything, my assistant will be just beyond the door. Try to eat something. Start small."

With that, he exited, leaving Darien alone with Rist and Evatra.

The room was silent for a long moment. Darien shifted, realizing suddenly that he wasn't fully dressed, and pulled the blankets around him.

"So," he said, voice hoarse. "What's happening? Any word on Cyprin? The other members of the Eldric?"

Rist shook his head, his dark hood swaying gently. "No. None of the scouts we sent have returned yet. It's possible Cyprin intercepted them, but unlikely. We should have news in the next few days."

Darien exhaled. "So what now?"

"There are two options," Evatra said, stepping forward. "One—we leave now. Just the two of you, with a small guard. The Cycle continues, and you collect the weapons quickly. The other two can catch up when they arrive."

Darien nodded, absorbing the thought. "And the second?"

A knock interrupted them as a servant entered, carefully setting a tray of food onto Darien's lap. He hadn't realized how hungry he was until he saw the bowl of steaming broth before him. He reached for it but hesitated, stirring the surface with a spoon to cool it.

"We wait," Rist answered. "The others should arrive soon. We leave as planned, fully prepared, with more knowledge of your condition and what supplies you might need."

Darien lifted a spoonful of broth to his lips, blowing on it before sipping. The warmth spread through his chest, washing away the lingering metallic taste of the tonic.

"I favor waiting," Rist continued, watching Darien carefully. "You need to recover. It would be foolish to rush this."

Darien scowled. Recover. He hated that word. He had spent his entire life training to be strong—to master himself and his body. And now?

Now, he was fragile.

"Do you agree?" Rist asked.

Darien didn't answer immediately. His grip tightened around the spoon, frustration gnawing at his thoughts. But the truth was undeniable. He wasn't ready. Not yet.

He gave a small nod.

"That settles it, then," Rist said. "Rest. The city would do well to see you. Word of your... prowess has spread. Seeing you among them would raise their spirits."

Darien made a noncommittal noise, barely able to stomach the idea. Prowess. The word felt like a joke. He hadn't been some great warrior—he had been a tool for a wraith. And now everyone was praising him for it?

Rist turned to leave. Evatra lingered.

She reached out, her fingers brushing against Darien's hand. He hesitated before squeezing back, grounding himself in the warmth of her touch. Without another word, Rist closed the door behind him.

"I'm glad you're okay," Evatra said softly.

Darien let out a small laugh. "Yeah. You too."

He immediately regretted how awkward that sounded.

Evatra exhaled a quiet chuckle, shaking her head. "Darien…" She hesitated, eyes flickering with some unspoken thought. "I've been meaning to talk to you. About us."

Darien's chest tightened. He knew this conversation was coming.

"What about us?" he asked carefully.

Evatra crossed her arms, shifting slightly. "We never talked about what happened back at the caves."

Darien studied her, searching her face. He had spent far too much time thinking about that moment. About her. About Kara. About everything he had left behind.

She held his gaze, waiting for him to speak first.

"Okay," he said finally. "What do you want to say about it?"

Evatra let out a breath. "I don't know," she admitted. "I just know that we've been through a lot together. And I don't want to ignore it."

Darien ran a hand through his hair. "Look, I have no idea where I'll be in two days. Or two months." He hesitated. "But I know I want you there."

A slow smile broke across Evatra's face. She stepped forward, reaching up to cup his cheek. Darien barely had time to react before her lips brushed against his.

He kissed her back, his hand moving behind her neck, pulling her closer. For the first time since the battle, the weight on his chest lifted, if only for a moment.

When she pulled away, she lingered, her forehead resting against his.

"Rest," she murmured. "You're going to need it."

With a final glance, she stepped away, disappearing through the doorway.

Darien sat in silence, his mind warring with itself. Kara. Evatra. Olympus. The Academy.

But in the end, none of it mattered.

Because before any of that—before love, before the past, before the future—there was Cyprin.

And Darien would not stop until Olympus was free.

Darien sat in silence, staring at the space where Evatra had just been. His heart beat a little too fast, his mind spinning between guilt and possibility. Thoughts of Kara pulled at him—of home, of the life he had left behind—but here, now, those things felt distant. The only path back to Earth lay within the mountain to the east. And with the Cycle changed, no one could know how long he would be in Olympus.

For now, he needed to move forward.

He exhaled sharply, pushing the tray of food aside. Sliding to the floor, he planted his feet and tried to stand. His legs shook violently. A wave of dizziness hit him, forcing him to catch himself against the bedframe.

Guess I'll stay here, then.

His body, warm from the broth and heavy with exhaustion, surrendered to sleep before he could fight it.

Darien woke to golden light filtering through his window, casting long, lazy beams across the chamber. Testing his legs again, he stood slowly, bracing himself for another wave of weakness—but this time, the tremors were less severe. His muscles still ached, but the stiffness was fading.

A knock sounded at the door.

"Come in," he called, stretching his arms as the white-robed doctor stepped inside, beaming.

"Good! Good! You're standing," the doctor said, setting his bag on the chair. "Come here, let me check a few things before you start running about the castle."

Darien let the troll prod at his joints and muscles, then sit him down to examine his eyes and ears with a strange, angled device.

"You're healing," the doctor finally declared. "Slower than I'd like, but healing nonetheless."

"Am I free to move around?" Darien asked.

The doctor nodded. "Yes, but take it slow. Your stamina won't be what it was before the battle."

Darien thanked him, dressed, and strapped on his sword. The blade was chipped and battered, bearing the scars of the battle. He made a note to find a smith who could repair it.

For the next two days, Darien wandered the city, much like he had when he first arrived in Olympus. But this time, he was different.

He had fought, bled, and nearly died for this place. He had seen its people at their strongest and their weakest. The ruins left by battle—collapsing buildings, shattered streets—were reminders of what they had lost. And what they had saved.

He passed citizens in the streets, their faces filled with gratitude. Many stopped him, thanking him for defending their home. Children pointed at him in awe. Warriors clapped him on the back. Darien responded politely, but it wore on him. He wasn't a hero. He was just someone who had survived.

Tired of the attention, he found himself in the city's reconstruction efforts, offering his strength where it was needed. Lifting. Carrying. Helping. He had just reached for a crate of stone when the pain in his head flared violently—sharp, searing agony exploding behind his eyes. The world tilted.

Blackness.

When he woke, he was in his room again. Again.

The doctor hovered beside him, frustrated but unsurprised. "Your body is still adjusting," he said. "You need to be more careful."

Darien swallowed his frustration. How could he help if his own body kept betraying him?

With his movement limited, he turned his attention to the castle itself. Its towering spires and ancient halls reminded him of The Academy. He wandered, exploring hidden corridors, tracing the tapestries that told stories of Olympus's past. He needed to understand this place. To understand what he was fighting for.

On the fifth afternoon after the battle, he climbed a narrow staircase to the top of a western tower, stepping out onto the high stone overlook. The wind hit him immediately, cool and crisp.

From here, he saw everything.

The sprawling city stretched out below him, its people rebuilding, healing. Beyond it, a silver lake shimmered under the afternoon sun. Silver Lake. He remembered its name now. The water rippled in the light breeze, mirroring the towering mountains beyond, their peaks dusted with dull-white snow.

Darien's chest tightened as he thought about his new condition. His limit. His weakness.

How could he complete the Cycle if a single headache could bring him to his knees?

A quiet rustle behind him. The hatch opened, and a familiar figure climbed up the ladder to join him.

"How did you find me?" Darien asked without turning.

"I looked for the blank space," Rist said, tapping his gloved finger against his temple.

Darien smirked. "Still can't feel me anymore?"

"It's not quite that simple," Rist replied, stepping beside him. "I can feel you, but I can't feel what you're feeling. It's… complicated."

Darien accepted the answer, exhaling as he turned back to the horizon.

"Do you think we'll make it, Rist?" he asked, his voice quiet. "Can we complete the Cycle this time after everything that's happened?"

Rist considered for a long moment before answering. "Yes."

His voice was cold, unwavering. Certain.

Darien turned to face him fully. "Why?"

"Cyprin sent an army, and we beat it," Rist said simply. "The disruption in the Cycle has been corrected. If Cyprin had more to throw at us, he would have done so already."

Darien nodded, but doubt still gnawed at him. "I hope you're right," he muttered. "But something tells me there's still more surprises coming."

They stood in silence, the wind tugging at their cloaks as they watched the city below. Waiting. Preparing.

Then—a sound.

A low, distant roar carried on the wind, coming from the northern edge of the city.

Darien and Rist exchanged a glance before hurrying down the tower stairs.

Evatra, Marenya, Oratrin, and Chorrun stood gathered in the castle's grand entryway. A small figure stood beside Evatra, clutching at her sleeve—Atreya. The girl's face was pale, her tiny fingers curled tight around Evatra's wrist.

Darien scanned the faces of the gathered warriors. Something had changed.

"What's happening?" he asked as Rist stepped up beside him.

Evatra gave him a quick, subtle smile—a reassurance meant only for him. But she kept her distance, their private connection still unspoken to the others.

"It seems the decision to wait has paid off," Oratrin said, nodding toward the massive wooden doors at the far end of the hall.

Darien turned, his heart thudding. Outside, he could hear cheers. Faint at first, growing louder, closer.

Marenya lifted her chin. "The others are here."

The doors groaned as they slowly opened.

Beyond them, in the golden afternoon light, two figures stepped forward.

Darien felt his pulse quicken.

The other two members of the Eldric had finally arrived.

The journey—the real journey—was about to begin.

He felt Evatra's fingers brush against his hand. He didn't pull away.

His gaze turned eastward, toward the distant mountains and toward where Cyprin waited.

His thoughts turned again to Torin, to the lives he'd seen lost. He thought of Velmark and the festival that the people so enjoyed. He thought of the new friendships he had forged and was now willing to fight for.

He hadn't forgotten his home. The Academy, his friends, even Kara and everything he had there with her. But fate, it seemed, had pulled him somewhere else, onto another path. Here in Olympus he had found something not just worth living for, but he had come to view this world as something he would fight for.

His thoughts turned again to Cyprin and the rage and anger he felt for the one being who wanted to strip all that away. His mind was filled with one, all consuming and purposeful thought.

I'm coming for you.

Pronunciation Guide

Aghemnon — AG-em-non
Altruis — AL-tru-is
Atreya — a-tr-AY-uh
Chorrun — COR-un
Cyprin — SIE-prin
Darien — DARE-E-un
Evatra — eh-VAT-ra
Evedra — eh-VED-ra
Evindor — EV-in-dore
Garik-GARE-ik
Hiranor — HEER-in-ore
Jodin — JO-din
Kara — CAR-uh
Laytri — LAY-tree
Lotry — LO-tree
Lystra — LIST-ruh
Marenya — muh-REN-yuh
Peronia — Per-OH-nee-uh
Ristvahkbain — RIST-vahk-bane
Scillan — SILL-uhn
Tahmer — TA-mer
Taitron — TAY-truhn
Taerrun — TARE-uhn
Torin — TORE-in
Totra-Dal — TO-truh-doll
Whyn — Win
Whytaren — WHI-tar-ehn
Zanarchin — ZAN-ar-kin

Author's Note

I began playing around with the idea for Saving Olympus in 2002, long before it ever made its way to the page in any serious way. I was twelve at the time and shared the first chapter with family and friends, who all spoke highly of it, encouraging me to continue. For fifteen years or so, I ignored them, always saying that someday I would eventually write Darien's story.

That someday finally arrived. Over the past few years, I poured myself into reworking those original words, expanding the world of Olympus, and refining the story through long conversations with friends and family. Seeing this book out in the world is truly surreal. I've lived with these characters for so long, and it's incredibly gratifying to let others see and engage with them as well.

Releasing this second edition has been just as exciting—and just as daunting—as the first. I wanted to improve the experience for readers, making the story stronger, the characters richer, and the pacing more immersive. It was a labor of love, spanning nearly two decades of my life, and I intend to see Darien's journey through to the end. He will face Cyprin—of that, I promise you.

As I continue writing the next part of this saga, I simply want to say thank you. You have an almost infinite supply of books to choose from, and I'm honored that you chose to spend time with this story. I would love to hear your thoughts and answer any questions you might have about Saving Olympus: The Dark Army. Please feel free to reach out through reviews or on my social media pages @RDWolfeBooks.

I hope to see you there.

Saving Olympus: The Spell Caster Excerpt

"Darien! Darien wait. Evatra!" It was Oratrin. The pair glanced at each other curiously before turning to walk towards him.

"What is it?" Evatra asked as they grew close enough to speak without shouting across the distance.

"The Queen asked me to find you after your visit with Totra-Dal. She has something she wishes to show you. She's gathered the other members of the Eldric in the vaults below. I'm to take you both there now."

"Lead the way then." Darien said and followed after Oratrin who led Darien through the door which, on all his previous attempts, had been locked at the rear of the grand entryway. They stepped into a dimly lit hallway that led to a spiral staircase that led into the depths of the castle. Darien began counting the steps only after he realized how unpleasant it would be to climb up the stairs again. They passed no fewer than four landings before finally reaching the bottom of the staircase. As they stepped onto level ground, Oratrin grabbed a lantern from the wall and a torch which held a smoldering ember, touching the two together and lighting the lantern and replacing the torch with the burning ember on the opposing wall.

"Come this way and be careful not to fall too far back. The passages here can be a death sentence if you find yourself lost in them." Oratrin warned and began guiding them through the halls and passages, making turns at unexpected times and unlocking doors into a new section of the tight corridors. The space reminded Darien a bit of The Academy. Long stretching halls with doors on either side leading into new areas waiting to be explored. He wondered if this was anything like what lay beneath his home and thought again about what secrets might be buried underneath the ancient school.

Several minutes later, they came into a room encircled by torch light, brighter than the unlit hallways they had followed Oratrin through, and causing both Darien and Evatra to shield their eyes as they acclimated to the increase in light around them. Eventually, Darien looked to the center of the room and saw a pedestal holding a small blue sphere roughly three inches across that cast a strange light into the air surrounding it, pulsing and whirling in a strangely familiar mode. Darien tried to think of what was familiar about the odd sound and rhythm of the object, but couldn't quite put his finger on it. To his left, Darien saw Marenya standing with Rist, Breyman, Airlyn, and Chorrun, the centaur who had served as Darien's guide on his initial journey to Farkland Reach before he had been captured by Totra-

Dal's marauders. Chorrun smiled at him, Breyman and Marenya watched them patiently, while Airlyn just looked annoyed.

"Thank you for joining us here, Darien." Marenya said in her soft friendly voice.

Darien nodded and turned his attention back to the strange blue orb.

"What's that?" Darien asked.

"That, is why I asked you all here." Marenya answered, taking a few steps toward the strange object. "We found this on the body of that thief Tahmer. When we found it, it was a solid black but this morning it began doing this." She gestured at the pulsing, glowing sphere. "We had it in a vault in an upper level, under much less security. One of the servants there heard the object and grabbed the satchel holding it. According to the others in the room, the orb fell to the floor and the poor soul reached down to pick it up. The man vanished without a trace."

Sounds of surprise rose up from around the room.

"This thing looks like the transitions that bring the Eldric to Olympus." Airlyn said wonderingly. "Could it be magic?"

"That," Marenya nodded in reply, "is our best guess. We have no idea as to where the poor soul was ripped away to, or even if he survived the journey, but that is not the most disturbing piece of information." Marenya began to pace around the room, silence and apprehension deepening the soft lines of her face with worry.

"After Tahmer failed in his plan," she continued, "we kept his body, thinking to see if Cyprin had somehow augmented him in any way. Our doctors and scientists tried to conduct their tests and experiments, but each fell ill on every attempt. Realizing that something was preventing us from performing any further tests, we quickly decided to burn his body and dispose of him, so that no other magic or evil could come from him. After several hours of him lying on the pile of timber, as we do for all of our race, we returned to find him lying on the stone slab beneath, surrounded by the ash of the timber, but completely untouched."

"How is that possible?" Evatra asked.

"Magic." Breyman rumbled, making them all jump at the rolling boom of his voice.

"I thought Cyprin controlled all the magic?" Darien asked, hoping this wouldn't give away the fact that he was still woefully ignorant of the details of Olympus, not having known about Cyprin, The Cycles, or even Olympus before arriving in the centaur village of Taitron weeks before.

"He does." Chorrun answered in a tone somewhere between awe and horror. The centaurs love of history and the story of Cyprin's rise to power clearly drawing his interest. "However, it seems that he may have imbued this orb, and maybe even Tahmer himself, with some kind of magic."

"That is what we have deduced as well, Master Chorrun." Marenya said, clearly impressed by the others skill of deduction. "There is more, however. It seems that at the same time this orb came to life, Tahmer's body, or Tahmer himself it seems, vanished."

Darien felt a wave of panic sweep over him. He had barely been able to hold his own against Tahmer in their duel for possession of the ancient sword, one of the Eldric weapons he and the others would need in order to re-imprison Cyprin. If it hadn't been for Rist, Tahmer would certainly have killed him. If he was alive again, by whatever means, that would almost certainly mean another fight. Darien shook himself back into the moment in time to hear the end of Rist's question.

"—do you have it secure?"

"We have the sword secured in an even more secret location than this," Marenya nodded, "with guards stationed along every portion and turn of the hallway, handpicked by Oratrin to be certain that no one stands a chance at acquiring it without facing dozens of men. There are also several passages they can use to send word back to the surface if there are any intruders. Rest assured, the sword remains safe."

"So what now?" Airlyn asked, her impatient tone bristling against Darien's ears.

A cold voice that sent a shiver up Darien's back answered him from the hallway leading back in the direction he and Evatra had followed Oratrin through into the circular room.

"Now the cycles end."

Everyone in the room turned to face the figure standing in the entryway. It was Tahmer.

"Get behind me!" Oratrin shouted at Marenya, jumping in front of her and drawing his sword, placing himself between the remaining member of the monarchy of the troll people and the deadly troll.

Tahmer didn't move, the mask that had covered his face when Darien had fought him in the courtyard was still in place, but a faint glow seemed to come from behind where his eyes were. The black eyes stared out at the group with hatred and amusement. In his right hand he held a sword, one of troll make, stained with blood. In his left, a cloth bound object, three to four feet in length with the hilt of a sword sticking out of one end.

He got the sword again!

Darien reached down to draw his sword from his waist but cursed when he realized he wasn't wearing it. He had given it to a smith to get repaired after the battle and hadn't gotten it back yet.

"What do you want, traitor?!" Marenya called to him.

"What was given to me by my master." Tahmer answered, pointing to the orb at the center of the room.

"Drop the sword. If you leave that, we will let you use that thing, and travel wherever Cyprin's black magic takes you." Rist hissed, a wicked dagger having appeared in one hand, and small bow like object with a bolt that resembled a crossbow in the other.

Tahmer laughed mirthlessly. "You'll let me? You can't stop me."

"Watch us," Darien answered venomously.

Tahmer's eyes flicked to Darien, and then to the orb. Darien instinctively knew what was about to happen and sprang into action before anyone else had even thought to move. He dashed towards the orb at the same moment Tahmer did. The pair rushed to close the distance, Tahmer sheathing his sword as his feet pounded against the gray stone of the floor, he reached out with his fingers outstretched trying to touch the magic before Darien could.

Darien wasn't reaching for the orb.